To M[...]

CW00495138

# THE MASTER'S SPIRIT

## BY

## ANDY FRAZIER

*Best Wishes*
*Andy [signature]*

All copyright: Andy Frazier 2022
Published by Chauffour Books

*For the love of a decent whisky!*

It was pitch dark when a faint sound echoed from a laptop computer somewhere in the room. Its owner swung bare legs out of bed onto a cold tiled floor, clicked on the light and padded over to the black machine, noting the daylight outside through a crack in the shutter. When he opened the lid a message suggested that an email had just arrived, its sender an auction house somewhere in China.

The heading read, 'New world record price for a bottle of whisky.'

A grin turned to a yawn, as the man stepped quietly out into a corridor, opening a glazed door to an already warm courtyard and a view to the Mediterranean Ocean.

# Chapter One

A dull glint of light illuminated squalling snowflakes, as Scott Donald pulled on the handbrake and peered through his windscreen towards the main window of Glenlachan distillery. Daylight seemed reluctant to show itself this morning, as he glanced at his watch and made a mental note of the time, 8.22am. Mid November, still dark, and already snowing?  He resisted the urge to write the words 'long winter ahead' on the steamed-up pane, instead opening the door and bracing against the cold knife-like blow that blasted his unshaven face. Since the rebuild he had only been up here in the summer, when the place was flooded with midges and tourists in equal measures, and the days seem to go on forever. The building itself was quite imposing, made up of two square barns joined together by a main entrance hall under a large pointed tower.

Pulling his hat down around his ears and raising his collar, Scott battled the hundred metres or so to the side door which was already unlocked and ajar. A figure met him in the doorway.

'Davie,' Scott nodded his head to the younger man. They were both familiar to each other, just acquaintances, as was everyone in these remote parts. 'What's so urgent it gets me out of bed at this hour, in this weather?'

For the first time Scott noticed how pale the boy was, his skin a light grey, stretched around frightened eyes, lips thin and cracked as he answered. 'It's the boss,' he mumbled, looking up to the roof and then down to his shoes.

'What aboot him?'

'He's dead!'

Scott took a breath, taking his time to reply. 'Dead? You sure?' He glanced up too and then around the dimly lit barn, the fading copper of the two giant stills just about returning the light, and the giant steel sided tank known as the mash-tun.

He composed himself before his next question. 'Which boss? Your boss? Or the Frenchman?'

'Charlie.' Davie's voice faltered as he looked up again. 'My boss, Charlie. Up there. In there. Down in there!' He nodded to the platform, and then turned away, a tear forming in his eye.

Half an hour later, the two men sipped warm tea in the canteen as Scott opened his notebook and started with the questions he had been forming. The two of them had been up the ladder onto the mezzanine platform, and Scott had used a torch to peer through the open square hatch down into the mash-tun. The large vessel had contained a soft mix of malted barley and water, which had an evil way of pulling you down like quick sand if you stepped on it. The mixture was known as grist in the trade and was stirred by agitators, rotating mechanisms inside, which moved it around slowly to extract the fermented sugar from the grains. Scott considered climbing down the short ladder for a better look, or maybe checking for a pulse but even from a few metres above, by the colour of the man's lifeless face, it was pretty certain he was dead. Instead he used his phone to take a few photos of the scene, the rising steam stinging his eyes and throat. The body was caught by the arm in one of the agitators directly below the lid, the remainder of it partly submerged in the grist. Thankfully the agitators would have sensors and cut-out if overly obstructed, or the mess could have been a lot worse.

It would take more than one person to raise the body back up through the hatch, but he would leave that to the crime-scene team so he sat for a few seconds regaining his breath and coughing before calling it in to the boys at Oban. His words were that there was 'no actual rush, the body wasn't going anywhere,' and that, in his opinion, it was an accident and there were no immediately suspicious circumstances. After confirming the body was really dead, the voice on the other end had told him to seal off the area and stay away, so Scott decided it perhaps best not to tell them that he had already poked his head in for closer look. Instead he told them to thank him not getting them out of bed too early, half-grinned and then ended the call. It wouldn't be the first time he had been cautioned just for using his own inquisitiveness. It was in nature of a rural job like his, working alone, that sometimes gave rise to ideas of taking the law into your own hands, especially when you actually were the law itself.

'So you last saw him at 6.30 last night?' Scott had gleaned this information during conversation with the lad but was now recording it in the correct order in his notebook. 'You left him to lock up?'

Davie nodded slowly. 'I took the tractor back home, as we had already discussed that there was a weather front coming in and it may make it easier to get here in the morning.' As if checking for his boss's agreement, he glanced up to the where the body lay on the platform. 'He said he would take the quad bike. He only lives...' He corrected himself, 'lived down the road, less than a mile, so he often walked it. But I guess he thought the quad would be handy if the snow drifted in.'

The two men glanced out through the main arched window, snow still circling around outside. Scott's gaze searched beyond the car-park, to see if there were any signs of the Oban officers arriving. He suspected it will take them all of an hour, and they wouldn't rush, based on the information he had given them. And the trek up from Taynuilt could be treacherous in summer, let alone in this weather, even in their police Land-Rover. He turned back to his routine questions.

'And you arrived back here at what time this morning?'

'Just after seven. That's my normal start time.' Habitually he glanced at his watch. 'I was a few minutes late but didn't think Charlie would mind too much. The quad bike was outside when I arrived. Pretty much in the same place.'

'So, Charlie normally started at 7am as well?'

'Yes, that's right. Sometimes he would be in a bit earlier, doing paperwork in the office.' A glance at a desk in the corner signified that this was his office, rather than the main room where the receptionists and summer staff worked.

'Well, he must have been in much earlier this morning. I'm nae an expert but I would say he's been dead for more than a couple of hours.' Scott thought for a minute. 'What would be his first job when he came in? Or last when he went home?' He looked up to the platform. 'Would he go up there?'

'No. That's what's unusual. He didn't really like heights. Especially not that one. You saw how slippery it is up there. He was always warning me, but generally it was me that did that climb.' Davie stopped, looking up again. 'And other thing,' he added, eventually. 'That lid would normally be closed.'

The cogs started turning in Scott's mind. For what seemed like a routine accident, something was starting not to fit. 'Davie. You said the quad bike was pretty much where you left it? Was it exactly where you left it?'

The lad stroked his chin, thinking. 'Well, I couldn't be certain but...' he tailed off, and then caught the policeman's eye. 'You think he never went home?' Davie gave this some thought before adding, 'I'm pretty sure I saw him leave, though. You can spot the lights up here from

Auchachenna and I reckon I saw some on road up here on my way home.'

'Lights from his quad, you mean?'

'Well, lights from something?'

Scott scribbled the words: 'Lights from something, at 6.30pm.' Could the something have been another vehicle arriving, before Charlie left? He underlined the word 'something' and stood up. 'Let's take a look outside. Snow seems to be slowing a bit now.' His mind whirred again. 'If there had been another vehicle, the snow would have covered its tracks.'

They checked the quad bike which still had the key in the lock. So many of these things got pinched every year that the insurance premiums had almost trebled, but still locals and farmers left the keys in the ignition. He thought back to his days on the farm where he grew up, not five minutes from here. They didn't have a motor bike back then, of course, just a horse and a couple of dogs to round up the hill. Things were so much harder back in the day, when he would run up the hills on foot until he knew every inch of the mountains, the old man shouting instructions from below. Yes, tough days, they were that. Which was why he had left the business, leaving his brother Fraser to run the farm. He would almost certainly have had at least one of these things, parked in the barn, probably with the key in it too. He brought his mind back to the present. If Charlie had gone home on it, and then come back later, chances are he *would* park it in the same spot. And the soft tyres on these things barely left any marks behind, especially on gravel tracks.

'So why would he come back?' He asked the question more to himself than to the young hand who worked there, but the lad heard.

'Maybe left the lights on? Or forgot something?'

They made their way back inside, Scott looking at the

tractor as they passed. It was a fairly new affair with 4-wheel drive, a flashing orange beacon fastened to the roof and a small loading-shovel attached to the front. Well at least it may come in handy if they got snowed in.

'Came back to turn the lights off and then decided to climb this ladder up onto the gantry?' Scott was already climbing the ladder again, gripping the cold steel handrail, as he spoke over his shoulder. 'Wouldn't come up here to turn the lights off, would he?' His foot slipped and he hung on with both hands before finding the rung again. 'Why else would he come up here, on his own, in the night?' He ventured over to the open lid again, looking down at Charlie. The face had already started to go purple as it cooled after the scalding from boiling water and brown liquid oozed from the mouth. His left arm was mangled where it was caught in the agitator which had ripped the sleeve from his shirt. The man was in his late forties, slim enough but probably more unfit than he cared to admit. He was just checking around the rim of the lid when he heard footsteps at the door and looked down to see two uniformed officers entering the building, stamping the snow off their feet. The taller of the two he recognised, as the man looked up.

'Suicide, is it?' he called up, his voice harsh west coast.

The other officer went to speak to Davie who was sitting staring into space at the table where he had left him. It was a woman who was quite short but attractive, once she unzipped her jacked and removed her hat. Scott could hear her muffled voice speaking to the lad in soft tones, before putting the kettle on.

'Must be easier ways to kill yourself, Jim,' he called back down to the officer. 'Than to climb up here and throw yourself into that shite?'

Jim Rettie was a man of the west, though and through. Schooled at the local grammar in Campbeltown, he had never moved very far in his 50 odd years. Unmarried, the life of a policeman suited him fine, with a bit of variety and a few perks. Scott had no idea how long Jim had worked for the Oban force, certainly as far back as he could remember, although during that time he suspected his pal had gone up a few sizes in uniform. It was generally agreed that Jim was a good copper and a good man and the two of them always got on fine, even if there was plenty of teasing to be handed out.

'Aye, far better to stick your head under the tap and slug down a few litres of the good stuff.' The man chuckled. 'Not that this is good stuff, so I heard.' Jim made his way up the ladder, his bulk testing a few of the rivets and the two men shook hands. 'A bugger of a day to do it, too, eh? Perhaps that's why. Long snowy winter, ahead, with vats full of whisky that won't make the grade?' He surveyed the area around this upper platform. 'See you sealed off the scene then, in your usual efficient way?'

Scott ignored the remark and then looked him in the eye, noting how Jim's hair had rapidly faded colour since he had last seen him. What was he now, 55, maybe more. 'Got a new partner, I spotted? Bit young for you, eh? Thought you went more for the older women,' he teased. 'From what I can remember of the Christmas party!'

A look from Jim suggested that little misdemeanour was best left forgotten. He was more old school, stuck a little too far in the past for modern policing and had never fully grasped the concept of being politically correct, especially when among his work colleagues. At his age most of them generally ignored his few faux-pas although they were always in the background as teasing material, particularly when spirits were low. 'So? Suicide? Or accident?'

Scott's face dropped to a more sullen look. 'I'm not sure it's either!'

The snow had stopped now and the wind subsided, as Scott leant on the bonnet of his Nissan 4x4 pick-up, smoking a roll-up. The warmer temperature in the building had been making him sweat as well as the sweet odour of the sugary fermenting wort getting into his throat and eyes. He looked back at the distillery as the threatening skies hung grey over its pointed roof. As a young teenager he had come up here, playing in the old stone building and wondering at the decaying steel structures that it housed. Back then the place was overrun with rats and he would take his terrier and a couple of mates and kill dozens of them, just for sport. The distillery had been closed for as long as he could remember, decaying as the roof started to cave in. Just another old warehouse, losing its history to the weather and a previous generation of whisky drinkers from the west. Then suddenly, like a swing in politics, whisky came back into favour with the youngsters. Within a decade demand for single malts quadrupled and a wave of younger entrepreneurs started to see the liquid gold's new worth. There were the big boys, of course, like Brown-Forman and the Japanese owned Beam Suntory, who had bought up old distilleries for their existing stocks, and then developed them as visitor centres. But it was a brave man with vision and a shed-load of money that had picked up Glenlachan for around a hundred thousand. Most of the locals ridiculed him of course, particularly as he was from overseas and therefore inherently stupid, and the jokes flowed through the pubs and along the valley, that the man believed there were thousands of gallons of whisky still in the place, although he had bought it unseen. Much of this was untrue, as Julien de Runcy was anything but stupid, having built himself an empire in the electronics business and sold out to the Americans before the crash. It was also untrue that he had bought it unseen, having had a number of experts look it over for him and plans drawn up and double checked. What now stood was a testament to the Frenchman's foresight and was hailed by the press and a few more tolerant locals as a masterpiece of architecture, incorporating the old and the new together in harmony. What was true, though, was that through all that time, in a tumble-down barn at the rear of the old building, some of the original Glenlachan whisky had survived.

Blinking at the reflection of the blue flashing lights from the SoCo vehicle parked near the entrance, Scott stubbed out his cigarette and walked round to the rear of the building. The quad bike was still there, untouched, but he felt that the unit should take a look at that too, just to check who else may have ridden it recently. As the snow melted on the ground he knelt down to check its tracks but there was little to give evidence of whether Charlie had left and returned on it the night before, or whether it had stayed put. He suspected there was little way of finding that out.

He had known Charlie, of course. Most locals did, or had at least heard of his reputation, as a drinker in the Kilchrenan Arms in the village. Scott would have been called to an incident back in the summer when what started out as a knowledgeable discussion about whisky between Charlie and two American tourists got a little heated, had he not already been at the scene. The younger of the Yanks took a dislike to the distiller's educated views on the subject and when he couldn't get his views on Scotch versus Bourbon to the top of the conversation had threatened to take Charlie outside for a kicking. Not the most popular man in the area, the locals had left Charlie to his own scrap and it looked like the man was against two-to-one odds. What they hadn't reckoned with was Scott perched on a stool at the far end of the bar, who raised his athletic frame and sauntered over between them. A few words were said, the men backed down and soon left, on foot once they had seen Scott's badge.

After that Charlie held the local copper in slightly higher esteem and had bought him a drink. During the next hour Scott had let the man speak, hearing how he was an expert of the highest order. His certificate as a Master Distiller from Herriot Watt University was mentioned numerous times, although those in the business knew there was no actual qualification of that name, just something that the more self-important distillers like to call themselves. He also bragged about an education at James Gordon, one of Scotland's most coveted private schools. The man had omitted the detail that his father had been distiller at a nearby distillery and thus the boy had had a 'local' scholarship sometimes given to workers in the area.

Their conversation had ended when Scott had got bored by hearing for the fourth time how Charlie was belligerently going to make the finest whisky ever known on the west coast, although it could never compete with that from Speyside. Scott had seen him a few times since, but only in passing, and he could quite understand why the man was not that popular with the locals from this remote area.

'Who had reason to kill him, though?' He said the words out loud and was quite startled when a female voice answered his question.

'Sounds like something a detective would say?'

Scott felt his face redden as he looked up to see the officer from Oban standing at the doorway.

She noticed his embarrassment and came over, holding out her hand. 'DCI Downs,' she said, her voice English and stern. 'Heather.'

Scott stood to his full height at least 6 inches taller than the petite officer, 'Scott Donald!' His face cracking a half smile. 'Local copper, local farmer, local busy-body!'

'Why shouldn't you be? It's your patch. Your case. We're just here to lend a hand.'

The way she said it was almost believable, but he had

been here before. 'Oh aye, I've taken Oban's hand in the past. And it's generally quite a heavy one.'

Her eyes narrowed. 'Look Scott. We have a job to do here, so let's hope we can all work together?' She turned back towards the door. 'We can start with a cup of tea. And you can fill me in on what you know about the case.'

Whilst her back was turned Scott raised his cheeks and mouthed the words, 'start with a cup of tea!' How so typically English. So this was Jim's new boss then? He hadn't mentioned that just now.

Heather, on the other hand, had been fully briefed on Scott Donald on the journey up from Oban.

A bright and popular chap, he had been in the job for over 10 years, with little or no ambition to move up or elsewhere. Son of a farmer, he and his brother had reputedly fallen out when their father had died, the older one inheriting the dairy farm on some of Argyll's better land down near the shores of Loch Awe, just a few miles away. With no prospect of work locally other than maybe working for his brother or in the evolving tourist trade, Scott had headed north to Inverness in his early twenties. From there he had worked on the oil rigs for a few years, believed to have been married and divorced, before coming home to Kilchrenan, and stepping into the role of local policeman after just a few months training, when old Ben had retired. Very much a loner, the remoteness of the job had great appeal and it had been mentioned at the station that he wasn't an enthusiastic team player. When he was a boy his grandfather had owned a small stone bothy half-way up the hill from the loch, with a few acres of harsh hill land. It had been bequeathed to him in his father's will and had lain empty for many years until Scott took it on and fixed up the house where he now lived, presumed on his own with a few farm animals for company.

The teacup was set before him as he sat in the canteen,

grateful that Jim had joined them to diffuse the situation.

'So, what makes you think it was murder?' Her tone was a little lighter now, although the question wasn't.

'Who said it was murder?' Scott tried his first defensive move, knowing before he said it that it would come straight back at him.

'Well, you did, actually.' She checked her notes and to Scott's horror she read the statement, 'who had reason to kill him, though?'

'Hang on, I said that to myself, it's a bit sneaky..'

Heather put her hand up to stop him. 'No-one is being sneaky. We just need to get some facts down.' He thought he saw a glimpse of a smile, as though she was teasing him. 'So let's start again. What makes you think it was murder?'

Jim butted in, to level the situation. 'You knew him, right. This Charles Edis?'

Scott was thankful for someone else to look at. 'I didn't exactly know him, Jim. But I had met him. He was able. And knew his trade. Brought in here by the owner for his reputation as a well-qualified distiller.'

'Ah yes, the owner'' Heather consulted her notes again. 'Has he been informed?'

'Yes, on his way, Ma'am.'

Scott looked taken aback. Did Jim just call her Ma'am? Bloody hell, he had never heard him do that to any woman before. She must have some hold on him. But what he said was: 'what, from France, in this weather?'

Jim grinned, 'No, he was in Snecky, actually. The young lad gave me his mobile number. Goes by name of John Luke, only spelt funny!'

'Snecky?' Heather raised an inquisitive eyebrow.

'Inverness, Ma'am. That's what it's known as by the, erm, locals.'

Scott smiled inwardly to himself. Jim might address her as Ma'am but he could still mock her Englishness. 'He's not the owner,' he said 'Not technically. Jean-Luc is the son of the owner. Cocky wee bugger. Bit of a lady's man.'

'And what's that supposed to mean?' Heather's tone was short and Scott saw Jim wince as she spoke.

'Aw, you know how the French men are. Like to think they are god's gift and all that?'

'Do I detect a hint of jealousy, PC Donald?' Heather's eyes flashed for a fraction of a second, and Scott knew he was being played.

'Jealously? Na, I got no time for that sort,' he sniffed. 'You might fancy him, though?'

Her eyes narrowed further until Jim broke the stare once again. 'Anyway, he's on his way. Will be here in an hour or so.'

During the next half an hour Scott filled the two of them in on what he knew about Charlie. He lived in a cottage just down the road, owned by the distillery, and had done since the Glenlachan had been rebuilt five years ago. Had a wife, Mary, and a daughter Shauna, who lived partly with them and partly with half the young men in the village. Scott had busted her a couple of times for drug offences but she had gone away with a caution. Charlie had previously worked mainly in Speyside distilleries, earning his Master's certificate whilst at Tomintoul. Jim had mentioned, just for the record, so far the tasting notes on the first few runs of whisky from Glenlachan were less than favourable.

Heather stood up as she saw a vehicle coming up the track outside. 'OK. Let's see what SoCo come back with. Scott, you get the job of informing the wife. Jim, you secure the area, and keep the press away from this. I'll go and see what 'God's gift' has to say!' They turned to see a dark-haired young man stepping out of a Black Porsche Cayenne 4x4 in tight slacks and very shiny shoes. Scott couldn't believe the man was actually wearing a beret!

# Chapter Two

'Och, alright. I can hear ya!' Scott blew on the flickering embers in the grate, adding some more old newspaper as they caught and flamed. He loaded another log of peat on the top and stepped back, narrowly avoiding a collie dog who was watching proceedings with the enthusiasm of someone at the movies. 'I guess you'll want fed as well, Beth, huh?' He patted her head and she spun round in a circle of delight. 'Let me go and see to that noisy lot first.' He pointed to the window and the dog immediately jumped up on the back of the old sofa and looked out into the night.

Pushing open a wooden gate, Scott did his best to shove half a dozen ewes out of the way, their horns digging into his thighs as the sheep did their best to knock him over. 'Gemma! C'Mon!' he yelled out into the darkness. Soon Gemma loomed into view, her long brown horns preceding her. He reached out and stroked her nose, before emptying a half sack of food into a wooden trough. The snow had all but thawed leaving the small paddock sticky underfoot and the hooves of his old Highland cow pierced the soil with each step until she nudged a couple of sheep aside and stuck her head in the trough. 'You'll keep me poor, you lot,' he muttered as he retreated back to the stone cottage.

Inside a single bulb hung low over a wooden table as wisps of smoke from the fire rose as if attracted to the light. Other than a few faded paintings on the wall, the cottage was sparse, with wood-clad walls and a low ceiling. Nearest the door a black granite work-surface stretched along one wall, above a shiny oven and some neat cupboards. On shelves above, modern white plates were neatly stacked, in order of size, lit by a row of bright spotlights. A wall-magnet attached to the grey metro-tiles tiles sported a range of sharp knives which again were arranged in order, as Scott pulled one down and cut into a piece of cold meat. 'No tin tonight, Beth. Got some real food for you.' He calmly dissected a lump of grey meat while the dog bounced up and down in anticipation. Scooping the lot into a bowl and adding some dry biscuits took more time than Beth could endure and she started barking, a high-pitched sound that went right through him. 'Aright! Gimme a minute!' He raised his voice a little too loud and the dog looked crestfallen for a second before resuming her dance until he put the bowl on the floor.

Opening the fridge, he looked at the contents for a few seconds, perusing the well stocked array of vegetables with some fresh meat shelved separately. Within minutes he had diced and seasoned a selection, stirring it into a casserole dish, placing it in the oven and setting the timer on its digital clock. Switching on the radio, he grabbed a beer from the fridge and settled into his old leather chair, socked-feet on the hearth, letting the sound of classical music wash over his day.

The shrill sound of a buzzer woke him an hour later, morphing from what had been a police siren in his dream until his nose confirmed it was just an announcement that dinner was ready, and he was in his own cottage, not pursuing thieves down a hillside.

As he ate his stew, he considered the day's events. They now had all the details on Charlie and had formally interviewed Davie and Jean-Luc, the latter who had taken exception to being treated like a suspect, but they were still no further forward as to a why a man had drowned in a vat of boiled malted barley. Scott had paid a visit to Mary to give her the bad news. At first she had seemed understanding, as though he was just arriving to mention some passing fact about someone in the village. It was when Shauna, the wandering daughter, came into the room that Mary broke down, sobbing in great waves of emotion that echoed around the ceiling. Shauna was more composed, even understanding, as she sat cross-legged on the couch wearing a long baggy jumper, her black hair tied up at the back and tinged with purple. She questioned whether it was an accident and he had said they hadn't ruled it out. All of them avoided the word 'suicide' as though it was never an option, although inside each considered the possibility. Something about Shauna's behaviour suggested that she may have known something but wasn't letting on, but then again, he suspected she had plenty of secrets she would never tell her parents. The girl definitely was a live-wire and, at times, he even felt she was coming on to him. She certainly had the attention of many of the boys around the area, including young Davie who worked for her father. Was there something between her and her father? Or one of her numerous conquests? Charlie was a man with a temper and his brash self-centredness could rub a lot of people up the wrong way. But enough to get himself killed?

And then there was the matter of why he would have gone up the ladder, somewhere he was not comfortable with going? Davie had admitted the mash-tun paddles sometimes got stuck but they could usually be sorted by hitting the red STOP button at the bottom, then reversing the mechanism a little bit, and starting again. There was no need to go and look in from the top. Anyway this mash was on the final sparge and almost complete, so keeping it moving wouldn't have been so crucial. The evidence, of course, led to Charlie intentionally going up the ladder to commit suicide and that was still the obvious conclusion to those with no more than a passing interest in this case. SoCo had said there had been a bang on the head but were pretty sure it hadn't been fatal, the only other obvious wounds were the mangled arm, and that is was a fair assumption that he was alive when he went in.

So, for it to be a murder, someone would have had to

persuade Charlie to go up the ladder and that would have taken some serious reasoning? Or a weapon?

Scott stood to his feet and immediately Beth was up too, at the door, running around in small circles. He glanced up at the clock on the oven. 8.28pm.

'Come on then, we'll just go for one, shall we?'

A low cloud had shrouded the road as he drove the 4x4 in the direction of the village, but he knew this one-mile journey like an old friend, having driven it a thousand times, man and boy. Beth watched the road too, from the passenger's seat, leaning sideways as he took the corners perhaps a little too fast. By his own rules she was supposed to ride in the back, as had her mother before her, but he was getting softer in his old age and it was a dark winter's night.

The Kilchrenan Inn had also become run down over the last few decades until bought by outsiders. Over the last year it too had been refurbished within an inch of its life, including a swanky new kitchen and restaurant which served delicious meals at city prices. Scott had eaten there plenty of times, being a man who not only enjoyed fine food but liked to cook it also. He particularly had enjoyed the shellfish risotto, made with local crayfish fetched out of the loch that very day. In fact, he had often poked his head into the kitchen and taken a few tips from the chef, a burly tattooed lad from Liverpool. Since he had moved on, Scott felt the food wasn't quite the same, but he never mentioned it. What had once been the old bar had been knocked through to become part of the restaurant area, which took away from the previous cosy atmosphere that he recalled from his youth. A time where the auld guard would have their specific place at the bar or by the fire at certain times of day or night, his father and grandfather included. Now there weren't quite so many locals but even at this time of year it still drew those that were resident in the surrounding area as well as a few day trippers from Oban and beyond. It was the restoration of the three bedrooms that had brought profit to this ancient coaching house. Furnished in tasteful splendour, a night's stay could cost near two hundred quid in peak season, and combine that with a gourmet dining experience for a couple of evenings and Scott wondered where the money came from, something that would take him a year to save up for on his salary. The wine list alone would be well out of reach of most of the locals.

Now it was more of a foodie place, dogs weren't allowed in the bar, so he pulled his truck into the carpark opposite and told Beth he wouldn't be too long. Through the window he could see who was in the bar, just as they could see him. It wasn't so much a they, as a she, who clocked him arrive and poured a pint of Tennants.

'Scott,' she said dryly as he entered, without looking at him.

'Hey, Jess. How are you?'

Jess made a point of not answering, just passing him the drink as he gave her a smile she didn't return. Her cropped hair glowed almost golden under the bar lights, over high cheek bones and a satin top cut just a little lower than most women felt comfortable with. Spangled earrings dangling to her shoulders reflected the light as she moved, setting her up as an almost stereotyped barmaid. It was an image she had worked on, but not how Scott had always known her.

There were only three stools at the bar and Scott took the empty one.

'Heard about Charlie,' said a voice from one of them. 'Pretty shitty way to go.'

'Aye, Dougie.' Scott replied, 'pretty shitty.' He sipped his pint. 'News travels!'

Dougie looked up from his pint, directly at Scott, his glasses slightly steamed, half covering his snake-like eyes.

'Aye. Always has, always will. Suicide, they say?'

Scott said nothing. Dougie was a local resident but, unlike Jess who was born in the village, he had come from further down the coast, turning up five or six years ago looking for work. A slim and fit young man, it soon transpired that he was good with his hands, as he started helping with repairs at the local campsite. Eventually he had rented a small yard in the village from where he chopped, sold and delivered firewood in Autumn, once the tourist season had finished. He had also done odd jobs around the area, including helping with the refurbishment of the pub. Usually dressed in workman's trousers with a dozen or more pockets, Dougie always pulled out wads of cash to pay for drinks and supplies and it was well recognised that his name was probably never listed in any tax office. A similar age to Scott, the two had never really got on, particularly when he started seeing Jess, much to her father's disapproval. That was over now. In fact, she was over them both, and back living at home.

'Charlie wouldn't do that.' This gruff addition to the conversation came from behind a newspaper. 'He loved himself too much to end it all. B'sides,' the large man slowly lowered the paper revealing a greying beard over a neckerchief tied around his neck. 'The man was chickenshit. He wouldn't have the guts.'

'Thanks for the character assassination, Dad,' Jess contributed. 'But maybe take it easy on the dead, eh?'

'Easy? Why should I take it easy? The man was a self-important prick. I never took to him alive, and I am sure not going to start blowing smoke up his dead arse!' He lifted the paper again, ending his involvement with the conversation that continued.

Dougie took the stand again. 'What you think, Scott? You think John's right?'

Scott picked up his pint, and a copy of the local newspaper, heading out towards a chair in the empty dining room. 'We are investigating it,' he quipped back over his shoulder. He refrained from adding, and you're all suspects!

For the next half an hour he skimmed through last Thursday's Oban Times, only stopping to fully read an account of a mountain rescue off Ben Mhor that he had been involved in. There was also a report on the Highland Cattle sales at Oban mart, which he skimmed though, noting that the trade was down a few hundred quid on last year. But the price of Scottish Blackface rams was making the headlines again. It never ceased to amaze him that one hill sheep could be worth a hundred thousand, when at the end of the day all it was good for was a bowl of stew! Draining his pint, he took the empty glass back into the bar and put it on the counter along with a five pound note.

Jess gave him a half smile this time, while giving him his change. 'How's Mary taken it?' she asked, her eyes showing hints of sympathy.

'Oh, you know, struggled to take it in, at first. Couldn't understand why he would be so careless. Shauna didn't help either, solemn thing that she is.'

'She's aff her nut, that one.' Jess shook her head so that her earrings rattled like wind chimes.

'Aye, she may be tonight.' He headed for the door.

'See'ya Scott,' Dougie called after him. 'I hope you catch the bugger!'

As he went through the half-glass door a shoulder bumped into him, knocking him backwards.

'Aw, merde. Sorry Monsieur.'

Scott looked into the narrow dark eyes of Jean-Luc. The man looked tired but at least he had removed that ridiculous beret. He could imagine what old John McCarthy would think about that garment.

The young Frenchman ignored him, his eyes focussed

on Jess behind the bar. 'Mademoiselle, ma cherie,' he gushed. 'Are you still serving your delicious food?'

Scott strolled away towards his pick-up, rolling his eyes. He knew Jean-Luc was staying at the hotel, as he often did. They had already asked him not to leave the area again until they had finished with the enquiry. Meanwhile he could chance his arm at chatting up Jess, if her old man didn't banjo him with a chair first!

# Chapter Three

Scott pulled hard on the steering wheel, the pick-up's knobbly tyres slipping on to the dirt, as he narrowly missed a head-on collision with the local milk tanker at the Annat junction, shaking him from his thoughts. The lorry would be heading down to his brother's farm at Inverinan and, by Scott's reckoning, coupled with the speed it was going, it was running late, probably trying to catch up after the snowy morning the day before. Today was like a different world though, as the clouds had lifted and the sun was even trying to peep over the Musdale ridge, casting an orange glow on to the slopes of Ben Cruachan to his right, as it towered over Loch Awe and the small hamlet of Kilchrenan. The late Autumnal colours really were beautiful this time of year and he never tired of admiring the arrays of brown and deep yellow that made up this magical landscape, a place that so many folks took for granted.

The distillery was in darkness when he got there, and he sat in his cab for a whole minute thinking. His night had been restless and he had been up early to mull things over. The more he considered the matter, the more convinced he was that there had been a murder in this village, the first for a very long time, and it didn't belong here. He had sat at the kitchen table, scribbling a list of suspects and motives then arranging them into a diagram, none of whom, he had to admit, seemed particularly plausible.

He had asked young Davie to meet him there at nine o'clock which gave him some time to check around outside. Since the snow had melted, the nearby stream, or burn, which in summer just trickled down the mountain and past the building was now raging with fresh water as it bulged and gurgled underneath a steel cattle-grid at the property's entrance. Water from this would be used to throughout the process, in essence making it the life-blood of the whisky itself.

Scott had no idea exactly what he was looking for although, with the snow now gone, there was a plethora of tyre tracks, each one overlapping the other. They had checked all the doors for signs of forced entry the previous day but nothing seemed out of the ordinary. Only three people had a key for the side door, and the front doors were electrically slid, operated from inside. The distillery itself was split into three parts. The actual place where they made the whisky was in the new building on the right-hand side, where the two giant copper stills lived, along with the mash-tun, four Douglas Fir washbacks (fermenters), a Porteus malt mill and a couple of stainless steel hot liquor tanks. The old building on the left had been restored and now housed the barrels, as well as a small grain store to the rear and the silo which stored the malted barley prior to milling commencing. Following a rather unique process of whisky making only used by Kilchoman and a couple of others, a percentage of local barley was delivered directly to the distillery and malted on site rather than being bought in from the larger malting companies. This required additional labour, as the soaked grains on the floor needed to be turned by hand on a regular basis, triggering it to germinate and thus converting the starch to sugar.

It was the central area that was the showpiece of the operation, consisting of a couple of administration offices, a main reception desk and a tearoom, as well as a sales area housing displays of bottles and artefacts about the original old distillery, along with the recent development plans and information on the region in general. Previously, the only spirit they had to sell was the first year bottled 'new make', a clear liquid that had been drawn off after one year to check its flavours which nobody really drank and people only purchased it as a memento. It had been on the market for a while, but the inaugural real batch of whisky was a recently bottled three-year-old Glenlachan, coinciding with an expensive marketing campaign. Cleverly labelled, Premier, which in French simply meant 'first', it made it sound like a premium malt. Hence it was priced up near £80, much higher than the competition, with the extensive price tag also meant to reflect the unique malting method under which it was made.

The centre attraction of this area were 'THE ORIGINALS!' When Julien had purchased the old building the rumours that there was still some whisky inside were proven to be true.

Formerly the old stone barn had been built in the 1890's. Back then it had been divided into quarters by thick stone walls and as the roof had caved in on one part, trees and vegetation had started to grow inside it. Scott recalled the inside of the barn very well from his younger days but he, nor anybody else, had ever given the rubble a second thought. It wasn't until they came to knock down part of the old store that a collection of 6 barrels had been discovered under the debris, which dated back to the 1950s. Whether Julien had been privy to this information or whether it was just sheer luck, nobody knew, although many suspected the former. The find was kept quiet for a while until a local news-reporter leaked the story and it made national headlines. By this time the barrels had been carefully moved and put on display. Again there were rumours ranging from *all the barrels were full of liquid gold* to *most were empty* through to *they were all full of rainwater*. The story fizzled out without conclusion and the clever Frenchman bided his time before enticing the press back again once the renovation had been near completed. He then invited a team of experts and distillers to a grand summer event where they would tap one of the barrels and declare its contents. The man who could best describe the whisky would be offered a job. Enter Charlie Edis, who hailed it as the best liquid ever, despite it not being from his native Speyside. With a handshake from the owner under the spotlights of the world's press, Charlie declared that he would recreate this vintage masterpiece within five years.

Subsequently, part of the barrel had been bottled, with some of those being sold off to private collectors for sums up to £4000 per bottle, although none had come up for auction. It was suspected that some of these collectors may have been disreputable and probably friends with the De Runcy. At this reckoning, a 200-litre barrel would be worth upwards of a million pounds, which was a figure that attracted a lot of column inches, fuelled by the flamboyant Frenchman who also declared himself an expert in such matters. And there were six of them!

Julien made an announcement that the other five would never be opened and would be retained as a national treasure in a 'stronghold' built in the middle of the reception area, where they were stacked behind bullet-proof glass and under spotlights and controlled climatic conditions.

All this information Scott had recalled from a few years ago and, at the time, was hailed as a good thing, bringing tourists in from around the globe to view what was potentially the most expensive liquid in the world. Money from the tourism had spilled over into the hotel, new bed and breakfast facilities, as well as the campsite, garage and other local businesses. Basically, the Frenchman had been a saviour in the area, to whom many indirectly owed their living. However, although a man of power and influence, all he was really concerned about was producing new whisky that could compete with the well-known brands, particularly those of the western isles of Islay and Jura. Until that point, he had little interest in visiting the area and left the day to day overseeing of it to his son, Jean-Luc.

Scott stood looking down the valley and could see a red quad bike approaching up the track. Beyond it, the milk tanker wended its way back to Taynuilt, now laden with profits for his brother's pocket. He could also see the hotel and the bulky outline of Jean-Luc's vulgar vehicle parked outside and couldn't stop himself from wondering if the lovely Jess had fallen for his charms. Later that day he would interview the man again, double checking his alibi for the night of the murder. Lighting a cigarette, Scott considered the relationship between the boss's son and the 'appointed' boss of this distillery. Had they disagreed about something? Had Jean-Luc been unhappy with the first whisky they had produced? It wouldn't be an excuse to kill Charlie though, surely? He could just fire him and get someone else? And anyway, the man said he was in Inverness that night and someone unquestionably would have noticed him there with that bloody hat on!

Thoughts of Jess ran through his mind again as the bike approached. Scott and her had been an item, back then. A perfect couple. Childhood friends, him returning after his time in the oil field, it wasn't long after his return that he had fallen in love with her. Together they modernised the old stone bothy, calling on her vision to use local materials and keep its originality, and his hard work to pull it together. Until it came to the kitchen, that is, which had come all the way from Italy at great expense. The Italians know how to eat, she used to say, they could show us a thing or two about cooking. Then Jennifer had returned and fucked everything up. Instead of explaining, and trying to make it right, he decided to try and give it another go with his ex-wife and things with Jess got out of hand. That was over three years ago and they had hardly spoken since apart from the odd Christmas kiss and her asking after the animals. Scott shook his head as though trying to clear her face from his mind and concentrated on the young lad circling the bike in front of the building. With no helmet on, Davie had his mobile phone to his ear, pushing back his straggly hair as he switched off the engine. 'Yes sir. I'll see you here.'

Scott strolled across towards him, still wondering at the words, *I'll see you here.* 'Who are you seeing here, Davie? Apart from me, that is?' He tugged the boy's hair. 'And aren't you supposed to wear a crash helmet riding that thing on the road?' He flicked his ear. 'Better watch yourself, there's policemen about!'

Davie looked at him sheepishly, saying nothing and unzipping his leather jacket as he climbed off the bike. 'You wanted to see me, Mr Donald?'

Scott looked him in the eye. 'Haven't you forgotten something, lad?'

The boy considered this. 'I think I told you everything yesterday?'

'The keys, Davie? The keys?'

Davie delved into his jacket pocket to retrieve a set of keys.

'Not those keys. Dim wit. The one for the bike?' Scott reached over and pulled the key from the ignition and handed it to him. 'Do you know how many of these quad-bikes get stolen in Scotland each year?' Davie admitted he didn't by shaking his head. 'Hundreds! That's how many. Makes far too much paperwork for me to deal with every time there is yet another insurance payout. But it's hardly a crime is it? When they are left lying around and ready to go?'

'Nobody's going to steal things around here, Mr. Donald!' He looked around. 'Not a soul about. See?'

'Nobody's going to commit murder round here either?' Scott glared at him now. 'But someone did, didn't they?'

The boy looked taken aback. 'You don't think I did it, Mr Donald, do ya?' His eyes took on a worried glaze.

'And why would I think that, Davie?'

As they walked to the building, Scott considered the words 'insurance payout', which had been one of the motives on his list that morning. But for insurance to pay, something had to have been stolen, didn't it?

Davie unlocked the side door, Scott making a note that it was a pretty solid lock, and switched on the lights. Inside, the distillery was eerily quiet, as he looked around. It reminded him of when he came up here as a kid, except with less rodents! There would probably be a cat in here somewhere. All distilleries had a resident cat, usually called Towser after the legendary Glenturret story of folklore about a cat who had supposedly killed hundreds of thousands of mice.

Since the discovery of the body, they had ceased production of this batch, as it would obviously be contaminated. At some stage the liquid would be siphoned off into the wash-tanks, and then disposed of.

Beneath him, the floor was of polished concrete, still barely marked due to the age of the place, with just the odd scuff here and there of dark rubber marks.

He climbed the ladder once again, peering down into the mash which had already changed in smell now it was no longer being stirred up by the machine. A quick calculation suggested it would be between four and five metres from the ground to the platform. Davie had followed behind him up the ladder.

'You load the barley into here with the fork-lift? Is that your job?'

'No, the barley comes in directly from the mill.' Davie considered the process. 'This went in on Tuesday.'

Scott ran his hands along the railing and then knelt down to the floor at the top of the ladder, running his hand over that as well. 'Do you have to have a licence to drive a fork-lift, these days?' A question he well knew the answer to.

'Took mine last year and passed it easy.' The boy looked proud of his achievement, 'I've been around these machines since I was a boy.'

'You would consider yourself a good driver then?'

'I'd say so, yes.'

'So, this scratch, here, on the metal floor. You do that, mister good driver?'

Davie inspected it. 'Not my doing. I don't lift the shovel up to here. No need to. The bin is filled with a pipe.'

'But it will lift this high, yes?'

'No idea. I never tried,' the boy glanced back down to the floor below. 'I guess so.'

Scott was hastily heading back down the ladder, pulling out his mobile phone as he went. By the time he got to the bottom rung, he was already in conversation. 'Morning Jim. Do you know if SoCo checked the forklift yesterday, it's in the..?' He raised an eyebrow to Davie, who pointed to the next building. 'It's in the grain area.' Scott nodded making his way through the barn door into the rear of the building, as Davie turned on the lights, the heavy switch making a dull thud. 'Thanks, get back to me as soon as you can?'

In the corner, a bright green solid machine on small rubber wheels which looked as new as the rest of everything else round here was parked against the far wall. Attached to the front were two long forks which were under an empty wooden pallet. Scott was bending down looking at it, when Davie arrived behind him. It was dim in this part of the barn and he took out his phone again, flicking on the torch. He was particularly interested in the left-hand edge of it and soon found what he was looking for, a small thread of blue material.

Making sure he didn't touch the rest of the pallet, he

pulled out his phone and was just about to take a photograph of the tiny cotton fibres when a text came through. It was from Jim Murray and simply said 'No, they didn't?'

Scott was just about to reply, asking Jim to see if they could confirm the cause of death when he heard footsteps in the other building. Davie had heard it too.

'Your next appointment?' he asked Davie, eyebrows raised. The boy just stood there. 'Well, go on then?'

Scott had guessed exactly who it was in the building and preferred to keep out of the way and let the two of them talk. For a while he continued to inspect the fork-lift which, as he had also suspected, still had a key in the ignition. Thoughts ran through his head. He was pretty certain that the fibres on the pallet would match those of clothes on the dead man, which led more or less conclusively to the fact that Charlie had been lifted up to the platform, either alive or dead, although he suspected the latter, or at least somewhere in between. Refraining from making a call and alerting their visitor, he sent another text through to Jim in Oban, suggesting they had new evidence and it was crucial that he knew the cause of death. Jim soon replied, 'Death by drowning, but considerable amount of alcohol involved!'

It was a common statement and also something of a joke amongst the force on the west coast. Many a death had been caused by someone drunk falling in the sea or a burn somewhere. 'Considerable amount of alcohol?' Had Charlie been drinking? One thing was for sure, he didn't climb that staircase so someone had put him up there using this machine.

He could hear voices coming from outside, and decided a little ear-wigging was necessary. Quietly he strolled within earshot. As he suspected, the voice was French.

'Of course it ees not a murder, don't be so stupid.' The

Frenchman was doing his best to stop Davie worrying but sounded almost a little too convincing. 'Charlie was a drunk. He stayed behind, drinking up my profits. I know he has been helping himself to my whisky since the day he started. This time he had one too many, and fell in the vat. It was bound to happen sooner or later. I should have fired him months ago. Now production has had to stop until this lot accepts that and stops romancing a silly situation into something it isn't.'

Scott struggled to hear Davie's reply through the thick stone wall but the Frenchman was nearer to the door.

'I don't care what they say, get that barley out of there tomorrow and get the bin and everything else cleaned down. I will oversee this batch of production. You take orders from me, not them. Understand?'

Jean-Luc's footsteps came back inside the door, so Scott showed himself and advanced. 'Ah, Mr de Runcy. I'm glad it's you. Can I have a word?'

'What are you doing here?

'I came to speak to you as a matter of fact. We were just checking out your alibi.' Scott made a show of pulling out his notebook. 'You spent the night in your apartment in Inverness, alone?'

'That's right.'

'Only we spoke the guy in the flat downstairs.' It had just been a phone call on the off chance. And there had been no reply. But Jean-Luc wasn't to know that! 'And he said he saw you go out.' He let this hang for a while, see where it led. It didn't take long.

'He was mistaken.'

'Maybe you popped out to pick up a carry-out or something?'

Jean-Luc took the bait. 'Maybe I did.'

'Do you live alone, Jean-Luc?

'I told you I did.'

'Only he said he never saw you return...'

'Look. Who is this prick downstairs?' The question came out a bit too venomous. 'I have never even seen anyone in that place.' He stared Scott in the eyes. 'This is bullshit! Your whole deal here is bullshit. Making up stories.'

'Stories?'

He turned to leave but Scott stood in the doorway. 'Listen monsieur, the police don't have time to go round making up stories. We have a dead body to deal with. One who died in your father's premises. As yet, all we know is the where, but we need to know the how and why. Wouldn't you like to know that? He was your best man. Put in place by your father to make the best whisky in the west?'

'The man was a drunk and a fraud!' Jean-Luc sputtered the words a bit too freely.

'A fraud?' Scott took his time to follow this up with, 'he had excellent credentials? I thought he was making top whisky for you.' Scott felt the presence of Davie behind him, so he closed the door. 'What makes you think that he was a fraud, Mister de Runcy?'

Jean-Luc backed down, perhaps regretting mentioning the subject. 'Let's just say he wasn't quite as good as we had hoped. His first few batches? Well, I've tasted better.' He pushed Scott's arm out of the way. 'Can I go now?'

Scott stood aside and opened the door, but Jean-Luc turned on his heels went in the other direction. 'I have some paperwork to sort out.' As he headed towards the offices, Scott followed him though into the reception area. Going through into an office the Frenchman turned back, eyeing him aggressively. 'The shop is closed for the winter,' he said, 'not that you could afford anything in here on a policeman's wages!'

'Costs nothing to look, though, does it?'

'As I said, the shop is closed.'

Scott ignored him and took a look around. A diamond shaped rack held a dozen bottles lying on their side on the wall nearest the main door. He took one out and studied the label. 'Premier. This was the stuff that the critics, Jim Murray among them, had said wasn't great. And now Jean-Luc had pretty much confirmed the same. How much did they have? He planned on finding out, but not by asking Jean-Luc. Something gave him the feeling that the man wasn't great with straight answers. In a smaller tub below the shelf, were a stack of miniature bottles of the same whisky. Scott picked one up and pocketed it, glancing up to check if the security camera was watching. It wasn't.

Next he made his way to the centre piece. The 'Stronghold of Originals,' a glass case which stood about 3 metres high in which six casks were stacked in a pyramid. He tapped the glass, as though it was a snake aquarium, which sounded pretty thick. Along both sides were laminated posters, one telling the history of the distillery going back to 1892 and how it was founded by the McKay brothers who farmed nearby. He had once heard his grandfather mention them, a couple of right hard-cases, who had bought their grain from a farm in the valley. They certainly looked the part, all beards and kilts and scowls. The other poster detailed the whisky in these barrels, showing photos of the original distillery, probably taken in the early 60s, and then the state it was in when the French had bought it, including photos of the old barn, just as he remembered it. Then of course, came the subject of price, suggesting that the six barrels were worth over one million pounds each, and how they were sealed in to be preserved for eternity. For all he knew, they *could* be full of rain-water! Nobody would ever know, would they? The casks were apparently made from Spanish oak, imported by sea through the port of Oban. Each one stencilled in black, showing dates of 1949 & 1953, the name Glenlachan, and a series of numbers charred into the wood on each end. He studied the floor beneath the casks, to see it was raised up on a wooden platform about 200mm high, covered in the obligatory tartan of these parts, along with a scattering of acorns and thistles for authenticity. There was a thermometer showing that the contents were on a constant temperature and a small plaque assuring of the ideal conditions in which the casks were stored, as well as the security of the glass. The whole thing did seem very well sealed. As he looked in he could see the reflection of Jean-Luc watching him intensely through a window in the office. Turning to give him a little wave, he left a five-pound note on the counter and went back into the building.

This time he turned his attention to the warehouse through a door to the left, in what was the front of the old distillery. Up in the rafters, oak criss-crossed beams supporting the roof were now aided by iron girders. A number of roof light widows had been added so the place wasn't as gloomy as he recalled it and all the stone walls had been whitewashed. On the racks on the floor were two rows of barrels, again with numbers and dates on the ends. Although the place was big enough for a thousand casks, he suspected most would be sent into a bonded warehouse somewhere, where they would lie and age under secure and perfect conditions until they were perhaps 10 years old. Only then would they be bottled, when the duty or tax would be due to be paid at that time. Whisky wasn't allowed to be called whisky until it was three years old and these, by the date on them were only two. This business was hard on the cash flow when all your sales were at least three years in arrears and some a lot more than that. Although the barrels looked new, Davie had mentioned that they were American oak, previously used to store Bourbon, the USA's equivalent to

Scotch whisky. Only they spelt it whiskey, with an e near the end, such was the difference with the English language across the Atlantic. Some of the barrels would be pre-sold, especially if the tasting notes were good. In richer circles, investing in whisky casks had become a bit of a trendy thing to do and he had read articles how actors, politicians and raconteurs had more than trebled their money in a few years. Gambling was alright, as long as you could afford to lose, that's what his mother had said when he had announced one day that he was going to Perth races for the day. His did lose and, as she predicted, he couldn't afford to. It taught him a lesson.

Julien de Runcy's gamble had paid off though, if those barrels were anything to go by. But if you could afford to leave six million quid sealed up, never to be opened, you maybe didn't need the money anyway? Does anyone have so much money that they don't need any more? Not that Scott ever wanted for much. He had paid for the work at the cottage at the time he restored it, and still had a few savings tied up in a safe bank, should he need a few repairs. He had never had it valued but had a reasonable idea of its worth, based on the sky-rocketing prices of properties around these parts.

Then his mind sprang back the words 'bonded and tax'. Would the owner of those old casks have to pay tax when they were bottled? And if so, at what rate. He made a mental note to check. Firstly, they had a murder to solve.

# Chapter Four

Oban was a wonderful wee place, dating back over 200 years as one of the main sea ports in the west, although the site itself claimed heritage back into the Stone Age. With under 10,000 residents, its population trebled with tourists in summertime and more recently had become an attraction for lovers of fresh seafood. The police station on Albany Street also felt the strain during those summer months and Scott had been drafted in many a time to help out on busier days or crimes that required more manpower. A lovely old traditional stone building with arch sandstone windows on the second floor which, from his recollection let in a lot of draft from the bay, it was the headquarters for Argyll & Bute, which covered a very large area of western Scotland. He had heard that a new Detective Inspector was about to take over, but yesterday was the first time they had met and, by his own admission, it hadn't gone well. Parking was at a premium, even in winter in this town, and he pulled into a space outside the station, putting his badge on the dashboard. Scott pulled a red windcheater over his regulation police issue woollen jumper and walked the two blocks, while admonishing himself that this needed to be a much better encounter. Maybe use the fact she had teased him a bit to start up some banter to get her more on side. He had plenty of charm if he needed it and his chat-up lines had usually worked over the years.

Her stern face at the entrance soon changed his mind and he found himself addressing her as Ma'am, despite her introducing herself the day before as Heather. As they entered a small room off the main corridor, Jim was already in front of a whiteboard, flanked by a younger officer who announced himself as just Bill. Facetiously adding, 'Young Bill, as opposed to Old Bill' and then pointing to Jim! An empty plate on the table offered confirmation that he had missed lunch.

By the time he had poured himself a coffee Heather was already in gear, keen to get on with proceedings. 'Okay, Scott. The floor's yours.'

Scott stood to the front of the whiteboard, still felling slightly intimidated. At the top he wrote the word MURDER, in capitals, then underneath it, 'Charles Edis, Distiller.' Bill stood up and handed him a picture of Edis which he stuck to the board with Blu-tack.

'I believe the victim was possibly semi or unconscious before he was raised on to the platform using a forklift and consequently pushed into the mash-tun.' He looked around at the other three, before continuing. 'As there were no wounds or signs of struggle, it may be the alcohol that caused this state.'

Jim said, 'So you think he got pissed, fell asleep, and then someone came along and hoyed him all the way up there?'

'Or, someone force fed him whisky, to get him drunk?' This was Heather.

Scott nodded. 'Precisely!'

'So, someone bears a grudge, catches him before he goes home at six o'clock. Feeds him some whisky?' Jim was walking through the scenario. 'Some not very nice whisky, perhaps?'

'I'm not sure the coroner could tell us exactly what type of whisky he had been drinking, but we can suppose it wasn't the four thousand quid a bottle stuff!'

'What about this fork-lift? Is it easy to drive? Can anyone do it?' Bill winked. 'Even someone like Jim, here?'

The other three let the joke fall but Scott took up the reply. 'Davie has a licence and, not to put too fine a point on it, he's not the sharpest chisel in the set! I assume

Charlie would have one too, although I haven't checked. But it's not that difficult. Just a few levers and pedals.'

'Assuming this is true,' Heather brought in, 'do we have any suspects?'

'I did draw up a list this morning, but it's just a list, with no substance.' He retrieved a crumpled-up piece of paper from his pocket and then started writing on the board. 'Jean-Luc de Runcy. His father owns the place, he likes to think he's the boss. He didn't get on too well with Edis and yesterday announced that he thought the man was a fraud.' He stopped writing and then remembered something else. 'Oh, and a drunk. He also told the boy that it was definitely not murder.'

'He told you that?' asked Heather.

'Well, no, actually. I heard that though a door.'

Heather gave him a sideways look and Scott recalled how he had accused her of being sneaky when she had written down his words.

'Motive, Scott?' Jim questioned.

'I've been thinking about this one. Obviously it's a bit tenuous but what if Charlie had been drinking when the murderer arrived. Let's say Jean-Luc came in and found him cracking into the bottle and they had a fight?'

'And he falls asleep and the French guy hoys him up into the bin?' Jim shook his head. 'Nah, got to be more to it than that. You don't just murder someone when they are having a kip unless you especially set out to do it? And anyway, didn't he have an alibi?'

'Alibi is a bit thin.' Scott scoffed. 'At home alone?'

'Have you checked it out?' Heather asked. 'Or is this you just making a case for disliking the man?'

'I spoke to one of our guys in Sneck...in Inverness, and they have been asking around but nobody saw him. There is a security camera in the building so we could check the tapes if I can have permission?

Heather nodded. 'Murder suspect. Don't see why not?'

'Right, I'll get on to it later.'

'Doesn't he have a girlfriend? Live in?' she raised an eyebrow. 'On and off, even?'

Scott chuckled to himself. 'Bidey-in you mean? I think quite a few come and go. I'll do some more digging on him.'

'OK, who's next on this exhaustive list?'

'Well, there is the young lad, Davie. Could have had a disagreement,' Scott was looking at his shoes. 'He drives the machine. Could have easily put the guy away.'

'You believe he is capable?' Heather enquired, knowing his answer.

'Nah, doubtful. And he's been quite co-operative. But we can't rule him out.' He had written Davie McLeod on the board. Now he put a cross next to the name.

Heather sighed. 'Who's next?'

'Well, there's a couple of locals that he used to drink with in the pub that didn't have much time for him.'

'Such as?'

'John McCarthy who runs the garage.'

'Jess's old man?' asked Jim.

'Yes. He was bad mouthing Charlie last night. He even said it couldn't be suicide as the man wasn't brave enough to top himself! Admitted he never liked him'

'Motive?'

'Still working on that one.' Scott replied. 'Planning on paying him a visit later. See if there is anything he can tell me.'

'And?'

'Local carpenter. Does a few odd jobs at the distillery. Shifty sort, never quite has a straight answer. Despite being told Charlie's death was suicide, his parting shot to me last night was 'hope you catch the bugger.'

Jim said. 'Sound's an odd thing to say. Especially if he is the murderer himself?'

'S'what I thought.' Scott wrote Dougie Cairns next to the others. 'Could have discovered something about Charlie while he was working up there?'

'Or Charlie found something out about him?' Bill added.

'He'd handle a fork-lift,' said Scott, 'no bother!'

Heather puffed out her cheeks. 'So, basically we have a murder. I have to announce that to the boss, and the press. And all we have as suspects are a man you don't like, and two blokes you met in the pub. Is this what you lot call policing, around here?' All three men looked at their shoes.

Only Bill answered her with 'No Ma'am.'

'Well, get out there, you two, and start knocking on doors. By tomorrow morning, I want more than hearsay!' She turned and left the room, closing the door a little too hard behind her. Bill followed, leaving just the two older officers.

'Were there any others on your list of primes?' Jim said, and then his face cracked into a smile as Scott's started to colour up.

Eventually he replied. 'Actually, there's a couple more, but they are female..'

'And you don't think a female could drive a forklift?'

'I never said that.' He swallowed hard. 'Please don't tell her I said that!'

Jim poured another coffee, Scott declining the offer. 'So, where do we start?'

'If you can deal with the alibi, I'll go and see the locals.'

# Chapter Five

Darkness was starting to close in as Scott pulled his pick-up outside the gated yard while a collie dog on a chain announced his arrival. A door to one of the buildings was slightly open with a light on inside. On the roof a plume of smoke confirmed that someone was home and keeping warm. Avoiding the dog, he didn't bother to knock as he pulled the door back a little further and peered in. The insides of the block-built barn were clad in timber and a couple of extinct calendars decorated the walls, showing the breasts of girls from the last couple of years. Beyond them Dougie stood hunched over a workbench, an arc light above his head lighting his work. Scott meandered across the floor which was littered with timer off-cuts and towards the stove.

'More snow coming in again tomorrow, so they say.' Dougie spoke without looking up.

Scott inspected what the man was working on. It was a long curved piece of wood into which he was carving the words "Abhainn a' Ghlinne Mhòir". A new line of work, Dougie?' he asked, casually.

'Anything to turn a shilling, Scott. You know me? Turn my hand to most jobs.' He looked down at his handiwork. 'Shame the stupid bastard didn't use a simpler name though? Why not call it "Loch View", like all the other folks do?'

Scott smiled. 'Everyone likes to blend in.' He stepped forward and touched the piece of wood. 'Nice grain.'

'American Oak!' Dougie held it up and looked down the curve. 'Barrel wood!'

''From a distillery?' He nodded. 'Got a few broken ones, eh?'

Dougie chose his words slowly. 'Some bugger caught it with the fork-lift. Went off like a firecracker.'

'The bugger being?'

'Yours truly, if you must know.' Dougie put down his chisel and pulled up his visor, taking off his glasses to clean them on his overall. 'No point in wasting good wood.' He turned to face Scott now. 'What can I do for you?'

'Well, that answers my first couple of questions. You do some work up at Glenlachan? And you can drive a fork-lift truck?'

'Didn't say it was from Glenlachan, plenty distilleries around here that I do a few jobs for.'

Scott glanced at a pile of similar wood in the corner, making out the dark crest stencilled on some of the pieces. Dougie saw him looking. 'OK, yes, an old cask from up the road! That what you came to ask?'

'When were you last up there, Dougie?' The question sounded as matter-of-fact as Scott could make it sound, whilst he watched the man's eye's through his glasses.

Dougie made a point of thinking. 'Day before yesterday, as it happens. Why?'

Scott moved back to the stove. 'What were you working on. Apart from smashing up barrels!'

'Fixing a broken lock on the barn door.'

'They had a break-in then?'

'Didn't say they had a break-in, just a broken lock. Spare me the detective work, please?'

Scott smiled to himself, recalling what Heather had said to him the day before. *'something a detective would say!'* But he was a copper and natural investigation went with the job title, and instinct told him there was definitely more to find out from this encounter. He continued, 'How did it get broken then?'

'You'd have to ask Charlie that?'

'Ha fucking ha.' He rubbed his hands down the back of his legs which were starting to smoulder in the heat. 'You never mentioned last night that you saw Charlie yesterday?'

'Don't have to tell you everything? Anything, for that matter?'

'You will if I take you in for questioning.'

Dougie's eyes flickered for a fraction of a second until he raised them. 'What do you want to know?'

Scott turned around, now facing the stove, studying the bare-breasted girl on the calendar. 'How was he? Charlie? How did he seem?'

'A bit pissed off, if you ask me.'

'Pissed off? Or pissed up?'

'Ah, you know Charlie. Always smelt of the stuff. Goes with the job, I suppose.'

Scott recalled that of Charlie. There was always a faint smell of whisky around him. A good disguise for an alcoholic. 'So, what was eating him?'

'No idea!'

Some people were better liars than others and if all people were as bad at it as Dougie was, police work would be a lot easier. He just raised an eyebrow at the man, intimating that this wasn't convincing.

'I think maybe he had a row. With the boss. The big boss.'

'What makes you think that, Dougie?'

'I heard them. Sorta.' The man was starting to squirm a little, knowing he was digging himself into a hole.

'On the phone?'

'Um. Yeah. Kind of.' He looked to the open door, as though someone might be listening.

'Sorta?' Scott enquired. 'Kinda? What exactly did you hear?'

Dougie puffed up his chest slightly. 'I'm not one to tell tales...'

Scott raised his voice. 'Tell me what you heard? Believe me, you would rather tell me than to a rather unpleasant policewoman!'

'They were in the office. And the boss was on the phone. Through a speaker, like. And I could hear Charlie getting a roasting from...'

'Wait a minute. The big boss. You mean the old man?'

'Yes. The big boss'.

'The 'they'?' Scott asked, matter-of-factly. 'Charlie and who?'

The man looked down at his desk, inspecting the letter G he had been carving. 'The other Frenchman,' he said with a sigh.

'Jean-Luc?'

'Yes. It was him who called me in to fix the lock.' He looked down at his boots now. 'Then, when I saw him last night he told me not to mention he was there..'

'Let me get this straight. Jean-Luc was at the distillery on the morning of the murder, arguing with Charlie.' He glared directly at Dougie. 'You were there also, replacing a lock which may or may not have been caused by a break-in?'

'So it was a murder, then?' Was all Dougie replied, getting back to work.

As Scott turned to leave he noted selections of steel rings in varying sizes, hanging on hooks from the ceiling. Lengths of new wood also lay across two trellises. He turned to the man. 'One more thing? Do you make barrels as well as breaking them up?'

Dougie glanced across the workshop. 'Hobby of mine!'

The collie dog started barking as he made his way across the yard to his truck, reminding him he should get back and feed his own one, as well as the rest of his animals. On his way back home, he mulled over the information he had just gained. Jean-Luc at the distillery in the early afternoon, when he was supposed to be in Inverness? Did he really think they wouldn't find out about that fact? And why hide it anyway? It was his place to come and go as he pleased. Arguing with his father on the phone? Maybe it was time they had a chat to him also. As he pulled in to a lay-by by his cottage, he could hear Beth barking inside once the headlights lit up the stonework. Gemma was waiting by the gate joining in with the demands. Scott ignored them a while longer, writing a text on his phone. 'How was the alibi?' He hit the send button and went to in feed the hoard.

# Chapter Six

Jim Murray stopped the frame, winding it backwards a whole minute and checking the footage again on a computer terminal in Oban station.   Behind him Bill looked on pointing a finger. 'That him?'

'That him? How many folks in Snecky wear a beret on their head?' He flicked the younger man's arm. 'Course that's him.' The clock on the slightly fuzzy screen showed 4.56pm as the figure of Jean-Luc entered through the door from a snowy street, stamping off the snow on the mat and heading to the elevator. He wasn't alone.'

'So who's that?' the two men watched as a second person shook off the snow from a large overcoat and stepped into the lift with him. As the doors closed, they embraced. 'That woman?'

'You sure it's a woman?'

Jim shrugged, 'based on what we have heard about him so far, it's a pretty safe bet?'

'So, who is she?' Bill asked. 'His statement says he was alone? A hooker, maybe?'

They slowly wound it back again, freeze-framing on the figure in a long dark leather coat, woollen hat pulled down over her ears. She never looked up and it was difficult to see her face. When Jim zoomed it in as close possible he could see a couple of gold studs in her nose and one through her lip. 'Interesting taste in girls?' he sniffed. 'If she is a hooker, that might make her a bit more easily identified.' When they moved it on, heavy black leather boots revealed themselves from under the long coat. Her back was to them as they got into the lift and embraced. She was a couple of inches shorter than the Frenchman, and very slim.

'Goth?' said Bill. 'Deffo. Probably got form.'

'What's a flash git like him doing with a goth, when he could have any woman he wants?'

'For a change, maybe? They can do some crazy things in bed those sort.' Bill grinned, as though talking from experience.

'And you would know, how?' Jim sneered.

'Just coz I'm a copper, doesn't mean I haven't been around!'

'Only woman you've ever been around is your mum!' Jim was laughing now. 'Now, go get the coffee's in!' While he was away, Jim fast forwarded the CCTV footage. 40 minutes later, the girl came back out of the lift on her own, still ducking her head as though not wanting the camera to see her face. 'That was quick, pal. I heard these Frenchmen are hot off the mark but bloody hell, you hardly got your money's worth, did you?' He watched the woman step out on to the busy street, tugging her hat down against the sleet outside. A while later another couple came in, shaking out an umbrella, the man pulling a key from his pocket and entering a ground floor flat, just in view. He wound it on again and another 25 minutes had passed on the tape before Bill came back in, carrying two styrofoam cups of coffee.

'Did I miss anything?' he glanced at the time on the screen.

'These goths? Fast workers are they?'

Bill looked quizzically at him.

'She was in and out, so to speak, in 40 minutes!' Jim clarified.

'40 minutes? Bloody hell. I know some girls charge by the hour but at least get your money's worth, pal.'

'Exactly what I...' Jim suddenly stopped the frame again.' Wait a minute! Looks like she's back for more!' The two men watched as the girl came back into the foyer, carrying a paper carrier bag. Steam coming from the top. 'Been out for a kerry-oot?' He checked the time on the clock. 6.25pm. As she stood and waited for the lift, they could see the digital number next to it showing it was descending from the third floor.

'Curry, or Chinese?' Bill asked. 'What do Frenchmen eat?'

'Cant think it would be snails, in Snecky. Curry I bet you?'

'You sounding a bit cocky there, Jim? Go a fiver?'

'Save your money, lad. Name on the bag, see?' he zoomed in and they both saw the word Rajah on the side of one of the bags. 'Keep alert, lad!'

Bill feigned an apology as they watched the girl disappear in the lift, it stopping at floor two.

For the next hour they wound the footage on, speeded up to treble-time. A couple of other residents came and went but nothing that seemed suspicious. Eventually, at 8.34am the next morning, Jean-Luc appeared in the lift on his own wearing his beret and leaving the building by the front door.

'Looks like a fairly sound alibi to me,' sighed Jim, still running the tape. 'Went in at 5pm, left at 8.30 next morning, pretty much as he said.'

'Except, he said he was alone?'

'Who's to say he wasn't?'

'You saw him,' Bill's voice raised an octave. 'He had a friend with him?'

'He did when he went in, admittedly.'

'Well, she never came out again? Maybe she had a lie in?'

'Not a lot of evidence. Perhaps she did.' Jim looked up from the screen. 'If you took a goth to bed for the night, would you admit it?' Then he smiled and added. 'Yes, *you* probably would!'

'So what's your theory? Guy goes in there with a girl, she goes out for food 40 minutes later, and then brings some carry-outs back?'

'Carry-outs? I only saw one bag didn't you?'

'So she goes out, gets dinner for one. Maybe they shared it?'

'Or maybe she lives in a different flat in the same building? Went to her place, ate her dinner in front of Strictly-come-Trancing and went to sleep in a coma on the sofa!'

'You saying we believe he was alone, Jim?'

'I'm saying we have nothing to disprove his alibi, son. No evidence to the contrary. And I am pretty sure if we tracked this woman down, she would back up his story.'

20 minutes later, Jim was on the phone to Scott, having relayed the information back to Heather in her office.

'Looks like his story holds up, mate. He couldn't have been there in Kilchrenan and Snecky same time.'

'Can you describe the girl?' Scott was asking.

'About five six, long coat, leather boots, bit of hardware through her snout. S'bout it, really.' Jim thought for a second. Oh, and likes an Indian. That narrow it down?'

'Can you get a freeze frame, and send it to my phone?'

'Now you're asking!' Jim coughed. 'But Billy whizz kid might be able to. Anyway, I could just about draw you a picture, it's that bland.'

'Well, send it as soon as you can. I might have an idea who she is?'

Scott ended the call and started the engine again, pulling back on to the road and heading to the village which seemed busy this morning. Tucking in behind the school bus he flashed his lights to let the milk-tanker through, which was followed by a tractor towing a trailer full of firewood, with Dougie at the helm. He put his hand up to the man who waved back. A few minutes later he pulled the pick-up into a space outside the local grocery shop, heading inside and waiting in a short queue to the till. Jeanie was behind the counter, chatting away to each of the locals about this and that whilst taking their money. It wasn't that she was nosey, or even a gossip by nature, just that it was the done thing to speak to everyone and any news soon spread, regardless of the truth or not. Two places in front of him, a man at the counter was in full conversation. 'Oh aye, terrible thing. Leaving a poor wifie and that young lassie an all. Should be ashamed of himself, doing a deed like that!'

Jeanie replied, 'I heard it was mur...' she stopped herself when she saw Scott standing in line, and changed tack. 'Anyways, things like that are aye a shock to a wee community like ours. Aye. Right you are, then, see you tomorrow!'

Scott waited his turn. 'Morning Jeanie,' he said brightly, as she coloured slightly. This woman had known him all his life, and ever since he was a wee boy she had never called him by his proper name, instead using the word he used to call himself as three year old. It wasn't as though she was trying to embarrass him, just a habit.

'The usual, is it, Scootie?' He nodded and she reached behind her, picking up a packet of rolling tobacco and placing it on the counter. He added the carton of milk he was holding and picked up a copy of the Oban Times. 'We heard about poor Mister Edis. Isn't it terrible? Such a horrible accident!' she lowered her voice to a whisper that could still be heard from the other side of the road. 'Was it an accident, Scootie?'

Scott leant over and whispered back to her. 'Aye, he just slipped and fell, Jeanie. Slipped and fell!' As he leant back he winked at her and she coloured up even more.

Then he raised his voice back to normal. 'Bye Jeanie!'

He knew it wouldn't stop the gossip, in fact if anything, it would spread rumours faster. But the last thing he wanted was the press picking up on a murder enquiry and stomping in from all parts.

Scott's next stop was only three doors down. As he walked in through the rickety door a small bell rung to announce him, doing a job it had probably done for 30 plus years, advising the owner that there was someone in the shop for him to ignore! Scott stepped behind the greasy counter and through a door marked private, into a large garage space, with an asbestos roof, half a dozen cars in varying states of repair and decay, and a workbench littered with tools. John McCarthy was underneath a raised car, a lamp attached to his head, as he whirled a spanner like a magician's wand.

'Time you retired, auld yen?' Scott said with a grin.

'Don't you bloody start!' came a gruff reply. 'Get enough of that from her!'

A short cough came from the far end of the workshop, one he recognised. He didn't actually know what he was going to say to John but persuaded himself it was the father he had come to see. Not the daughter.

'Time you listened to her then, eh?'

'Unless you have come to bring me business, kindly bugger off elsewhere with your infinite wisdom before I sling this seven-eighths in your direction!'

'Well, my pick-up will need booking in for a service, and I think the front half-shaft is rattling again. But, for now, I could just do with a word, please.'

'Socially, I guess!' John put down the spanner and ducked his head from under the ramp, the lamp shining in Scott's eyes.

'Aye, if you like. Must be brew time, surely?' Scott heard Jess cough again. Brew time was the man's word for

'Woman, get the kettle on' around these parts of the world that were still left in the last century. She was no feminist, he knew that, but she did resent being the tea-lady, as he knew she could wield a spanner as well as any man.

The two of them went into the shop and leant on the counter. Scott started the awkward conversation. 'When did you last see Charlie Edis?'

'That what this is about, eh? Word is, someone put him in his own drink?'

Scott raised an eyebrow, waiting for the answer.

'Last week. Came in here, wanting me to fix a bearing. Said it was urgent.'

'A bearing on what?'

'One of the machines up at Glenlachan. In the mash-tun.'

'Did you do it?'

'Sure I did.' Jess put two cups of tea in front of them and her father picked his up. 'For a price.'

'What day was that, John?' Scott was scribbling in his notebook.

'Sunday morning. 8am.'

'Anyone else there?'

"Nope. Charlie met me there, showed me the problem. Fortunately, I keep a few bearings in stock so I took a spare with me and switched them over.'

'How long were you there?'

'As long as it took.' John looked him in the eye.

'How long, John. Come on, I have a job to do here!'

'Let's just say I charged him four hours.' John sipped his tea again, resisting the urge to wink. 'Tricky those bearings!'

'Any you saw no one else?'

'Nope. Did the job, went home. That's it, pretty much.

Next, I heard a few days later, Charlie is face down in the very bin that I had been working in.'

'You didn't much like Charlie did you, John?' Scott looked him in the eye. 'Why is that?'

'Man wasn't as clever as he thought he was. Not as charming either. Lecherous old bastard!'

Jess poked her head round the door. 'Who's a lecherous old bastard? Good coming from you two!'

'Charlie Edis. He came after you, didn't he, Jess? Man was nearly old enough to be her father!'

Scott raised his eyebrows to this comment, waiting for Jess's predictable answer. 'I can look after myself, Dad. And I told you, back off talking ill of the dead, eh?' She retreated back into the workshop, wiping her hands on her green overalls. Scott couldn't help but watch her curves as she went. He took a deep breath.

'Did you notice anything else, out of the ordinary? About Charlie? Or the distillery?'

John shook his head, and Scott was putting his notebook away when he added. 'Oh, there was one thing.' He stopped himself. 'Oh, doesn't matter.'

'Go on,' Scott encouraged him.

'A tractor arrived, with a trailer full of barley. Driver was cussing because he couldn't get into the barn.'

Scott looked up to the ceiling. He had a good idea who would be cussing with impatience. 'My brother?'

John nodded. 'Was nothing to do with me so I ignored him. He must have got in eventually after a bit of banging and crashing, he reversed in, emptied the load and left.'

'And Charlie never came back, before you left.'

'Nope!'

# Chapter Seven

'Well that explains the broken lock then,' Jim said, as the two of them sat in the cafe in the village. 'You think we should go and pay Fraser a visit?'

'All in good time.'

They ordered lunch, Scott going with a lorne sausage sandwich and another tea, Jim opting for pie, beans and chips.

'So, you just came through here for lunch then?'

'Aye. Pretty much!' he smiled. 'That and the chance to interview a goth!'

'Aha, Casanova strikes again.' Scott teased him, making a show of brushing down his hair and the twiddling an imaginary moustache.

'What is a goth, anyway? I know there are a few in Oban, like. What does it stand for?'

'Och, it's just kids wanting to be different. They use some historic cult religion to worship the darker side of life. And probably the darkness. I dunno. I think it's just a ploy to get noticed, to be honest. And have attitude. Have you heard the music they listen to?' Jim shook his head, eyeing his meat pie from both sides. 'Fucking hellish row. That's what it is. Would make your ears bleed to death!'

'But you think this picture is Edis's daughter?'

'Not 100 percent sure. And there's plenty of this tribe around Snecky. But I would suspect so.'

'So, the Frenchman is seeing to her. A bit young for him, don't you think? What's he, 30, 31?'

'Around there. And she's twentyish?' He grinned at Jim. 'Opposite way round to you then, mate!'

They took Jim's marked police car to the Edis house, as

Scott thought it made the visit seem a bit more official. Mary met Scott and the door. Her eyes were puffy and hair not quite as tidy as it should be, as she dusted down her skirt. Scott told her it was Shauna they had come to see.

Mary looked flustered. 'She's not been in trouble again, has she?' Scott said nothing, so she continued. 'She out. At work, she said. Down at the campsite.'

'The Mills' place? I wasn't aware she worked there.'

'Oh that girl seems to have jobs everywhere. One minute the distillery, the next a campsite. I can't keep up with her.' Scott just nodded and thanked her.

He got back in the car. 'News to me, but our lass seems to have a number of jobs. Unless that's just what she tells her mum.'

Jim started the engine. 'Where do we go from here?'

'Is it down to the loch, I fear!' Scott sung out the words which caught Jim by surprise. 'Haircut 100!' he added, just for clarity. Jim shook his head in an 'I have no idea what you're talking about' way and turned the car around. As they headed down the hill, Scott sung out the rest of a verse from the song 'Love Plus One'. On a clear day like this the view from the road down to Loch Awe was stunning, as the water panned out below them, shimmering in the sunlight. Across the loch, Portsonachan Hotel, picked out in white against layers of autumnal orange of the forests beyond, spread its lodges along the shoreline. The road swung to the left and hugged the shoreline for half a mile or so, past the occasional private jetty with a small boat moored up and rugged down for the winter.

Ardnashaig campsite had been built in the early eighties, nestled on the side of the loch with its own wee beach and jetty. It wasn't the most salubrious campsite in the area, consisting of a dozen or so mobile homes, many of which had seen better days. To the loch side there were a row of pitches for mobile homes and campervans which were becoming more popular of late and beyond them a field for pitching tents. A brick-built toilet block was locked up for the year and there was one small blue tent at the far end that looked like it would blow away in a light draft, let alone the winters in the west. Jim swung the car around towards the main office, a white pebble-dashed flat-roof square building with large windows and an ice-cream sign outside. Beyond it a row of tiny lodges, all joined together, opened onto a lawn which was three weeks in need of cutting. A small privet hedge separated what constituted as a garden for each one. The whole property had been bought the year before by an English couple who had spruced up some of the paint-work but not really had the money to outlay for a full refurbishment. Inside the small office, Harry Mills, sat at a desk, typing into a computer in front of a giant panoramic picture of the bay and surrounding hills. Just why he required the picture of such a beautiful scene when he had pretty much the same view out of the window in front of him was anyone's guess, but it did look welcoming.

London born and bred, Harry's had been an existence behind a desk for over twenty years during which time he had dreamt of the outdoor life and the Highlands of Scotland. Using all the money they could muster, they moved north. It soon dawned on him however, although the scenery was much better, a life juggling, people, ground, buildings and more importantly finances still required hours and hours of paperwork which, in the absence of the money to employ staff to take it on, all boiled down to him. He looked up as the two policemen entered and did his best to smile. 'How can I help you gentlemen?'

'Mr Mills?' Scott showed his badge. 'Does Shauna Edis work for you?'

'Shauna?' He sounded surprised. 'Yes, she does some work here during busy times.'

'Is now a busy time?' Scott made a point of looking to the empty car-park and the rows of keys on a board behind the desk.

'Got a few in, yes. We like to stay open to catch the later trade. Still a few walkers around until winter really kicks in.'

Scott was going to add that he knew all about that, having been involved in a mountain rescue of Ben Cruachan more times than he cared to consider. Most of them well underdressed for their endeavours and, he would also add, the biggest number of them English. Before he could relay any of this, a door opened behind Harry through which entered a woman also underdressed for this time of year.

'Liz Mills,' she put out a hand to shake. 'Officer?'

'Donald. Scott Donald.' Liz was older than Scott, perhaps mid-forties, but in good shape, as her tight canvas jeans and cropped top was keen to purvey. Dark hair cut into a bob framed her smile as she oozed just a little too much charm in his direction. Unlike her husband, Liz was a people person through and through. She had held down a few temp jobs over the years, often using the skills she had learned at a young age to intimidate her way in, charm skills she had learned from her father who had been a smiling but ruthless travelling salesman. At school she had had an affair with her art teacher who was some years her senior, just to improve her grades. He had thought it was love, of course. They all did. Those were the lessons you learned from a salesman. Make folks feel good about themselves and offer them what they want. The pay would always follow. Yes, Liz knew how to play men, and play with them too, which she often did, sometimes out of boredom but more often for sport! Scott caught the reflection of Jim's face, his mouth slightly open at the sight of the vision.

'What is it we can do for you, Scott Donald? Have you come to arrest my husband for being a fat lazy bastard?' The word 'bastard' didn't quite fit with the image but somehow she made it sound genial, as though she had just thrown him a compliment. Scott was half waiting for her to hold her hands out and ask him to arrest her in some sort of comedy moment.

Scott had heard about the couple, just from hearsay in the pub, particularly from Dougie. There had been rumours of some nocturnal activity at the camp site through the summer and he suspected much of this would revolve around this woman who exuded sex appeal in abundance.

'Is it about Charlie? That poor man! Such a horrible thing to happen.'

Scott was quite surprised at the statement. 'Were you a friend of Mr Edis?'

He couldn't help notice her make a fraction of a glance at her husband. 'We'd met, yes.'

Scott was trying to place her accent, somewhere in the Midlands maybe, he wasn't great with English locations. 'Actually, we are looking for Miss Edis. Does she work here?'

'Shauna? Work?' the reply came a bit too sudden. 'Yes, she does some cleaning for us, in some of the chalets.'

'Is she here now?'

'I'm not sure,' Liz admitted. 'She comes and goes.'

'Comes and goes. To work?'

'No. Not to work. She has a chalet here. Well, rents a chalet here.'

'You're saying she lives here?'

'Not all of the time. As I said, she comes and goes. The place is rented for six months. We let a number of them go like that, through winter. Usually local workers. Husbands thrown out.' She glanced at Harry again. 'Folks needing to hide from their suitors, parents, enemies. Even you lot!' She actually winked at him. 'It pays a few bills.'

'Mind if we check, Mrs Mills?' Scott glanced up to the keys on the board again.

'Call me Liz, please.' The charming smile was back again. In fact, it had hardly been away. 'Number seven.'

Scott returned the smile, and stepped outside the door, Jim following. He leant against a waste-bin, just out of eyesight, surveying the place while he rolled a cigarette. From inside he could hear the two arguing, Harry raising his voice. 'What you want to tell him we're harbouring folks on the run for? Don't we have enough problems without encouraging the law to start sniffing around?'

Jim's pulse was starting to come back down to normal as he checked the numbers on the row of chalets. There were lights on in more than one of them, and a couple of cars parked behind the building. 'A right little hornet's nest we have here. Would do some buzzing if we decided to kick it, eh?'

'Och well. We will if we have to. But let's keep the profile down just now. If there are wrong-uns here they're better staying put where we know where to find them, rather than sending them running again.' He drew on the cigarette. 'Why would a young woman choose to stay here though? Hardly alive with nightlife, is it?'

'You heard what Liz said. Hiding from her parents, maybe?' Jim sniffed. 'Except she told them she works here?'

'Well, she does, sometimes.' Scott stubbed the cigarette out under his foot, watching a young man in a suit leave one of the chalets and get into a shiny estate car.

Jim clocked him too. 'And who says there is no night life, here, eh?'

'Come on, let's go see what the lass has to say for herself?'

The two men wandered past the rear of the row of chalets. Each had a small back yard with a single entrance door, roof sloping towards the back. A cat lounged in the last of the sun while it set over Ben Cruachan as they eyed a small pink bicycle with tassels on the handlebars outside number four.

Number seven had a maroon Toyota Yaris parked in the space at the back, on fairly new plates. Scott squeezed past it, rattling a spooky looking wind-chime with witches on it as he did so. A purplish glow shone through the frosted pane as he chapped the door. It was a full half-minute and he was about to knock again when it opened.

It was difficult to describe what Shauna was wearing when she opened the door and stood there eyeing the both of them with defiance. Her black mane of hair was pulled over to one side of her head and she wore a black leather band tight around her neck. Below that both men averted their eyes from her exposed cleavage which was just about wrapped in a very tight top with leather laces threaded through it. She had some sort of dungaree outfit below that, with denim braces over her shoulder which would have hardly been required to hold up some very tight black jeans that looked as though they had been attacked by a hedge trimmer! Somewhere in the mix were some black fishnet tights although it didn't feel right to dwell on them. Her feet were bare, toenails blackened, as were her fingernails and lips, which pouted. Although Scott had seen her the day before, and a few times over the last year, he hadn't witnessed her in full regalia like this. Beyond her the room was shrouded in purple haze and a smell of marijuana drifted out.

Inwardly Scott smiled to himself, imagining Jim's reaction on meeting his first real-life goth. 'Hi Shauna,' he said. 'Can we come in?'

As she stood aside, each of the men felt glad the other was there, as they stepped along a narrow passageway towards the main room. To the left a sink and microwave constituted as a kitchen, and a bathroom through an open door on the right displayed a line of garments that they didn't care to dwell on either. Once in the room a giant black poster on the only blank wall displayed a few skeletons around the words 'My Chemical Romance'. Scott wasn't sure if that was the name of a band or an admission of drug addiction, or possibly both. He had half expected to see a skull over the fireplace but was quite relieved when there was just a mirror above a gas fire. It reflected the pretty girl standing behind him, and a further door which he suspected led to a bedroom, although judging by the outside dimensions of this building, it wouldn't be very spacious. A laptop hummed on a low table, portraying geometric shapes on its screen, each morphing into something different every ten seconds. The other wall was pretty much all glass, offering a relieving view down to the loch and the beautiful countryside beyond. He gazed out towards the east, marvelling at the golden glow that was starting to brighten the landscape all the way down the loch and across to Oban as the sun set behind them.

When he had taken enough time to make the girl feel a little uncomfortable he said, 'Where were you the night before last, Shauna?' He turned to watch her eyes as she formed the lie he expected was coming.

'The night my father was killed you mean?' She drew in a deep breath that raised her cheekbones. 'I was in a flat in Inverness!'

Scott turned back to the window again, resuming his observation of the landscape changing colour, giving him a chance to think. Well at least she was brave enough to admit it, although he suspected bravado was something she didn't lack. The question of why she was there didn't really seem relevant at this point and nor did the: Why hadn't you mentioned it when I saw you yesterday? The one he led with was 'Were you alone?' and even this seemed a stupid thing to say.

'What do you think, Scott?' she smiled and her eyes seemed to drill into his reflection. 'You don't mind if I call you Scott, do you?'

'It's not for me to guess, but I would say not.'

'Bingo!' she pulled out a packet of Rothmans. 'Mind if I smoke?' She lit one, before offering the packet. 'Want one?'

'Were you alone?' Scott turned and repeated the question although she had all but answered it already.

She blew out smoke, this time in Jim's direction as she offered him the packet and then pulled it away even before he could refuse. 'No,' she almost purred. 'I don't like being alone.'

Scott wondered why a girl who didn't like being alone lived in a tiny place like this, miles away from civilisation. It wouldn't take too much speculation that she didn't spend much of that time just in her own company.

'Jean-Luc was with you, all night.' His turn to smile. 'Oh, I shouldn't be guessing here, should I? But the night is closing in, and Jim here has a long drive, and I have animals to feed, so let's get on with it shall we?'

'I thought you'd never ask,' she purred.

'Shauna. We can do this down at the station if you prefer. Or you can tell me if Jean-Luc was with you all night, and perhaps why he told us he was there on his own?'

'Yes, he was there all night. Unless you saw him leave? I didn't!' She pulled on the Rothmans again. 'And as to why he denied me being with him, well you'd have to ask him that. Although I suspect he didn't want his girlfriend to know about us.'

'Which girlfriend?'

'Touché!' she made a motion of fencing him with an imaginary sword.

'He has more than one?' Scott made himself look foolish with this question.

'Perhaps it was one of your old ones, Scott. Who knows how many women a man like that can steal?'

The last comment hit Scott in the stomach like a sucker punch and he decided this interview was over. There were plenty of other questions he wanted to ask her, about her relationship with her father, and her work at the distillery, and what other work she did, but decided that he had had enough of her teasing for one day. He signalled to Jim that they were leaving and was about to ask where he could contact her if they needed to when she pre-empted his question, reaching into her back pocket and pulling out a couple of cards, handing one to each of them. It was shiny and black and it was still warm from her body heat. It simply had the word Shauna written on it in purple curly script, above a mobile phone number.

'If either of you get lonely,' she whispered, and then pulled a sexy grin.

Jim was certainly glad of the fresh air as the two of them walked down to the jetty by the loch. 'Bloody hell, man! Talk about being eaten alive!' he half-grinned at his partner. 'Are all goths like that?'

Scott re-ran the interview in his head. Not that it had been much of one, just a few simple questions. According to Jim's assessment of the CCTV footage, she had arrived at the apartment in Inverness with Jean-Luc at around 5pm. Even in that hotshot 4x4 it would be more than a two-hour drive, which presumably would have put him leaving the village not after 3pm. He had sent her out for food at 6pm, and then he had left in the morning around 8am. Scott had visited the Edis place early afternoon that day and Shauna had come in around the same time. So why didn't he bring her home with him? Did she stay there for a few days at a time, maybe? Or had slept in, and then got the train down to Oban, after her mother had phoned her to tell her about her father. Even if she had, she would have struggled to get back to Kilchrenan by early afternoon. Or had she left the apartment by another entrance, him not wanting the CCTV to know she had been there?

'Jim, was there another entrance?'

'What, to this place?' He started to squint around in the fading light.

'No. To the apartment block, in Inverness?' He raised his eyes. 'Did you check?'

'No, I didn't check, but I can. Why?'

'Jean-Luc has a watertight alibi that he was with this girl all night in his apartment. But we never saw her leave with him in the morning?'

Jim looked confused. 'You mean she wasn't there all night?'

'Or he wasn't!' He started to walk faster back to the car. 'Get on the phone to Snecky. Get them to check for a back entrance to that place. I have a feeling we are being played.'

# Chapter Eight

'Ladies and gentlemen, welcome to the prestigious annual Scotch Whisky Awards.' Dressed in evening jacket and dark tartan trousers, James, the society's chairman, addressed the assembled crowd. 'This year we welcome three new judges to our twenty-strong panel, who have worked tirelessly,' a ripple of laughter circled the room, 'to select winners in our list of categories tonight.' Behind him, twenty men and woman walked on to the stage and stood in line under the powerful spotlights. Among their number were most of the movers and shakers within the whisky industry throughout Scotland and other parts of the world.

The Whisky awards had been a long-standing institution which had more recently moved to Glasgow's Hilton hotel and was one of the biggest nights on the whisky calendar. Upwards of thirty circular tables were arranged throughout the room, each being hosted by different distilleries with their guests who had being finely dined at a suitable price.

Jean-Luc had a table of his own, hosting a number of friends and their wives. These included some mates of his own age and a pair of older gentlemen who speculated in the whisky world, with profits from their Glasgow property empire. He felt his phone vibrate in the breast pocket of his dinner jacket and lifted it out to discreetly check the screen. It was a number he didn't recognise so he pressed the red button and put it away. Shortly it buzzed again and he felt a glare from one or two on the table as he checked it again, seeing that the last caller had left him voicemail. This time he switched it off.

'Tonight, the first category to be announced is for the newcomer, an award that shares this honour with some quite salubrious names such as Arran, Kilchoman and Wolfburn, all of whom have received it in the past and gone on to become household names in the industry. Tonight's short list are, Kingsbarns, Fife. A small cheer went up from the far side of the room. Ardnamurchan, from the West Highlands, and Glenlachan from Argyll.

Jean-Luc was already getting to his feet as the chairman said, 'And the winner of best newcomer is Glenlachan.' He made his way to the stage and graciously accepted the award, asking for the microphone.

'Merci, thank you, ladies and gentlemen. Some of you may know we recently had a tragedy at Glenlachan when we lost out Master Blender in a fatal accident. This is for 'im.' He raised the trophy to a ripple of polite applause and returned to his seat. A few people around him congratulated him on the success, including a former international rugby player he didn't recognise. Back at the table one of the older men lent across, shaking his hand and suggesting that the award would certainly be good for business. The other older man just proffered him a wink.

The road was quiet on his way back to Kilchrenan, and Jean-Luc switched on his phone and listened to a message from Scott Donald of the Argyll police constabulary, asking that he report to Oban station the following morning. It was gone midnight by the time he reached the hotel and he was extremely tired when he opened the door to his room.

A darkly dressed figure standing near the window gave him a fright as he said, 'Bravo, mon fils. Vous avez bien fait!'

*Well done my son. You did well!*

# Chapter Nine

'Would you like a coffee?' Bill waved a styrofoam cup in front of the Frenchman who pulled a face.

'No. Your Scottish coffee is shit.'

Bill sniffed the cup. 'You can say that again,' he grinned, taking a sip.

Scott joined him in the small interview room, sitting at a desk opposite while Bill stood against a wall to the rear. Posters on the walls depicted how to avoid drug abuse and other subjects that were supposed to piqué the interest of suspects as they sat in here awaiting their fate, or thinking through lies and stories they would tell the police interview.  On the table a recording device sat with a blue light on, the owner of many a real piece of evidence, when someone let something slip that they hadn't meant to. Stuff that could be analysed, used and reused in a court of law.

He pressed a button so the light went red.

'Interview started, 10.07am, Monday 18th November. Officers Scott Donald and Bill Young in presence with Jean-Luc de Runcy.' He stopped and looked at the man, with his brown eyes and dark features. Somewhere in the back of his mind he imagined this man entwined with Jess and tried hard to override his annoyance. 'Did anyone offer you a coffee?'

'Is it an offence if I declined?' he answered, flippantly.

Scott took a deep breath. 'Jean-Luc, for the record could you state where you were on the night of Sunday 14th November?'

Jean-Luc glanced at the recording machine. 'I was in my apartment in Inverness. I have already told you this?'

'Who were you with?'

This time he sighed. 'I was with Shauna Edis.'

'And can you tell us why when we asked you on the morning of Friday 15th, that you said you were alone?'

'I didn't want to get her into trouble?'

'Trouble. What sort of trouble.'

On the table Jean-Luc's mobile phone vibrated and he glanced at it before considering the question.

'With her mother. Her father didn't like me seeing Shauna. He was very angry about it.'

'Angry. In what way?'

'He warned me. Told me to stay away from her.'

'Did he threaten you?'

Jean-Luc took a breath. 'The man was drunk!'

Scott nodded. 'And when was this? That Charlie Edis threatened you?'

'On Thursday. The day he died. That is why I didn't mention Shauna. I knew what it would look like.'

'What would it look like, Jean-Luc?'

'You know, a man threatens me, then gets killed?' He looked up to the solitary light bulb hanging over the table and then at his phone which buzzed another WhatsApp message. 'It was already well-known that he didn't like me.'

Scott let the words hang in the air for a while, checking notes from a bundle of papers in front of him. Eventually he said. 'Is there another entrance to your building, in Inverness?'

For the first time the man fidgeted but said nothing.

'Only we know that there is,' Scott looked the man in the eye. 'A fire escape, which can be accessed from the third floor?' Jean-Luc still said nothing so Scott continued. 'An exit that is not covered by CCTV. The same exit that Shauna used to leave the building on Friday morning?' he glanced to his notes again. 'We also note from the CCTV footage that the elevator went to the third floor after Shauna went out to get food at 6.05pm?'

Bill spoke for the first time. 'How was your curry, by the way?'

Scott glared at him and then turned back to Jean-Luc. 'Was that you, in the elevator, leaving the building through the back door while she went out front to distract us?'

Jean-Luc put his hands flat on the table. 'Can I call my lawyer?' As if on cue his phone vibrated a message.

'Maybe that's him,' said Bill, flippantly, walking over and picking up the device, reading the list of callers who had recently left messages. 'Popular today, aren't we?'

'If you must know, those are people congratulating me.' The Frenchman pulled his chest in a little. 'On our success!'

'And what success would that be?' Scott enquired, just to appease the statement.

'Last night we won an award. For our whisky. Best newcomer! Now, please may I call my lawyer?'

Scott stood up and spoke to the machine. 'Interview paused, 10.15am.' As the two of them left the room Jean-Luc was aware that he was still being filmed and that probably the other officers were watching him from behind a window. They were.

Jim spoke quietly to his superior officer. 'Award? For that stuff? I thought everyone said it was shite. Didn't he say it himself?'

'You're supposed to be the expert?' Heather stood up from her chair at the window, and brushed the creases from her skirt. 'Not my specialist subject. Can't stand the stuff!' She had been watching Jean-Luc intensely for 15 minutes and he seemed credible enough. Even if he had left the building by a side exit, they had no evidence of him being at the distillery at the time of the murder. Scott was so convinced this was their man she guessed he was ready to make an arrest. She may not be a local here but she suspected his lawyer would have their measure and have him out in no time. Scott met her at the door and she told him as much. 'Nice work in there. But are we any further forward?'

'Well he hasn't denied that he left the building, has he?'

'The law doesn't work like that. Well, not where I come from anyway!' She stared him in the eye. 'We need a confession? At least, that he left the place. Or preferably to murder! So we can wrap this up?' She turned to head down the narrow corridor back towards her office and then stopped and sighed. 'Or at least some more evidence, Scott? Isn't there some other camera somewhere that picked him up?'

'We're working on that.'

'Well, you'd better be quick. His lawyer will have him out in about 30 seconds.'

Scott went and sat with Jim, watching the man through the glass. Jim repeated what he had just said to Heather. 'How the fuck did that whisky win an award?'

'Have you tried it, mate?'

'Nah, I can't afford stuff like that on my salary!' His smile faded away. 'You?'

'Not yet. But I do have a sample we can test. Picked it up the other day and not got around to opening it.' He grinned at Jim. 'How's your taste-buds?'

'Was top of my team at uni, I'll have you know.' He tapped his nose. 'Best in Argyll! Even if I say so myself.'

'We'd best give it a try then, over lunch.' Scott winked.

'Aye, in the name of research.' They spotted Heather coming back down the corridor and he hissed in a whisper. 'Meanwhile, better get some evidence sorted if we are going to nail down this sleazy bastard!' Jim raised his voice so she could hear. 'We're looking at the traffic cameras. Black SUV like that, can't be too many around in Snecky?'

'Narrow it down to around 6pm? If he made it back down to the distillery that night, he'd need to get a shift on.'

'Lawyer's here,' Heather quipped, 'a good one too!'

Scott looked at the man in his expensive shoes but didn't recognise him as Heather led him past. 'Bloody hell, has this guy got a time machine or something?' He shook his head. 'That suit must be a Weegie, would take him a couple of hours to get here from Glasgow?'

Jim watched him go. 'My guess he had him already on route. Shauna must have warned him we were on to him. Got his reply lined up.'

'OK, I'll go back in, you round up those traffic guys, and fast.'

Half an hour later, as predicted, Jean-Luc had signed a couple of forms and was walking out of the door of the station.

# Chapter Ten

Set a couple of streets back from the harbour, Scottish pubs don't get much more authentic than Aulay's Bar on Oban's Aird's Crescent. During summer months an exotic display of hanging flowers welcomed tourists into its crowded rustic front bar, complete with wooden decor and bar lunches. To describe the other half of it as a lounge was a tad overstating it but, particularly in winter, it tended to a bit quieter. Scott looked up at the masses of paintings of ships from a past era, almost wallpapered together on one wall while another was decorated with pub sports trophies denoting achievements, both past and present.

Jim returned from the bar with four glasses, three of which contained a centimetre of golden liquid, the fourth being empty. He also had a plastic litre bottle of water under his arm. 'Right then chaps, let's have a little test shall we?'

Bill looked at the glasses and up at Jim. 'What are we celebrating? You retiring at last?'

Jim glared at him. 'I bloody would if I could. But this government says I got another decade to do yet!'

'To be fair, Jim. All governments agree that we need to work till we're old.' Scott picked up one of the glasses and held it to the light. 'If only to pay for the youngsters to have an easier life!' The last comment was aimed at Bill but it washed over him.

'Can someone tell me what's going on here then?'

Jim took the glass back from Scott and placed it back on the table. 'This, my boy,' he told Bill, 'is a lesson.' He mixed up the glasses until even Scott couldn't tell which was the one he had just picked up. 'Right, two single malts. One blend, and one..?' He looked to Scott who produced a miniature from his jacket pocket, the bottle that he had picked up and paid for in Glenlachan distillery two days earlier. Jim checked the label, unscrewed the top and poured the contents into the empty glass. 'And one prize-winning three-year old.'

Turning to face the light, Jim held up the first glass and swirled it around for half a minute, eyeing the liquid. Then he held it under his nose and gave a great sniff, inhaling the fumes deep into his throat. He placed the glass back on the table and Scott picked it up, doing the same.

'Islay,' he said, recognising the hint of TCP that accompanied peaty whisky, as Bill spluttered after his inhale.

'Now man, don't get too far ahead of yourself. Let the boy try as well.'

Jim was already on to glass number two, again taking the scent deep into his lungs and saying nothing. The three of them went around in turn again, and then Jim took a tiny sip, analysing the taste before pouring in a tiny splash of water into the glass.

'Water?' Scott raised an eyebrow. 'I thought you connoisseurs took it neat.'

'That's where you are wrong.' He swished the liquid around. 'We nose it neat, to get all the aromas from it, get a wee taste of it neat, but then water opens up the flavour, ya ken?' he offered the glass to Scott.

'Better go easy, I'm driving.'

'That's why you get first taste. I'll mop up, don't you worry!'

Scott took a tiny sip and swirled it around in his mouth, placing the glass in front of Bill. 'Definitely Islay, west coast, peaty. Laphroaig or Lagavulin.' he continued.

Bill concurred and Jim drained the glass. 'Laphroaig,'

he said, licking his lips. 'God's own nectar. A real man's drink.' He reached for the next glass. 'Well done. Although it is probably the most easily recognised whisky in the world.'

The next glass the two novices found harder to pin-point.'

'It was harsh on the nose', Bill was keen to impress, 'but much softer with water.'

'Aye lad. A dash of water certainly helps.'

The third one they all tasted and agreed it was much smoother, softer flavours. Scott even pointed out hints of vanilla.

Then came the last glass. They all nosed it again, and then went through the tasting. 'Bloody hell!' was all that Jim said, and his face showed he didn't mean it in a nice way.

'Right. We had a Laphroaig, hard peaty strong, west coast whisky. Followed by a Whyte and Mackay table whisky, straight out the optic, although some around here would sup it from a brown paper bag at under a tenner a bottle. Then we get a super smooth Aberlour, straight out the Spey River. Lots of flavour but not strong enough to put hairs on your chest!' He picked up the empty miniature bottle, checking the label again. 'And then there's this stuff that I wouldn't even put on ma chips!'

Scott tucked into an egg sandwich as they walked back to the station, the other two chomping on chips, with extra vinegar to soak up the smell of whisky. 'So you're saying that the Glenlachan three-year old is not good enough to win a medal?'

'Aye, that I am!' he chucked a chip to a scrounging seagull. 'And wouldn't be if you kept it for another ten years either! Lord knows who was on that judging panel?'

Jim's phone rang and he rested the chip packet on a waste-bin while he fished it out of his pocket. Within seconds, his eyes lit up. 'That's braw. Send it through. I'll be at my desk in five.' The same seagull grabbed at the packet now and he batted it away with his fist before turning to Scott.

'We got him, at the Raigmore roundabout! 7.30pm!'

# Chapter Eleven

It was surprising how much traffic the A85 main road carried as Scott set-off home from Oban, stuck behind a lorry carrying concrete. As the days were getting shorter and shorter when the road pulled inland from the sea for the first few miles, he could already see the sun starting to go down. When the road opened out the expanse of Dunlaridge bay to his left, with its modern marina, was already taking on a golden luminescence. Rather than race to overtake the slovenly vehicle, he pulled his pick-up on to the side of the road for a few minutes to think. Rolling a cigarette, he admired the tall masts of expensive boats moored up in the water below him, just like a giant car-park, all paying fees for their winter stall. Some of the more expensive ones, or moreover the ones with wealthier owners, would be lifted out of the water and stored on dry land for the period. In fact the Marina had been extended over the last few years and was now one of the biggest and smartest on the west coast. He had heard rumours that Jean-Luc had a yacht out here somewhere but he didn't know which one. If it was anything like his car it would be flash, that was for sure. Stepping out into the sea breeze he leant on the bonnet, breathing in the spectacular view and considered the afternoon's proceedings.

The video of the Raigmore road wasn't particularly clear, as it had been a dark and drizzly night, but they were certain of the number-plate and the time. Unfortunately winter rain had been thick with snowflakes and it was impossible to see how many people were in the car or identify who was driving. Despite numerous phone calls they hadn't been able to reach Jean-Luc or his lawyer since both of them left the station, which was quite frustrating, if not alarming. But the most interesting thing was, if the Frenchman had been heading back to Glenlachan distillery to commit a murder what was he doing at Raigmore which was at least a couple of miles in the wrong direction? This in itself bugged him even more than the fact that Glenlachan whisky had just won an award for which, according to his sources, it was unworthy. That wasn't really a crime was it? But it did open up perhaps another motive. He checked his watch as the sun submerged itself on the horizon and set off again.

As he neared Connel some of the traffic indicated left to continue up the coast towards Fort William via Glencoe and he hoped the truck had gone that way too. The cantilever construction of the steel bridge was over 100 years old and at the time, along with the Forth Rail bridge which had been built by the same company, was one of the longest rail bridges in Europe. It was subsequently adapted for a road as well and this evening, as it spanned the quarter of a mile estuary, the low light picked out its silver paintwork against the backdrop of the gilded Highlands beyond.

After the junction, the main road turned inland, passing the Falls of Lora, a tidal set of rapids that was a mecca to kayaking enthusiasts in spring, and hugged the shore of Loch Etive with its black water shimmering in the evening light. Through a clearing he could see the moon already starting out on its night journey, round and full, ready to replace the golden aura with its traces of silver. Such a contrast to just a few nights ago when winter threatened to set in for its long four months, tonight was maybe the last time he'd see this road at its best, as he wound the five miles or so towards Taynuilt. There would be a frost tonight, that was for certain. Once he turned off the A85 the journey got a lot slower, climbing steeply in single track through the wooded hillside that closed it back into darkness. His headlights picked out a red deer with her fawn that jumped from the road to the safety of the bracken beside it. Although only a further five miles, this stretch of road made up over a third of the journey time from Oban, but Scott just took it in his stride, a journey he had done a million times before. Oncoming headlights heralded a vehicle approaching and he pulled into a passing place to wait for it, the driver of the twice daily milk-tanker peeping his horn as a thank you. Up to his left a track led towards an open quarry that was used to supply stone to repair most of the roads in this area. A few heavy machines sat in darkness, as the moon glinted off the steep stone face above. Then a chicane of bends let you know the road had reached the summit and it started its descent again. As a boy this was the best part of the journey, when you could let the brakes off and coast your bike down round the sharp bends, cooling off for a mile or two until the loch spread out before you. Scott drove on a bit more cautiously these days until the lights of Glenlachan loomed from the right-hand side.

He checked the clock on his dashboard, 5.35pm and, assuming they would still be open, swung the pick-up into the tarmac turning and up the short road to the distillery. His tyres rattling over the cattle grid could well announce his arrival to whoever was inside and he looked around for Jean-Luc's car but there was no sign of it.

As well as the quad bike there was, however, a van parked near the side entrance. Scott studied it for a second, pulling his pick-up closer before stepping out and poking his head inside the building. Noises were coming from the barn to the far side and he stood and listened to what sounded like barrels being rolled along the concrete, as well as a distant low hum.

'How many more?'

Scott recognised Davie's voice, calling from a distance.

'Another one, at least!' This shout was unmistakably Dougie Cairns, 'In about half an hour! Go get the kettle on, I'll see to it here!'

Scott squinted into the darkness, past the stills to

where there was a light on in the next building. Shortly Davie came out through a doorway from the barn and entered the offices, flicking on the main light. Scott let him go and waited till he heard the kettle start to boil and the boy close the door to the lavatory, before creeping quietly across the main floor to the doorway to the barn. Adjusting his eyes to the light, he focussed on a hosepipe across the floor towards the area where the barrels were laid in rows. The other end of the pipe trailed towards a door in the interior barn wall that he hadn't noticed before and he looked around, before heading over that way to get a closer look. A set of stone steps led down to what looked like a cellar. In all the years he had been coming here as a boy he had never realised there was a cellar in the place.

That was the last thought he had, after a heavy blow caught him on the back of the head and the lights went out. And pretty much the same one he woke up with five minutes later.

Around him the building came slowly back into focus as a hammering ache ticked away at his skull. He put his hand up to feel a wet towel wrapped around his forehead and stains of blood covering his fingers. Resisting the urge to shout out he realised he wasn't tied up and had no other injuries that he could feel.

Behind him a voice said, 'I am so sorry, Mister Donald. I am so sorry I hit you. I thought you was a murderer, Mister Donald.'

Scott raised his hand for the apologies to stop, and climbed unsteadily to his feet, looking directly at Davie. 'Bloody idiot,' he growled. 'You could have killed me!'

'You shouldn't creep around in the darkness like that. Not after what happened. I thought you was the murderer coming back to do some more murdering, Mister Donald. And then,' the boy looked like he going to cry, 'then I thought I'd killed a polis man!'

Steadying himself against an upright barrel, Scott

glanced around again. Something was different. The sweeping sound of a broom materialised into Dougie who was cleaning up the floor and whistling a tune. He saw Scott and grinned. 'Oh, you back with us then? Poor lad thought he'd done for you. How's the head? He must have hit you pretty hard, you've been out for a good while.' He looked hard at Davie. 'Well, don't just stand there, eejit. Go and get Scott a cup of tea.' As the lad scurried off, Dougie added. 'Anyway, what were you doing sneaking around in the darkness?' He pulled a small flask out of his pocket and offered it to Scott who accepted the gift.

'I might ask you the same question?' He took a swig, his second taste of whisky that day. Swilling it round in his mouth, he sniffed the top of the hipflask, and then took another pull. It certainly tasted better than the stuff they had tried earlier.

'I'm just helping the boy out. He had to clear the mash out and needed to move a couple of barrels.' Dougie took up with the broom again, sweeping grain dust across the floor towards the store behind the barn. 'Your brother's coming for it, later.'

Scott perished the thought of seeing his brother, especially with a thick head like this and the thought of him teasing him about being a copper and being sneaked up on by a young lad. He and Fraser had never really got on, even as kids. The man had an awkward streak in him and always seemed to revel in an argument, even when he was wrong, as he often was. He had a nasty streak too, which he often enforced with bullying fists. Scott's eyes focussed on the barn in front of him and the scene he had walked into a few minutes earlier. Walking around the barrels he noted that they were all sealed, but he could have sworn there was a pipe leading into one earlier. He traced his memory to the other end of it and the door in the barn wall. It was little wonder he hadn't seen it before as it was now covered by a sheet of hessian that draped over it from the beam above. 'What's down there?' he asked, impatiently pointing to the wall.

'Down there? Nothing really. Just an old cellar.' Dougie blew his nose on a dirty looking handkerchief. 'A few rats and that!'

'Has it always been there?' he stopped and considered the absurdity of the question, as if they would have just dug out a cellar in the last year or two. 'Usable, I mean.'

'I guess it got cleared out when they rebuilt the place. Couldn't tell you, exactly. I never really came in to the old place. It's damp, though. Stinks in fact.'

'You were running a hose pipe down there earlier?' Scott tried to picture it, going down the steps and Dougie's voice at the bottom above a humming sound.

Dougie's eyes went upwards for a second before he answered. 'Yeah. The water's getting in. It does when the burn's in full flow.' The man went back to his broom. 'We were pumping it out. Weren't we Davie?'

Scott turned as Davie offered him a steaming cup of tea. 'Yeah. Pumping it out, that's right.'

He sipped tea, feeling his head thumping again. 'Pumping it out to where, Davie?'

Dougie answered the question for him. 'Just outside onto the gravel. Silly I suppose, really. Pump it outside and it'll just drain back in again, I guess.' He shrugged, continuing his work.

Scott considered this and recalled a conversation he had heard earlier. Earlier being maybe ten minutes ago but seemed much longer. The words, 'another barrel!'

Outside he heard the rumble of a heavy vehicle crossing the cattle grid and guessed it to be his brother arriving for the grain. He decided to let his investigation of the cellar wait until daytime.

'I actually came here to find your boss. Has he been here this afternoon?'

Both men shook their head, although Scott couldn't be sure this wasn't them just denying it and obeying orders as they had done before. As the tractor circled the barn, so Scott made his exit through the side door and headed down the hill to the village. Glancing into the car-park of the hotel he noted there was still no sign of the Porsche before wending his way through the bottom of the village to his cottage. When he got there, another car was parked outside.

# Chapter Twelve

'How long you do you think you can get away with this for.' Jean-Luc sat on a cold rock, staring out to a landscape lit by moonlight from a vantage point high up above the old quarry. Its reflection ran the whole width of the loch now, like a white line on an otherwise jet-black canvas. It wasn't his native Bretagne, but there were some similarities about being in the far west of the country, the way its ruggedness became untameable if you went far enough.

Opposite, a man stood wrapped in a heavy coat, taking in the same view, his grey hair showing silver in the light. He spoke slowly, in French. 'Get away with it? It's you they are after, I think?' The older man pulled a sarcastic smile. 'I'm not the one running away?'

Jean-Luc stood and pulled his hands under his armpits for warmth. Now the clouds had dispersed, the temperature dropped like a falling stone. 'Running away, to protect you, Papa! It's you that has done wrong. You can't remain invisible forever? These people will look for you.'

The smile had gone now, replaced by a look of power as he faced up to the younger man. 'Oh, but I can,' he snarled. 'By tomorrow morning my work here will be done and I can be back home and untraceable.' His cold eyes bore into his son's. 'Nobody will know I was even here! Not even them.'

Jean-Luc sat back down again, the granite almost icy beneath his denim jeans, and sighed. It was a good thirty seconds before he spoke again. 'What should I tell the police?'

'About the whisky?' he sniffed. 'Nothing to tell. We

employed an expert. We made some good spirit. It won an award. Now it stays in the barrel for two more years until they forget about it. End of story?'

'Except the man who made it is dead.'

Julien raised his voice. 'I made it!' he shouted. 'It was me. I made the whisky. In my own distillery! I am the master!' The words echoed down the valley, as though the old man's ego was commanding an audience. 'That man was just an employee. That man...' he dropped his voice again. 'That man was my man. He did what I told him to. And you will do the same.'

'He was murdered, Papa? The police believe he might have been murdered!' Jean-Luc stayed still, focussing on the moon itself now. 'They are looking for me because they think I killed him.'

'Nonsense. They have no proof. The man always drank too much. And he stole from us. He drank too much and fell to his death. They have no proof of anything else. And they never will.'

The son stayed quiet a moment longer, looking at his father's silhouette. 'And the other ones?' he said softly.

'I'll take care of them when the time is right,' was the simple reply.

# Chapter Thirteen

'How long have you been waiting?' At last a bowl of food had managed to contain Beth's excited barking long enough for Scott to speak. It wasn't just the food and her master's return that had triggered the dog into such a frenzy, but the visitor herself. And this was a very special visitor. So much so that she had known where the key to the cottage was, let herself in, found some old newspaper, sticks and matches, and lit the fire in the grate, while Beth helped by adding her exhaustive commentary.

'Oh, about three years!' Jess gave him that smile, the one that teased him to his core. The same one she had used as a child, when she had one over on him and was about to pounce. He recalled the time when the two of them were no more than eight or nine and she had hidden his bicycle and then pretend to help him look for it. 'Why don't you call the police,' she had teased. For half a day they looked around everywhere for it but, once they had looked in his granddad's barn and not found it, she went and moved it from its hiding place leant against the stone dyke in the fold-yard and put it in the barn! An hour later in between fits of giggles she gave him a clue and suggested maybe he hadn't looked hard enough in the barn.

'And to what do I owe the honour?' He opened the fridge, checking the contents.

'I needed to speak to you.' Jess recoiled a bit, as though not quite sure how to approach the subject.

Scott pulled out a pack of chicken thighs and raised an inquisitive eyebrow. 'Can it wait until dinner?'

'Why, are you going to poison me, again?' The smile was back once more, the one he so adored but also feared for its seductive powers. When she looked at him like that he remembered his love for her, and how she could wrap him around her little finger whenever she wanted. Then his heart sank at the recall of the vindictiveness she showed when she had thought he wasn't treating her right. Back then, maybe he could have handled it better, when she accused him of sleeping with Rachel he went off on one until she retaliated, bashing him with her fists as she had done when they fought as kids. Although he would never admit it, this was not just the only woman he had ever really loved but, apart from his grandmother, the only one he had ever feared.

'Aw, come on. We're not still calling that one?' he smiled back, playing with her emotions and gauging the reaction. 'It was just a stomach bug. And too much wine!'

'I was sick for two whole fucking days, Scott!' Her eyes narrowed for a second and then she burst out laughing. The laughter broke the ice. This woman could still smile when she was mad at him but when that laugh came, it was from the heart. And the one thing he believed his childhood friend had was a great big heart. 'You were a terrible cook, back then though.'

'Back then?' he grinned. 'I'll take that as a compliment!'

She shook her head. 'Sorry, can't stay though. I will make it another day, I promise?' Then she noticed the blood on the back of his head. 'Are you alright?'

He pulled his hand up to the lump and shrugged. 'Just a small misunderstanding! I'll be fine.' He opened an eye-level cupboard. 'A glass of wine then?' before she could reply he was already reaching down two large glasses.

'Alright. But just a quick glass. I have to get to work

tonight.'

'New Zealand Chardonnay okay?' He knew the answer to that one. In fact these days, despite its price tag, it was pretty much the only white wine he drunk, and always kept one chilled in the door of the fridge. Until he had gotten back from the rigs, he hadn't known a Chardonnay from a shandy, such was his lack of sophistication of the subject, but she had taught him, slowly and surely, in the same way she had taught him to cook, and he was forever grateful for those lessons. Pouring the wine he encouraged her to sit at the table. 'What's on your mind? Got some pub gossip for me?'

'It's my Dad, actually?'

Scott looked genuinely surprised. Her Dad was one of the strongest men he knew, both physically and mentally. 'Your Dad? Is he OK?'

'Yes. I think so. I dunno, really.' She took a sip from the glass. 'He's been acting kinda strange.'

'In what way?'

She ran her hand through her cropped hair. 'Oh, just, secretive. Like he's up to something. Like, he knows something?' she sipped the wine again, a gulp this time, and then nodded the glass towards him. 'This is good by the way!'

'Cloudy Bay!' Scott puffed his chest out slightly. It was a bottle he had been saving for a while. At nearly twenty quid a pop he couldn't afford to drink it regularly. 'Have you questioned him about it?'

'You know what he's normally like. Quick with an opinion. Ready to offer his ten-penneth on just about any subject. Well, lately he clams up, like he's worried about saying something he shouldn't. Maybe it's nothing, but I would say he is hiding something.'

'To do with Charlie Edis, you think?'

She nodded, as though answering would put her in a

bad light with her father.

'There was certainly no love lost between them.' Scott answered. 'He made no bones about that.'

'Not just about Charlie's death, but with Jean-Luc as well. Everyone really. Like he's disinterested in it all. Which is so unlike him?'

Scott agreed that was most unlike the John McCarthy that he knew, but then used the sentence to open up another subject.

'Jean-Luc and him don't get on either? You do though, don't you?' It was a hard question and he knew he shouldn't have said it. In another situation he was likely to get the wine thrown in his face but he thought she may restrain herself as she was on his turf.

'Don't you bloody start,' was all she said, raising her eyebrows. Scott stared into her eyes as she did so and felt a massive pang of relief. He would have reached across and kissed her were it not inappropriate, especially as she seemed genuinely worried about her father. But the way she said it confirmed his belief that she had rejected Jean-Luc's advances, despite what Shauna had said.

'You think I should question him?' he searched for an easy way to say it, but couldn't. 'Officially, I mean?'

'To be honest, I'm not sure you would get any more answers out of Dad than I would. You know what a stubborn old brute he can be when he wants to.'

'So, why come to me, Jess?' The question was an official one now. A police matter was a police matter.

'Let's just say that a few of them might be up to something.' Glancing up to the clock on the oven, she drained her glass and went to stand.

'A few of them? A few of who?'

'Well, I wouldn't trust old snake eyes, for one. They are definitely sharing something that neither of them want to talk about. And I wouldn't be surprised if fat Harry and his promiscuous wife weren't in there somewhere!'

'You sound like you're two steps ahead of me.' He took her hands as she stood up. 'As always!' Inwardly he considered 'old snake eyes' as a reference to Dougie and again his heart skipped at how scornfully she considered the man.

'Maybe I'm putting two and two together and getting the maths skewed, but something doesn't seem right. That's all I'm saying. And, whatever it is, it has to do with that distillery.' She patted Beth on the head as she made for the door. 'Thanks for the wine, Scott. And for listening.' She was just about to give him a peck on the cheek when he turned her face towards him and made the kiss real, enjoying the moment.

'I promised you dinner,' he said quietly. 'And a promise is a promise, OK?'

Jess pulled away from him. 'Sure. But I'm late, gotta go!' A rush of cold air filled the room as she opened the door, Beth following her outside.

'Just one other thing,' he asked. 'Have you seen Jean-Luc? We are looking for him!'

Jess stopped in her tracks, whipping around. 'What makes you think I would have seen him?' Just the way she said it. The way she looked at him took him back to their childhood again. As though she herself knew more than she could let on.

'Oh, no reason. I know he had been staying at the hotel, that's all.'

She climbed into her battered old hatchback and he watched her head back up the hill, wondering at the real purpose of her visit. Had it been to tease him? Or seduce him? Or something a little more complicated, like a warning?

A noise behind him made him jump and he realised it was Gemma up against the old stone wall outside the door wanting her evening meal as well. Absentmindedly he fed the animals while he pondered the brief conversation they had just had. It certainly had dawned on him that some people were not telling him the whole truth but he thought that was just him being cynical. Most folks clammed up when being interviewed by the police, cautious not to incriminate themselves even if they were as innocent as a new-born fawn.

The day before he had drawn up a list of suspects and since then had interviewed all of them in a systematic fashion, but to no real avail. Apart from a thin slither of material in the forklift, there was no more evidence other than Charlie Edis had either killed himself, or been drunk and fallen in the vat. There was one more person to speak to though, but that could wait until morning.

As the fire crackled in the grate, Scott pulled out the crumpled list again, glanced at it for a minute or two and then put together a pan of chicken and vegetables that would have been enough to share. It was still cold in the sitting room and he switched on an electric radiator to take the chill off until the fire did its job. Then he went through to the larger bedroom, flicking on the switch that brought on three rows of spotlights that dazzled his eyes. Quickly he tapped on a bedside light and knocked the main switch off again, before putting on another similar heater in the bedroom. Then he stripped and headed for the shower, waiting for the water to run hot before stepping in. Beneath him the tray ran crimson with blood as the head-wound re-opened and spilled some more, but the warm water felt good on his body and he let it flow for a half a minute or so before soaping his hair and applying a towel to stem the flow. In the mirror he considered his athletic frame, noting that the years were starting to make themselves known and that he was maybe getting too old to be clouted on the head in the name of duty. Lesser men on the force would claim a few days off for such an injury but that wasn't really his style. He might be rapidly approaching forty but he wasn't there yet. And anyway, it was only a number. As he dried himself he considered that somewhere some boffins must have an equation or algorithm that compared your muscles with your age and divided it by some variable, multiplied that by how many injuries you had had to come up with a life expectancy number. You could possibly even find the answer on Google if you looked hard enough but it didn't bear thinking about. At what age did you start looking over your shoulder? Scott's father had died young, well relatively so, anyway. His mother was now in a home, tucked away and tucked up.

The thought led him on to John McCarthy, a man with plenty of advice to hand around, but also a man in whom you felt there was plenty more, left unsaid.

# Chapter Fourteen

Ardban farm had been a smallholding since the 18th century, nestled on the edge of Ardban Bay, about three miles south west of Kilchrenan. To reach it you followed the single-track road through thick woodlands, keeping Loch Awe on your left until you went over a cattle grid that rattled the hub-caps off the tourist's cars. It wasn't a busy road as it didn't really go to anywhere that couldn't be reached by better ones, but it was picturesque and more recently attracted the odd campervan who may stop and overnight park at its side with a view of the Loch. Once you passed the cattle grid you were on Ardban land until you crossed a further one which said you weren't. Scott's grandfather had taken over tenancy from the Duke of Argyll before the Second World War and then added some better acres at Achachenna a decade later. By East and Central Scotland standards Ardban was hardly high-quality grazing land and it certainly wouldn't be fit for arable produce or the massive combine harvesters that gobbled up crops like Pacman, but over the years the thin soil had been turned and cultivated into decent grassland that would provide for a small herd of dairy cows as well as the inherent sheep that grazed the rougher hills. The land at up at Auchachenna was different though. At least twenty acres of that was under the plough and, back in the day, the milk would be bottled for the locals and sold either at the farm gate or through the shop in the village. Now all the produce was bought up by conglomerates of dairy processors who mixed it, treated it and processed it into cardboard cartons that would keep it fresh for half a week or more. The farm's fifty-odd cows were contained by means of an electric fence that not only ran the perimeter but also dissected the fields in criss-cross patterns which varied according to the season, always leaving a main track back to the farm buildings so they could make the trip twice per day to be milked.

Scott parked on the grid itself, watching the hybrid black and white beasts lumbering out to a pasture after their morning drain-out to munch what sparse seedlings there were left this time of year. With winter fast approaching this would be one of the last few times they saw or tasted fresh greenery for three months or so, instead being corralled into a couple of large airy buildings with dry straw underneath and steaming silage at meal times, scattered with the remnants of barley that had had the single malt squeezed from it! When he was younger Scott used to feel sorry for the cows at winter housing time but as he got older he suspected a life without their natural diet and space was probably far more preferable to the harsh west coast winter weather on their backs. Plus it gave the ground chance to breathe and recover its composure, without a thousand hooves per day rotovating it up into clarts that stuck to your legs like toffee. At the back of the throng his brother Fraser followed, perched on a red quad-bike which was idly ticking over, with a disinterested sheepdog making the trip for company. Beth sat up on the seat by his side, viewing the dog with interest and occasionally curling her lip up to show two rows of perfect canine teeth. A few years older than Scott, Fraser had a much more rugged appearance, not helped by layers of grubby attire that suggested the washing machine was broken down and a flat cap that he was rarely seen without. He raised a forefinger on his handlebar in recognition of his sibling, without making eye contact, and continued slowly on his journey up the hill through the trees. Once he was gone Scott fired up the pickup again and drove down into the farmyard and parked behind the old farmhouse, obscuring his view of the loch.

He knew Annabel would offer him tea, biscuits, even breakfast if he wanted but declined to go to the door, instead waiting patiently until his brother returned, checking his mobile phone. An email from Jim had suggested that the image that had been stilled from the traffic camera in Inverness contained two figures in the front. This would shake the theory that Jean-Luc had headed out on his own, leaving Shauna in the flat with her curry. That was, of course, if it were Shauna in the vehicle with him. Then there was a text from Jess simply saying, 'Go easy on him.' He was just replying to that one with a smiley faced emoji when he spotted his brother coming back onto the yard on the bike.

Scott stepped out and faced him, reeling at the smell and recalling it was probably what he whiffed like when he was a teenager. 'Fraser,' he said and offered a half smile.

'Scott. Don't see you back home much these days.' He pulled his cap back to scratch his head and Scott noticed how far back his hairline had receded since he last saw him. 'You here for breakfast. I am not sure if we...'

Scott put up a hand to decline. 'Just for a quick chat, that's all.' He rolled a cigarette to signify that he didn't want to come into the farmhouse, somewhere he hadn't been for more years that he cared to remember.

Fraser made towards the back door of the house, leaning against the wall to remove his waterproof trousers and wellingtons. 'Shoot.'

'You were up at Glenlachan this week?'

''Up there most weeks at present. Those boys seem to keep making batch after batch.' He smiled at Scott. 'Which suits me fine. Sell em barley at top dollar and buy it back for tuppence.'

'Sunday? You were up there Sunday.'

'If you say so?'

Scott noticed the obligatory hole in his brother's sock as the boot came off. He ramped up the conversation. 'You do know the man is dead, don't you?'

'What of it? Nothing to do with me. I don't take my orders from the blender.' The other wellington came off with a popping sound. 'Only from the boss!'

'What was your relationship like with Charlie Edis?'

Fraser chuckled out loud. It was a sound he had always made when stating something obvious and vindictive at the same time; a natural trait of his. Always looking for the upper hand and then making sure everyone knew about it. 'Edis? He wasn't worth having a relationship with, was he. Not unless you were a woman, anyway. The drink got to him way too young. Women and booze! The death of any man, if you ask me?'

Scott felt his hackles rising. It wasn't just the mess and hard work that made him leave the farm. He could have coped with that all too well. It was his brother's attitude. Always so quick to judge. 'Just answer the bloody question, Fraser!'

'I hadn't much time for him.' The man's face reddened. 'Bloke was a dickhead. Full of himself, bragging all the time. Usually half full of whisky, too.'

'Why did you break in to the barn?'

Fraser stood up in his socked feet, one hand on the door handle and raised his voice. 'Who says I broke in?' he glared at his brother. 'That what you doing here is it? Come to arrest me for breaking in?'

Scott stayed calm. He knew when he had him rattled. For all his brother might be a bully, he had always known how to wind him up and get him mad. 'Just doing my job, Fraser. Checking out all the facts. A witness says you broke the lock, with your tractor.' He walked a few paces nearer so he could catch his sibling's expression. 'Well? Did you or didn't you?'

Fraser relented. 'I was running late. Edis was supposed to meet me there and open the doors. I phoned him when I got there and there was no reply. I assumed he was either asleep or out with his fancy woman.'

'And which woman would that be?' It was news to Scott that Charlie had been anything other than a family man. But then, a daughter like Shauna must have got her genes from somewhere.

A sadistic smile crept across Fraser's face. One he saved for victorious moments. 'You don't know do you?' He slapped his hand on his knee and a cloud of dust dispersed on impact. 'Call yourself a copper. A man gets killed. And you don't even know who he was shagging?' The chuckle was back again. 'Bloody hell bruv. You are supposed to uphold the law? I'm surprised you can even uphold your own trousers.'

Scott tried very hard to resist the urge to step forward and punch the man squarely in the face. 'Who?' he demanded again, in a calm and collected manner. 'I might not be Chief Constable, but withholding information is still a crime!'

Fraser had the door open and was stepping inside. 'Liz whats-her-face. Her down at the campsite.' The door slammed firmly closed behind him.

His mobile phone dropped off the dashboard as Scott rattled back over the cattle-grid much faster than he had arrived. It was not so much that he was in a hurry, just that whenever he met with his brother it always left him in a rage that he had never quite been able to control. To his right the expanse of the loch opened up again and he decided to take a few seconds to cool down, pulling the pick-up to a halt. Dark clouds were rolling in across the water and the wind whipping up a storm which nearly took the door out of his hand as he opened it and stepped out, pulling his collar up and strolling to the shore. Small waves were washing up piles of leaves on to the shale stones, splashing cool fresh water across his face. When the rain did come, he suspected it would fall as snow on the higher ground up near the distillery as it had done a few days previous.

'Come on then?' he called to the dog who responded by hurling herself off the seat and charging down to the shoreline. He watched her go, feeling the guilt of never walking her enough during winter, unlike in the summer months when the two of them would scale a mountain most weekends. One of the blessings of living in this part of the world was that there was no shortage of hills to conquer. Known as Munros after Scottish mountaineer Sir Hugh Munro, who sadly never climbed all of them, there are nearly 300 mountains over the height of 3000 feet in Scotland and many of them on the west side of the country. In fact the sport of 'peak-bagging', as it had become known, was growing in popularity with over 6000 members now enrolled in the Munro society, an exclusive club who's only joining criteria was to have climbed every one of them. Attempts at this, of course, posed a problem to the local forces of which Scott was only too well aware. One of the finest of these mountains, and the one he was looking at right now was Ben Cruachan and its neighbouring Stob Daimh. Although not quite making it into the top thirty hierarchy, at 1126 metres it still very much kept its head in the clouds. Today its lower slopes were white with snow and he suspected it would be coming down hard at higher altitude. He hoped there weren't idiots up there scaling the ridge walk this morning for a glimpse of the reservoir, even in their expensive hiking gear.

Somehow, the roar of the wind seemed to fuel his anger rather than curtail it as he stared across the loch. He knew Fraser would be smugly tucking into a farmhouse breakfast, probably bad-mouthing him to his wife at the same time. It shouldn't bother him, he knew that, and he had walked away from the battle a long time ago. But, one way or another, the wounds just re-opened themselves at will.

Shaking his head, he turned back to the last fact, the only fact actually, that his brother had divulged. Why hadn't Scott known about Charlie Edis and Liz Mills? Assuming it was true, despite it seeming quite an unlikely match. Was that what the locals were all being close lipped about? Why should a secret like that stay under wraps when the village was rife with gossip about just about anything and everything? It wasn't as though marital affairs were scarce in these rural parts. Quite the opposite, he suspected, although gossip was not one of his strong points. What had Fraser said? Call yourself a copper and you don't even know who is shagging who?

Absentmindedly he picked up a flat stone and skimmed it across the rippling water, watching it fade after just a couple of bounces. In the distance Beth was investigating a rocky outcrop, her tail wagging frantically. She'd probably find some dead animal, and then roll in it profusely until she smelled hellish, stinking out the truck until they got home and washed her down.

'Beth!' he called out. 'Come on, we've got work to do!' She couldn't hear him through the wind, so he trudged his way along the slippery stones until he was in earshot. Reluctantly she obeyed and was soon bouncing on to the passenger's seat, not smelling as bad as she might.

In his mind, his day was already mapped out to be pretty busy but he added a further trip to the campsite to the list before pointing the truck back along the loch and up to the distillery. As he climbed the hill snow was already starting to fall and he was glad of the vehicle's four-wheel drive. It was incredible how the weather could turn so fast in this area, often experiencing the cliché of four seasons in one day; another reason why Ben Cruachan demanded more care than most.

# Chapter Fifteen

The lights were on in the building as Scott pulled up the track to Glenlachan. Again, there was no sign of the Porsche Cayenne and they had had no contact from Jean-Luc since the previous morning. It would be up to Heather whether they would issue an arrest but, as yet, she still wasn't convinced he had done anything wrong, despite Scott thinking otherwise.

He pulled the pick-up near the main door, so he wouldn't need to walk quite so far with the snow coming down. He made his way to the glass door before recalling that the visitor centre was closed this time of year. The side door was unlocked, once he made his way along the slippery path to it and he welcomed the warmth from inside. He decided to call out from the doorway, remembering what happened the last time he visited unannounced. 'Hello. Davie?'

The lad soon appeared, looking as flustered as ever. 'Hello, Mister Donald. Are you alright?' He was looking at Scott's head, which now had a baseball cap over it. 'I really am sorry about your head.'

Scott didn't think he looked that sorry but he didn't say so. In fact, the more he considered the evening before, he wondered how Davie had made it out of the toilet and around behind him without him hearing him. Had the attack been innocent? 'Mind if I take a look round?'

'He's not here, if that's what you are looking for. I came into work today but have nothing to do. I need some more orders. I have phoned him!'

'You and me both, lad.' Scott immediately made his way to the large hessian sheet hanging from the wall of the barn. Questions were already forming in his mind. Why keep this door covered up? Maybe just to stop the damp coming through? He folded back the sheeting to reveal the heavy wooden door, only to find it padlocked securely. Something just didn't feel right. He called Davie over. 'Why lock this door, Davie?'

The boy looked at the lock and then back at Scott, thinking. 'I dunno. It has always been locked. Nobody really goes down there!'

'But you were in there last night. Or at least Dougie was. Round about the time you tried to crack my skull?' His eyes bored into the lad who shifted uneasily. 'The key, Davie. Where is it?'

'I dunno, Mister Donald?' Maybe Doug has it. 'I'm...'

Scott had got hold of him by the lapels on his jacket, quite surprised at the strength of the lad considering how thin he was. 'Look, I've about had enough of this all innocent '*I dunno Mister Donald* shite.' He shook Davie for effect before raising his voice. 'Now get me the key to this fucking door before it becomes my turn to knock you out!' Davie bristled and tightened his stance, showing a more aggressive streak but he was no match for Scott who yanked his arm behind his back. 'Now!' he shouted.

'Alright, alright! I heard ya.' Davie's voice had changed slightly, speeding up. In fact his whole demeanour had altered, as he shook himself free. 'It's in the office. I'll get it.' Something about the way lad spoke suggested that he wouldn't get it at all, but was about to run, so Scott followed him closely, ready to nail him to the ground when he tried to bolt. When they got into the office, Scott closed the door behind them as he watched Davie take a small key from his pocket and unlock a drawer under a wooden desk. He reached inside and Scott found himself saying 'Easy, Davie. No sudden movements.' Maybe he had been through too much training or watched enough detective series but Scott had a suspicion that the boy would pull out a gun from the drawer and was quite relieved when he saw just a set of keys in the lad's hand. He still made a point of checking the drawer himself though just in case a weapon was on show. Davie chucked the key to him and he flinched before catching it and then saying, 'You're coming with me, lad.'

'I'm not going down there. There's rats!' Davie had reverted back to the frightened boy that Scott thought he was, but he wasn't buying it this time.

'Well tuck your trousers in your socks, then.' He pulled a grin. 'Stops them running up your leg and biting yer baws!' In his mind Scott had pictured the boy letting him go down the cellar and then locking the door with him inside. Nope, he wasn't buying that trick. Whatever there was down there, they were going together and this boy had some serious explaining to do. He opened the door from the office and pushed the lad in front of him as they entered the bigger barn and then pulled the curtain back again.  Before he undid the lock, Scott looked at Davie again. 'I'm going to give you the benefit of the doubt lad. Unless you have something to confess right now, I am going to believe that you have done nothing wrong. OK?' His eyes narrowed. 'And that you are helping the police with their enquiries, willingly.' He turned the key, removing the padlock and sliding back a stiff steel bolt. 'But if you wanna run?' He looked him in the eye, questioningly. 'I'll catch you, arrest you and charge you. Understood?'

'What with?' yelped the lad, but Scott was already pushing him inside the dank doorway. Although it was musty, there was also a smell of disinfectant. That and whisky. As he switched on the light, a single bulb revealed the stone staircase that Scott had seen the day before, leading to another illuminated space below. 'You first?' he said egging the lad on and then pulling the door closed behind them and fastening it with another bolt. At just over of six feet, Scott being the taller of the two had to duck his head under the stone archway as they descended the steps.

All in all, it was about four metres square and the air was thick and very chilly. A couple of single light bulbs, one hanging in each archway of the ceiling, did nothing to give the place a welcoming feel. Scott pulled out his phone and switched on the torch, shining it into the corners and ducking his head from arch to arch. Now and again he flashed it up at Davie who was looking nervous at best as he said, 'See. Nothing here!'

Scott considered this but had already started to realise that the lad had not been very forthcoming with the truth of late. 'No, nothing here,' he repeated. 'Not even any water?' He shone the torch down on to the cobbled floor. 'In fact its remarkably dry considering it was flooded yesterday?' The boy said nothing.

It wasn't the floor that took his interest though, but a few stone blocks in the ceiling, which looked considerably newer than the rest of the ancient stone that he suspected dated back over a hundred years. Tapping the blocks with his knuckle and then comparing to the other stones, these three definitely sounded hollow. He pushed the torch up close, checking around the edges until he found what he was looking for. A pair of hinges, barely visible. Again he glanced back to Davie who was fidgeting. 'Come over here, lad. Where I can see you.' Davie moved until he too was under the newer stones.

'And are you going to show me how this opens, or do I have to smash my way in?' He was considering retreating back up into the barn to get a crowbar he had spotted in the grain store when Davie reached past him. A smaller stone at the far end turned sideways, revealing a handle.

'You'll need to help,' Davie said, resigning himself to the fact that Scott had found what he was looking for. While he stood under the stones, placing both hands on the ceiling, Scott released the handle and a panel above them opened a fraction. 'It's bloody heavy,' Davie grimaced under the weight and Scott helped him lower the panel, about 50 centimetres square until it was hanging vertically on its hinges. The section was made of 25mm plywood and faced underneath with stones that had been cut to a similar depth and fastened on to it with screws from the top side. The whole cover had looked very realistic and he suspected nobody would ever notice it unless they were looking closely. Above the panel was a cavern of maybe a metre cubed and there was even a folding wooden ladder hooked up the one side.

Scott's next question would have been to ask what part of the distillery was above this cellar but he had already figured out a few minutes earlier that it was directly below the main foyer. As he shone his torch up into the gap, he could see another wooden platform on its top side. A brass tap was fastened to it, with small brass pipes spreading out like a manifold to each corner. Fastened to the side wall he could see the machine that was making yesterday's humming sound, an electric pump about the size of a tennis ball with a flex cable leading from it to a plug socket on the ceiling. The whole area wafted with the sweet smell of whisky.

'Well,' he reached up, unclipping the ladder and folding it down to the floor. 'What have we here, Davie?' He grinned at the boy. 'What *have* we here!' The ladder just about reached to the cobbled floor and it was quite a squeeze for Scott to get through the gap and climb the couple of metres so that he could reach the ceiling above. He tapped it with his knuckle and realised it was hollow above. Looking down at Davie below him he asked, 'What happens if I turn on this tap?'

Davie simply said, 'I wouldn't advise that you do that.'

Scott considered his words and decided that it was time the lad did some talking. Five minutes later the kettle was on and the two of them sat in the warmth of the canteen. Scott had sent a brief text to Jim in Oban simply saying: 'Developments at the distillery, will call you later.' Now he had his notebook out and was filling in the time and date. As Davie returned to the table with two cups of tea he eyed the lad and then let out a half smile. 'Thanks, son.' Then, taking a deep breath, he added. 'OK, let's start with you?'

The boy removed his hat and sighed. 'What do you want to know?'

'Your full name, address, some history, that sort of stuff.'

'Am I being officially interviewed?' Gone was the worried demeanour now, replaced by something more confident and co-operative.

'Yes, you are. Now we could go down to the station in Oban and do this officially, or you can offer the information in a voluntary manner. Up to you?'

'Let's get on with it, then.' Davie just sipped his tea as though lubricating is voice. 'David Robertson, born Hamilton, Glasgow, nineteen years ago.' His eyes went back into his head as he recalled the place. 'In the schemes. Laighstonehall.'

Scott recalled Laighstonehall, one of the more notorious blocks in that area, and the rough lads that patrolled it. It had been nicknamed Wine Valley in the 80s and had a pretty tough reputation. He encouraged the boy to continue.

'Didn't do too well at school. Didn't do well at anything really. Never had a dad. Joined in one of the local gangs. Spent a few years on the dole and got in a bit of bother. Me Mam had a habit, but I stayed clear of the stuff. Saw this job advertised, thought it might suit me to be away from all that shite for a while.' He looked up from his cup, almost apologetically. 'Changed my name to McCleod, plenty of them round here. Got use of a caravan down behind Collaig house. Kept my head down, did what I was told.'

'When was that?'

'Just over a year ago. Last September.'

Scott was writing without looking up. 'You got a record?'

'Is it important?' he sniffed. 'Nobody has asked me about it.'

'Well, it is definitely illegal. Changing your name to hide a police record. Won't take me many seconds to check.'

Davie sighed. 'Yes. Just the once. Me and a few lads boosted a Merc. Got away with a caution but I guess it will be on file somewhere. Didn't think it would look good in an interview so hence the name change.'

'And adopted a simple image?'

'Look, Officer. I just kept my head down, did my job.' He cradled his cup in his hands. 'Learned a bit as I went. Took my pay.'

'Girlfriend?'

He nodded. 'I seen Shauna a few times, but she was too sharp for me.'

Scott drained his tea and stood up, taking a look round the room. Outside the snow had calmed down again and was already starting to melt.

'OK, so let's move on to your work here. And your relationship with Charlie?'

'Charlie was alright!' The lad said abruptly. 'A bit lazy. And had too much to say. But he was alright with me. Sure he made me do all the dirty work. General dogsbody, but I didn't mind. We were a team, and he was the boss.' Davie sighed again. 'When he was sober.'

'What about when he wasn't?' Scott took the chair again, going back to his notebook. 'How often was that?'

'Quite often,' Davie continued without looking up. 'Especially lately.'

'Why lately?'

'He didn't tell me everything but he was starting to get pissed off with the place. With the job. Complained that the grains weren't right. That the water was wrong. Any amount of excuses. And Jean-Luc piled a lot of pressure on him to get the whisky perfect, every time.'

Scott let that subject sit for a while and changed tack. 'What about his personal life?'

'What about it?'

'Well,' Scott thought it best not to mention what his brother had said and see if this interview backed that up. 'Did he mention it? His life at home? Mary? Shauna?'

'He wasn't keen on me seeing Shauna if that's what you mean?'

'I was more concerned with if he was seeing anyone?'

'You mean Liz? Oh, he saw her alright.'

'Regularly? Up here at the distillery?'

Davie looked down at his shoes. 'Not during the daytime. Not often, anyway. But she would often arrive. In the early evening.'

'You saw her?'

'The odd time. She didn't know that though. Just spotted her, out the back, waiting til I went home. It was a secret, but not very well kept. Drunk folks can't keep secrets, can they? That's what my Ma used to say.'

Scott agreed with this statement. 'Who else knew?'

Davie stood up. 'I don't know. A few folks.' He took a few steps towards the toilet. 'Mind if I...?'

'On you go.' Scott wrote the words Liz Mills and underlined it in his notebook. The fact his brother had been right on this one irritated him but he let it go. He had a couple more questions on the subject: one, whether her husband knew and: two, whether she had been there on the night of Charlie's death? Giving both some consideration he decided to ask her those two questions. Hearing the toilet flush he waited to confront the lad on more pressing matters. 'So. You want to tell me about this cellar?'

# Chapter Sixteen

Jean-Luc watched the coffee in his mug swill slowly from side to side but without quite reaching the edges. There was something about the motion of being on the water that was both soothing and irritating at the same time. It wasn't the most salubrious of boats, not by super-yacht standards but the *Jeanneau 32* did have a reasonable level of comfort and enough room to move about below deck when the weather turned rough. Not many people lived on their boats on this side of the earth and his was never that intention either. He just needed somewhere to get his head down and keep his distance from the world for a day or two until he could work this thing out.

Running his hand over the back of his seat he admired the craftsmanship of the cabin's intricate interior woodwork, which oozed style and panache right down to the chromed hinges and handles. The two rows of long white leather seats would pull together to form a decent sized double bed, if the need arose. In the centre of the fold-leaf table he could see his distorted reflection in the stainless-steel pillar that underpinned the main sail. Beyond the cabin was a further bedroom, the one which he used, its double bed tapered towards the stern and neatly laid out with towels and white sheets. During summer he would have a maid and cleaner in each day to make sure everything was perfect, especially when he was entertaining. Those months were taken up with clients who masqueraded as friends, as well as a few of his fellow French pals who would make the trip over by light aircraft. Each would be accompanied by a pretty girl and if not, Jean-Luc had a list of plenty on his phone, some who came along just to enjoy the food, wine and highlife, others who charged a hefty fee for the honour of their company. Up on deck there was seating for four, or six at a squeeze and room on the bow for the girls to sunbathe, if the weather allowed. He considered the boat's official model name, the *Jeanneau Sun Odyssey*, to some people it was a contradiction in terms with the west coast of Scotland. But then, up here it wasn't about the blue skies, but the rush of the westerly winds that changed and challenged on every journey. He had named the boat Jouer Sur Mer, literally meaning 'play on the sea.'

On good days he would head up the different lochs, each one surpassing the next with their never-ending beauty where the mountains met the water. Loch Linnhe, past the Island of Lismore up to the inlet at Ballachulish and the valley of Glencoe, once a famous battlefield, and then on into the serenity of shelter in Loch Leven, where the waters could be as crystal blue as the shores of the Caribbean. If the winds were right, he would occasionally tuck in behind Lismore and into the bay at Port Appin where a trip ashore would be rewarded with a meal in the fabulous Pierhouse Hotel with its cosy dining room or outdoor covered terrace serving seafood to die for. From there he could negotiate his way into Loch Crennan, again into much calmer waters once away from the open sea. These were the days he lived for, pitching his wits against the elements as the sails rippled and strained to keep his path. Of course, these modern yachts had all the toys on board where a computer would do the work for you, if you so wished, but he still liked the feel of that four-foot steering wheel under his grasp.

Although they would occasionally fish, he had a 'tame' fisherman in two or three ports where a man in oilskins would wheel on a whole box of fresh plaice and local langoustines caught the night before and layered with crushed ice. The electric fired portable stove he had on board would grill just about anything with precision but when the sun was out he preferred a stainless barbeque using dried driftwood he bought from a man in

Oban. Being a Frenchman, cooking was in his blood and his natural skills in the kitchen were the envy of many, something that fed his desperate ego.

He sipped at the coffee, attempting to focus on the daily newspaper on the table in front of him. But each time his mind got hijacked by the events of the last few days. He thought of Shauna, a pretty girl, ten years his junior, and her beautiful slim body and how she liked to tease him with it. And about how he had used her, paid her, to stand in for him as an alibi. Then there was the death of Charlie, the incompetence of whom he despised, especially when he bragged about the prowess of his nose and taste as though he was some sort of genius of the spirit world. Well, he was with the spirit world now, full of spirit, as it happened! Jean-Luc pulled a smile at the irony of the way English words always courted each other, even in death. But the subject of his death hadn't made this week's local paper's deadline and he assumed from that the police hadn't called it in. They would be still looking at angles and needing an arrest before they would admit it was murder. As his father had said, they had no proof. Jean-Luc knew he would need to turn himself in shortly, maybe this afternoon, maybe tomorrow if they hadn't worked out where he was already. Then they could go through their farce of an interview again, taunting him with false information in an attempt to trip him up on his own words, their words, their English words. Rather than worry him this made him think about the language again, and its modification in this part of the world. A world where a whole new language had unintentionally been preserved for centuries, often using completely different words for everyday things such as bonnet for a hat and lum for chimney, as well as some of his favourite ones such as crabbit and skulduggery, the latter sounding like something a pirate would do! He was guessing that would be what best described what his father had been up to these last few days. Probably for most of his life, if the truth be known. Never a person to sit still, the old man would always have some scheme on the go, never quite illegal but always sailing close enough to the wind to be controversial at best and downright immoral at most. Skulduggery, ha, yes that was him. Sailing close to the wind, there it went again, a reference so apt for this situation. He glanced out of the porthole window where the wind rattled the masts of a hundred or so other boats. There was no way he was going out in this weather either. The water may be little more than a light swell hidden here in the bay behind Dunlaridge Head but he knew what was just around the corner.

The waves would get bigger, that was for sure!

He made a decision and pulled out his mobile phone.

# Chapter Seventeen

'Let me get this straight?' Scott was doing his best to take the information in and understand it, before he wrote it down. 'You are saying that you have been instructed to siphon whisky from the old barrels, and store it elsewhere?'

Davie nodded without repeating himself, as though this was just another part of his job description.

'Correct me if I am wrong, but the whisky in those barrels is supposed to date back five or six decades. And worth thousands.' Scott glanced down at his book. 'If not millions?'

'Don't ask me,' the lad shrugged. 'I don't touch the stuff. Had my share of that shite when I was in Glasgow. It does weird things to me!'

'So, you didn't taste what was in them?'

'Oh, I took a sniff, when Charlie offered it. Don't get me wrong, I could tell one from another, when it was pointed out to me. But once I had a taste,' he gulped for effect, 'that burn in the back of my throat gave me such a jolt I nearly threw up.'

Scott recalled the whisky tasting he had done with Jim the day before. How each one smelled completely different once you put your mind to it. But drinking it neat? He had to admit, they all had a similar effect. Like trying an Indian curry that was too hot? The menu could identify all sorts of ingredients to you, but all you got was that hit of chilli that could only be quelled with a cold beer. He said, 'How often did you do this?'

Davie thought for a moment. 'Three, maybe four times, that I was involved in, anyway.'

'Just you and Charlie?' Scott asked. 'Or were there

others helping?'

'Dougie Cairns was there a couple of times but the big bosses never got their hands dirty with the day-to-day stuff.'

'Day to day stuff!' Scott whistled through his teeth. 'Day to day stealing of millions of pounds worth of whisky!'

'Nobody was stealing it, though?' Davie pulled his cap down on his head. 'Just moving things around. That's what Charlie said. Moving it around...' He stopped, thinking.

'Moving it around and what, Davie?'

'Moving and mixing! Those were Charlie's words. He used to say, never mind the 'movers and shakers,' we are the movers and mixers of this world.' Davie had his eyes closed, mimicking Charlie's North East accent. 'See that certificate on my office wall, lad? Master Blender, that's what it says. Move it and mix it lad. That's what we do! Good with the bad, bad with the good, get the recipe right lad and they give you a medal.'

Scott stood to his feet, intrigued by what he had just heard. As though the world of alchemy had just opened up its pages. 'So, where did you put it? This stuff you didn't steal?'

'You can't accuse me of stealing anything!' Davie stood up too, his tone outraged. 'I just helped the men do their job!'

Scott repeated the question. 'Where did you put it?'

'Special barrels. New ones.'

'New ones?'

The lad nodded. 'Yeah!'

'Why new ones?'

'Search me.' He looked Scott in the eye. 'You'd better ask the bloke that made them.' Davie headed towards the door.

'Oh, I will,' thought Scott. 'Go on, then,' he nodded towards the barn. 'Go and do some work.'

It took Scott another ten minutes to write down all he had just heard in some sort of assembled order after Davie had left. As he read the notes back through he looked at the names he had underlined. Jean-Luc, Liz Mills, Harry Mills, Dougie Cairns. Then there was the next person on his list to visit that morning. Was he in on this too?

Before leaving he wandered into the main foyer, spotlights coming on automatically as he entered, giving the place the glistening brightness of a shopping mall. For a while he studied the large pyramid of barrels on the centre stage, sitting innocently sealed in their glass case to be admired by many. He wondered how much whisky was really in them, and what sort of whisky it was. Then he followed through to the barrel storage barn, meandering along the four long rows of wooden barrels, each with marks and logos from a previous life, when they would have stored port, sherry, rum or even bourbon. That was all part of the process, so Jim had explained. Store that neat stuff in oak that had once stored something else and everything changed flavour. Like putting tea in a cup that had just had vinegar in it. He tapped a couple of the barrels with his knuckle, not quite knowing what sound he was looking for, but assuming they were full - of something? One barrel piqued his interest, as it was discoloured slightly more than the rest. Below the name Glenlachan, a tiny squiggle was carved lightly into the wood. Scott pulled out his phone and took a couple of photographs of it and then pocketed it again. It may just have been a scratch, or it could possibly be some initials. 'D' and 'C', perhaps?

Pulling out his car keys, he made his way outside where the whiteout of the snow had given way to the kaleidoscope of a brown-stained world. Through the swirling wind the roar of the burn made its presence known, delivering this morning's offering off the slopes of Ben Cruachan back down to the loch once more, like one of those ornamental garden ponds that run in endless circulation as long as there is something to pump it around. In this case, nature was the biggest pump of all.

As he drove he considered pumps in general and how effortlessly they could move liquid from one place to another as long as the pipes were connected correctly. 'And probably back again,' he heard himself saying to Beth who had woken up and was licking his hand. When he neared the village the snow was gone while the sides of the roads teamed with fresh water heading into thirsty drains. Still keeping an eye out for the Porsche, he passed the Inn and shop before finding a space outside John McCarthy's garage. He glanced at his watch and then dialled Jim's mobile number, knowing that if he left it any later the man would be off out for his daily pie.

'Whit like?' replied the answer on the fourth ring.

Scott considered where to begin and was just about to start with the first fact of the day about an affair between the deceased and one of the women Jim had been lusting after the day before when he spotted John leaving the garage and climbing into an old Land-Rover Discovery. 'Call you back,' he said, ending the call. McCarthy hadn't seen him in the car-park opposite and pulled the vehicle out on to the road, its tailpipe rattling as he gunned it downhill. Scott started the engine and followed, keeping his distance. At the right-hand junction at Annat, the Disco went straight on without indicating, opening up the throttle as the narrow road straightened out towards the loch ahead. The snow might be gone but the road would still be greasy and Scott struggled to keep pace with the old 4x4 and its V8 engine, expertly tuned and driven by a man who had been around fast motors all his days. When he saw the brake lights come on up ahead as it neared

Ardnashaig, he pulled back and let McCarthy turn up into the campsite. 'Oh well,' Scott said out loud again. 'That's two visits in one then.'

Rather than following him in, Scott pulled his pick-up on to the grass at the side of the single-track road, feeling his wheels sinking into the turf. Whatever John had come to do or see, he seemed in a hell of a hurry. 'We'll give him a few minutes to get settled then, shall we,' he said to Beth, who was looking out of the side window at a few distant geese on the loch, her pink wet tongue hanging out as she panted. Scott picked up his mobile again and hit the redial. Jim answered, sooner this time. As he started to reveal the facts he had learned that morning the reception wasn't great and he found himself repeating sentences a few times. At one point Jim had said 'Randy old bugger,' which made him smile when he thought how Jim had drooled like his dog when he had seen Liz Mills yesterday. He explained about the cellar and the barrels, checking his notebook. He read out the words Davie had said when he had mimicked Charlie Edis. Movers and Mixers.

Jim stayed quiet for a few seconds, thinking, before saying, 'There'll be records, surely? They have to keep records of what whisky goes into which blend.'

Scott shrugged. 'I guess so, but unless we can prove there has been a crime I don't see how we can get access to that without a warrant?' Beth added a low pitch growl to her panting as the nearest of the geese stepped onto the bank no more than ten yards away. Scott guessed she would bark any minute and decided to move on. 'Speak to your boss. If the Frenchman doesn't turn up then who's to stop us going in and taking a look for ourselves.' He fired up the engine. 'Talking of which, I assume we are looking for him today?' he asked, sarcastically. Predictably Beth let out a series of barks, baring her teeth at the creature outside the window that was getting nearer. He ended the call and drove the pick-up slowly towards the campsite as she jumped into the back seat and carried on her glare through the rear window. Near the entrance a row of five or six flag poles rattled incessantly in the wind, the first one stridently displaying a flapping Saltire which was frayed at the edges. Next to it a three-inch strip of white material was all that was left of a George Cross that had probably been retrieved by locals. It wasn't that the English were unwelcome in these parts, more that they were just about tolerated as long as they fitted in and perhaps brought something in the way of wealth to the party. A quick internet search on his phone had shown that Harry and Liz Mills had bought this place in April the previous year, at the start of the season and had done 'a lot' of upgrading and renovations to the pitches as well as the chalets, according to their website. The upgrading he suspected was just a coat of paint and to replace a few rotten boards here and there.

Scott scoured the car-park from inside of his truck, as he idled at the entrance. As well as the two cars that had been there the day before, which he assumed belonged to the owners, he noted a white van he recognised from being at the distillery the night before, belonging to Dougie Cairns. The battered Discovery was parked further up the tarmac road near the chalets and he could just make out Shauna's Yaris in the distance. 'A right little gathering we have here then, eh,' he said to Beth, considering the names of suspects he had underlined in his notebook not long before. He couldn't help but consider how cosy it would be if they were all in bed together when he walked in but put the thought from his mind. Rather than sneaking in to see what he could spy or overhear he decided to take a drive around the place and give them chance to get organised, pulling the pick-up into a low gear and turning the radio back up.

On the dashboard his phone buzzed through a text message and he took a quick glance at it. '*Meet me for dinner at the hotel, 7pm? Jean-Luc.*'

'Well, well,' he mouthed the words to himself and then sung the verse of a song he had just heard on the radio. 'I wasn't expecting that!' Then he considered the text for a few seconds before answering. Jean-Luc was back, and had something he wanted to say. Would this be an admission of guilt? Of murder? Had it taken him twenty-four hours to work out a story in his defence? To start with he wrote the words, 'Where are you?' but then deleted them again as he didn't think they would get an answer. He considered replying with 'can we make it in Oban station this afternoon?' but again he thought that was unlikely to happen. Assuming the word 'hotel' referred to the Kilchrenan Inn, he just wrote 'Sure' and hit the send button. He hoped Jean-Luc was paying.

Pulling into the campsite, Scott noticed a single security camera fastened to the main building as well as what looked like a wi-fi antenna, as he skirted the perimeter along a greasy track past a some square concrete patches where campervans and mobile caravans would park, each one displaying a number on a low peg at the side. From the level round by the loch the track rose slightly when it turned inwards and he was soon back on to tarmac again as the first of the mobile homes took pride of place on a corner plot. Raised up on metal jacks it reminded him of some of the cars he had seen in the outskirts of Inverness that had their wheels stolen. The structures did in fact have wheels but they were so undersized they made the whole thing look foolish. Like a child drawing a lorry out of proportion. The outside was clad in white plastic, moulded to look like wooden boards, and there was an apex over the door which pretended to be a porch. Along its front a layer of wooden decking was surrounded by railings that rattled precariously in the wind and looked like they could take off at any minute, leaving the owner a perilous chance of shuffling off the edge and plunging the four feet to the grass below! Some garden furniture had been wrapped up in tarpaulin which too was rustling its way to freedom in the western blow. A small plaque at the door announced that this one was imaginatively named Loch View, either a display of cunning irony or a denotation of the intellect of its owner. Beyond it, a further dozen or so of these creatures lumbered on their rusting raised standings, each one no doubt trying to exceed their neighbours with the same garishness that Scott suspected they would be using on their housing estates back in Glasgow or further afield. At the end of the row the tarmac met a T-junction before a high hedge and Scott swung the pick-up left and then left again, down into the alleyway where the concrete chalets sat joined together in parallel monotony. At the bottom of the row was a low roofed building with large wooden framed windows that lacked insulation against even the summer weather. Although there was no light on inside as Scott crept slowly past and he could see a number of people talking, holding a meeting of some sort. Dougie Cairns spotted him through the window and stopped talking mid-sentence, as though the policeman may be able to lip-read his incrimination. Scott tugged on the handbrake and pushed open the door which was offering more than enough resistance against the gale coming in from the loch. He stepped on to the tarmac, allowing Beth to jump out too, who immediately rushed across to Loch View and chased a rabbit to ground under its chassis.

It was Liz who welcomed him at the window with a smile and her hands in a questioning T signal. He nodded and went around to the side door, pushing it open and stepping in out of the wind. Inside the air was musty, as though the underlying dampness had given up disguising its presence. He glanced at his watch before looking around. 'Morning all,' he said, in an almost a comedy fashion.

Liz busied herself in the decrepit kitchen, throwing a teabag into a yellow patterned cup and topping it with boiling water, her slim shape once again clad in figure-hugging material that cut into her curves at the seams. 'We have been waiting for you,' she said, turning with the cup and stepping towards him in her heels.

Dougie was standing holding a similar cup, his elbow resting on the wall, checking his mobile phone as though disinterested in the visitor. John had perched his large frame on a fairly meagre chair that looked like it had once been in a classroom and was possibly due for the skip before it did the dastardly deed of collapsing under the weight of a tourist. On the wall behind him a flat screen TV stood unused for some time, harbouring a layer of dust and a few cobwebs that entwined around its multiple leads. Below that, what looked like a football table was covered with a sheet that reached the grubby lino floor. An old wardrobe stored upwards of a hundred paperback books, their sun-bleached spines faded to illegibility as the shelves bowed under their weight. Scott suspected their pages would be so yellow you would need sunglasses to read them. 'Just the three people I wanted to see,' he said brightly. He nodded to McCarthy. 'I didn't know you were in the tourist business too, John?' The large man said nothing, his bearded face expressionless and his stubborn eyes glaring out. Scott took a sip of the scolding tea and then set it down on a table by the window where most of the putty around the pane had fallen out, so it rattled rhythmically. 'Right,' he said, raising his voice slightly. 'Who's going to tell me what's going on?'

# Chapter Eighteen

To access the pontoon at Dunlaridge Marina you first needed to open a metal framed gate that required a swipe with an exclusive membership card that denoted you either owned or had business with a one of its boats. This was in place not so much to keep the tourists and day-trippers out and prevent them from ambling along the rows of floating wooden platforms admiring the decadent vessels that collectively they would never afford in a fistful of lifetimes. To some it was seen as of a barrier of prudence where the 'haves' could cavort on their decks, popping corks and laughing vulgarly, just far enough away from the prying eyes of the 'have-nots' to be seen, heard, and envied. The real reason for the barrier, of course, was for safety and, more importantly, for the marina's insurance. These days, health and safety executives were none too keen to let the uninitiated even walk too close to the seafront, let alone traverse a treacherous platform without a high regulation handrail to cling on to. The still waters around the boats were hardly in themselves a killer although it wouldn't be advisable, in fact it was forbidden, to swim even in the shallows, partly because of the chance of being crushed between bow and pontoon, but also due to the pollution spewing from a hundred diesel engines and the occasional toilet that left a layer of colourful grime on its surface.

Dunlaridge was owned by a father and son pairing named McLaren, but it was the son, Ronni, who ran the place. Himself a product of Scotland's public school system, his pride was in his meticulous attention to detail and he firmly believed that the growing success of the business was down to that coupled with his choice of staff, which numbered into dozens in peak season. In summer he lived on an old wooden yacht which he had taken two years to renovate since he had claimed it from the marina after it had sat in a mooring for nearly a decade, paying no rent. Going through the correct channels it was assumed that the previous untraceable owner must have died and Ronni had subsequently purchased it for next to nothing. Having not only a free mooring for his newly rebuilt craft during summer, he also had access to the lifting gear to bring it up on to the dock, where he could work on it during the quieter winter months. Now it was in a giant hanger, sitting on a steel frame that supported it in four places, keeping it upright while he worked on some modifications to the old wooden galley kitchen. On this wintery day there was nobody else at work as far as he was aware so the noise of what sounded like someone dropping a lump of concrete caught his attention. At first he ignored it but then his curiosity got the better of him, as he considered it may be a door banging in the wind or maybe even a boat blowing over on the dock.  With a heavy sigh he climbed out of the boat and down the ladder to the ground.

Outside the gale had increased its power and the noise intensified, once he opened the steel door from the hangar, to an ear deafening level. Still unable to pinpoint the source of the noise he glanced back up the hill and could see the tail lights of a car pulling away from the marina. A quick walk around still didn't identify anything and he was just about to go back inside when he noticed a dark shape in the water about halfway along the second pontoon. Ronni strained his eyes to see and battled his way against the wind, barely upright, towards the gate to the pontoon. Thankfully he kept his security key-card on a ribbon otherwise it would have taken off across the yard as he unlocked the door and stepped onto the platform to take a closer look.

Although still some twenty feet away, as a trail of red bloodied the water around the shape, it was fairly evident that this was a body.

Out on the main road a dark Mercedes pulled into a layby near Connel Bridge, its driver removing a pair of gloves. The man checked himself in the mirror slicking back his hair, replaced a black signet ring on his little finger and hit the accelerator heading south.

# Chapter Nineteen

'On my way!' Scott ended the brief call, put his phone back in his pocket and drained his tea cup, heading for the door. 'This will have to wait,' he said over his shoulder. 'But I still need to speak to all three of you later.'

Pulling out his keys he nearly forgot about Beth as he jumped into the driver's seat and started the engine. Thankfully she wasn't far away and she jumped in beside him pretty much as soon as he called. His wheels spun on the gravel as he headed out onto the single-track road, hitting the accelerator as hard as he could. Jim hadn't furnished him with much detail. Just said that they had a phone call and it involved a body. When he rounded the corner towards Annat a tree was lying in the road and he skidded to avoid it. This would be a treacherous journey and he took it a bit easier after that, slowing through the village and climbing the hill heading for Taynuilt where the slushy snow lay in tracks.

Half an hour later he could see flashing blue lights in the darkening skies as he followed the A85 from Connel towards Oban. The entrance to the marina was cordoned off with yellow police tape so he pulled the pick-up into the upper car park next to two other marked cars, zipping up his jacket as he ducked under it. Heather met him, her face pale and solemn, the wind messing with her hair while she tried to keep it from her face. Scott looked beyond her where Jim and Bill Young were down near the water.

'Any ID?' he asked her.

'We're still waiting for the crew from Inverness to arrive, SoCo are bringing divers with them.' The collar of her jacket flapped in her face and she held it down. 'Nothing positive, yet, no.'

'So, the body's still in the water?' Scott was already heading down to the quayside but Heather put a hand on his arm.

'Jim has an idea who it might be, Scott.' She took a deep breath. 'You're not going to like it.'

He stopped mid stride. 'Go on?'

'Victim is face down in the harbour but from first impression he thinks it might be the Frenchman you've been looking for!'

Half an hour later, heavy rain was lashing against the window as Scott watched the police divers working methodically to retrieve the body from the choppy waters. It hadn't been an easy task as access from the pontoon had been obstructed by the boats moored along it. Opposite him Ronni stared blankly at the scene through the window, nursing a cup of coffee, saying nothing. From the dockside, Jim waved his arm, a signal that at last they were bringing the body out. Scott had been interviewing the marina's owner and had established that Jean-Luc did have a boat there and had been on it recently. Pulling his baseball cap down hard he left the canteen and faced the elements outside as the wind cut into him and stung his eyes. Still only mid-afternoon it was as though the wind had swept the light from the skies as a grey hue hung around, darkening the mood still further. By the time Scott reached the pontoon the body was already lying there, face downwards with a few straggles of seaweed hanging from around his ear. One of the Crime Scene Investigators, a pretty girl with bright green eyes by the name of Rose was bending over the corpse, her white overalls rustling in the sea breeze. He held his breath when she turned the body over and then set his sight on the man's face. There was no mistaking that nose, and although the eyes were barely open, they definitely belonged to Jean-Luc de Runcy.

Scott felt a burning in the pit of his stomach and was

rather glad he hadn't had lunch that day as he turned his back to the scene. A burp involuntarily arrived in his throat and he felt the taste of vomit as the flash of a camera lit up the air around them. While the flashes repeated he caught sight of Jim who was still grimly looking down at the body. Catching his eye, he nodded to him to step away from the others.

'Well, that's that search over then?' Jim said with a hint of irony.

Rose was already speaking about what she had found, her colleague using his phone to record the conversation. 'White Caucasian, mid late thirties.' She bent down and touched his open jacket with a gloved hand. 'Single wound to the right side of the chest, possibly from a bullet.'

'Christ!' gasped Scott. 'Poor bugger's been shot.' He considered the news headlines while he listened to Rose continuing her diagnosis.

'Aye. That'll get the Super out of bed.'

Scott kept his voice down. 'I had a text from him,' he said. 'Wanting to meet up.' He couldn't help but stare at the body again. 'As though he wanted to tell me something?'

Jim thought about this for a few seconds. 'To confess, you think. To Edis?'

'I dunno. Maybe.'

'Or to confess to us who did do it,' Jim continued. 'And got himself killed for his troubles.'

Scott pulled in some more gulps of air, just about keeping himself from throwing up. 'One thing for sure,' he said eventually. 'I can tell you at least three people who didn't do it!'

'Narrows it down, I suppose,' Jim nodded. Scott pulled out a plastic packet to roll a cigarette but in the strong wind he thought better of it. 'You want to get a cup of tea?'

he asked.

Jim was nodding and they were on their way up to the canteen when Heather caught up with them. Scott informed her of the text and she acknowledged it with a nod before saying. 'Gun shot. That's probably going to pull in the CID from Inverness.' She had to shout to be heard as the three turned their back to the wind. Her eyes were on Scott. 'Please tell me you have an idea who did this?'

'Not a Scooby?' he shrugged. 'I mean, no Ma'am, I don't. Not yet anyway.' He glanced at his watch as the light started to fade, approaching 5pm. It would be a long night. 'You got any dog food down at the station, Jim?' he sighed.

An hour later the whole main office at Oban Police station had been set up as an incident room. On a long wall the whiteboard that had been used before had been cleaned and re-written. Two rows of chairs were laid out, some already occupied and the place smelled of strong coffee.

Scott was putting the finishing touches to the wall display. The picture of Charlie Edis was now pinned high on the left side above the word 'drowned', with arrows down to the list of suspects they had originally penned in two days earlier. Principle name on that list had been Jean-Luc and he had written the word DEAD under it in capital letters which in any other circumstance would have looked a little too dramatic. Beside that were three more names. Dougie Cairns, Davie McCleod ne Robertson, and John McCarthy. To one side, more names of Liz Mills, Jess McCarthy and Shauna Edis were also added, as though the girls didn't warrant an accusation of murder but could well be involved somewhere.

On the right-hand side of the board, Jean-Luc de Runcy took centrepiece. The photo was one that had been used as promotion for Glenlachan a couple of years ago and Scott studied it and, compared it to the last time he had seen his face, pale and puffy, a string of seaweed added here and there. The man had been handsome in a Gaelic sort of way, dark features, piercing eyes under a strong forehead. So far the board was a pretty comprehensive but that was about where the trail ran out. He was writing 'Who would want this man dead?' when the door opened and two uniformed policemen entered, along with Heather Downs, who had tidied up her appearance.

She introduced the smaller of the two as Andrew McClatchie, Deputy Chief Constable, a man in his fifties who either paid some serious attention to his appearance or had someone to polish his buttons for him. 'The Chief apologises he couldn't make it in person,' he said, holding out his hand. The voice hailed from Scotland's North East area, a deep guttural sound sprinkled with something upper class and overly intellectual. Scott guessed that a single murder didn't warrant the chief missing whatever function he would be attending that evening.

The other man was your typical redheaded Scot, a man of a similar age to Scott and aptly named as Sandy, or DCI Lawson as he was being introduced as. Six foot two, broad shoulders and well-muscled, with a jumble of facial hair that was in need of a tidy-up. He suspected the man spent his weekends in a kilt. The two of them had met a couple of times before and although a smile was forthcoming Scott could remember that here was a man who, when it came to his job, liked to have the upper hand over his peers and who would gladly find a way to take the credit, whether it was due or not. Lawson hailed from Aberdeen where his family had a long association with fishing around the port of Peterhead.

'Sandy. It's been a while.' Scott said, 'You'll get lost over here in the wilds.'

'Fit like, Scott,' he muttered, in a broad voice that didn't sound like it wanted to be there.

132

Other introductions were made by Heather, as though she was hosting a cocktail party but in a professional way. Bill Young squeezed Sandy's handshake a little harder than necessary, as the two men eyeballed each other in faint recognition. The deputy straightened his tie and dusted down his uniform before saying a few polite words. 'Right, that's the welcome party over. We all know why we're here, to lend a hand. So, let's try to get to the bottom of this as fast as we can, eh chaps?' If Heather took exception to being referred to as a 'chap' she didn't let it show. Instead she nodded to Scott who took the floor in front of the board.

'OK, we are pretty certain we are looking at one murder here, and possibly two. Our original suspicions were that the first murder had been committed by this man, the second victim. Unfortunately we never got chance to prove that and now a confession won't be possible, obviously.' Using a cheap biro in his hand he pointed to his three suspects. 'If we can start with the first death, all three of these men had contact with the deceased within a few hours of his death, which occurred on Sunday evening.' As Scott recapped the circumstances of Charlie Edis's demise, he noticed Sandy was scribbling in an A4 notebook. 'We have a full report written up,' he said, irritably. The detective didn't look up, as though his notes would be far more valuable than whatever these amateurs had put together.

Over the next half an hour Scott mentioned what he considered to be some illegal goings on at the distillery but it would require an expert in that subject to confirm what was and what was not permitted within the law as well as the whisky industry itself. He also mentioned that he was in the process of speaking to two of the men on the suspect list when the second death was called in. Finally he revealed about the text he had received from Jean-Luc about arranging a meet up that evening. 'We have reason to believe, if illegal moving of whisky was going on, it could have an impact on both victims, and thus lead us to our killer.'

Sandy muttered, 'Who is?'

'Who is what, Sandy?' Scott replied, impatiently.

'Who is your killer?' He put down his pen and looked up to the board. 'You have systematically told us who didn't do this, so I was waiting for you to get round to who did it? Then we can move on a bit further, don't you think?'

Scott glanced at Heather who was looking at her shoes, and then to the Deputy Chief Constable who was staring at him rather expectantly, and he squirmed slightly, trying to hide his embarrassment. It had been a perfectly reasonable question where the answer of 'I don't know,' would no longer fill the void. He looked to the back of the room for a second.

'It has to be to do with the whisky.' Seeking Jim's encouragement, he bore on into the darkness. 'We. That is my colleague and I, believe that the whisky being produced at Glenlachan distillery was well below standard.' His foot involuntarily fidgeted, scratching an imaginary itch on his other ankle. 'And yet, it has just won an award.'

'And you know this, how?' This was Heather questioning.

'We tried it,' he replied, which solicited a snigger he was expecting.

The senior officer, who had remained silent up until now, took the opportunity to throw in a question. 'A whisky just won a top award, I presume judged by experts? And you say it wasn't good enough. Good god, man! Who am I supposed to believe here? Are you claiming to be a connoisseur, officer?' The man was going red in the face. 'Firstly we have a dead man that may or not have been murdered and you can't decide which, while a bunch of locals have you running around in circles about it. Then your main suspect gets killed and you have absolutely no idea who did it.' Scott was sure he could see a smirk on Sandy's face, as though he was enjoying every second of this. He turned his eyes back to the senior officer, partly in defiance, who continued. 'And now you tell us that your humble opinion on the quality of malt whisky is worth more than a panel of paid professionals?' He retreated slightly, and Scott hoped the worst of the bollocking was over, until he added. 'Looks like we got here just in time, eh, Detective Lawson?'

'Yes, sir,' Sandy said, hiding his grin from the superior man but not from Scott.

Scott went for broke now, trying to defend his suggestion. 'Sir, it is my belief that the whisky had been switched, and that Jean-Luc was in on that, Sir.' He pulled his chin back in, realising his tone was bordering on aggressive. 'And I believe that may have been what got him shot and killed.' He was about to leave it at that but caught Jim's eye who seemed to be egging him on. 'The distillery is also home to some very good whisky, Sir. Some whisky worth a lot of money. And we have evidence that it has been moved around although no clue yet as to where or why. But it could have easily found its way into a bottle that was put before the judges.' He stopped letting the idea sink in.

Jim broke the silence. 'Or some money found its way into the judges' pockets?'

'Yes. Or that,' Scott followed with. 'But either way, I think this is what got De Runcy killed.'

He was quite surprised that Sandy chipped in, almost endorsing his argument. 'So, if whisky was getting 'moved around', as you put it, the first victim was the master distiller, he would have been party to whatever was going on here?'

'Almost certainly!' Scott referred to his notebook,

turning to the page where he had interviewed Davie. Seeing the date written at the top of the page, his mind said, was that really only this morning? He read out, 'MOVERS AND MIXERS.' And then looked up. 'That's what he had described himself as to the boy. Move it and mix it. That's what I do.'

'What's the background on this distiller?' Sandy asked.

'He hails from your neck of the woods. Came with a long list of credentials. Appointed by the boss himself.'

'And they all checked out OK?' A simple question from Sandy which again felt barbed, as though he knew the answer.

'Not yet, no.'

'Not checked out OK?' Sandy asked, innocently. 'Or not yet been checked out?'

Scott stood his ground, glancing at the senior again. 'We hadn't had cause to double check out his history until now. There was no real reason to suspect foul-play. Not until this morning. And, since then, I've been slightly busy.'

Heather stood up and came to the screen, taking over proceedings in her officer's defence at last. 'Bill, get me everything we can find on Charlie Edis. I want his school and college records, his past employers, work colleagues. Let's find out how kosher this distiller really was?'

Bill stood up. 'Yes Ma'am. I'm on it. '

'Jim,' she continued, 'find out exactly where our Frenchman had been for the last twenty four hours. Who he'd seen, spoken to. Phone records. Everything. See where that leads us.' She stopped, looking at the Super, as though for clearance. 'And then take a look at that judging panel. See if anything comes to light there?'

'You're with me, Sandy,' she added. The deputy nodded, as though they had already agreed something together. 'Let's look at this with some fresh eyes, see if we have missed something?'

Here we go, thought Scott, Sandy picking holes through what we have given him, and then putting it back together and taking the praise. He realised Heather was talking to him, 'Scott, you get that dog back home, and then grill those suspects of yours? I know they potentially had alibis for this second crime but doesn't mean they didn't kill Charlie Edis. Find out what they were up to.'

She turned to the deputy chief who looked suitably impressed with her leadership. 'Sir. The father of victim will be here shortly. He is the boss of this operation. I would rather you spoke with him if possible.'

McClatchie looked at his watch. 'What time's he due?'

'He's driving up from Glasgow airport, now sir.'

The deputy sighed. 'Is there decent hotel around here? Sort a couple of rooms out for Sandy and I please?'

# Chapter Twenty

Liz had taken control of the meeting again after Scott had left the room. 'Sounded like something serious,' she said, putting his empty mug in the sink.

John McCarthy said, 'How much do you think he knows?'

'About us?' Dougie shrugged. 'I'm not sure the man could find his own arse with both hands!' He checked his phone again as though expecting something.

'Well, without Charlie's word, we need to stick to a story.' Liz turned round to face the other two again. 'Poor bugger,' she took in a sharp breath, eyes to the yellow stained ceiling. 'Never deserved that. Never deserved to die.'

'He drank too much!' Dougie said, with more animosity than the statement deserved.

Liz flew at him, her sharp heels spiking the cheap lino on the floor as she took the three or four strides to reach where he was standing. The man recoiled a bit, taken aback as he smelled her perfume first-hand. 'He was a good man!' she snarled, pink lipstick showing on her teeth. 'Worth two of you, you rat's knob!'

Dougie pulled a sadistic grin. He had been called a few things during his time on this earth but couldn't recall being called a rat's knob before. 'Alright, keep your knickers on!' He was going to add 'If that's possible for you!' but decided that might solicit a slap, or worse. 'I'm just saying. He drank too much, and fell in the mash-tun. That's all. No need to get all defensive. We all know you two were at it!'

John winced even before the words had quite completed their journey out of the man's lips, when the flat of one hand cracked around Dougie's jaw. This was briefly followed by a second blow from her other hand, a commendable left and right. He was ready to pounce if Dougie responded but the smaller man pulled himself backwards, gripping the table with one hand. 'Bloody hell!' was all he said.

Silence filled the air for a good half a minute, while Liz and Dougie glared at each other. John broke it with, 'Can we all just calm down? Scott,' he sighed, 'the copper, will be back. He'll want to know where we all were. He will ask what Charlie was doing. With the whisky? He'll dig. And fish. And cheat.'

'Aye, just like he did with your daughter!' spat Dougie, unwisely redirecting his anger.

John just glared at him, with a look that could easily end in more pain than he had just received from a woman. He spoke slowly. 'We need to tell him what he wants to hear. All three of us! Davie has spilled a few beans but the rest of them can stay nice and snugly in the pan, OK?'

Liz went back to the sink, wiping down the surface and hanging the discoloured cloth over the tap. 'What about the others?' she said, quietly.

# Chapter Twenty-One

Andrew McClatchie sat patiently in the interview room as he listened to the commotion in the area next door. A man was speaking loudly, making demands, both in French and English. That was the thing about the job, once you reached his level. All the others could pick up the slack, and deal with the criminals, victims, even calming the loved ones. All you had to do was soak it up, make sure they stayed in line, and pass on the credit of their work, through your own desk, to pacify those above you.

Peering at some papers in front of him, he looked up as the door opened. Heather poked her head through. 'The victim's father is here now, Sir.'

'Ah, yes.' He stood, straightening his uniform once more. 'Send him in.'

The first thing you noticed about Julien de Runcy was the aura of authority that surrounded him. Dressed in an expensive leather overcoat, over jeans and a navy-blue crew-neck jumper, his frame was slim but fit for a man of his age. A full head of hair, swept back but not yet fully grey complimented a beard that was tightly cropped, barely covering his perfectly square jaw. Despite addressing one of the most senior law officers in Scotland, De Runcy immediately took control of what should have been a rather difficult situation for the man and McClatchie's confidence waned slightly as he offered him a seat.

'Have you found out who did it yet?' the Frenchman said, staying standing.

'Er, I'm sorry Mister de Runcy,' the officer shifted uneasily in his chair. 'We have only recovered the body a few hours ago. Did someone get you a coffee?'

Again, Julien ignored the offer. 'Where is the body?' he insisted.

'The body has been formally identified by one of our officers who had interviewed him the previous day.' The deputy tried not to sound too callous. 'And is now in the...' he coughed, rethinking the word morgue he was going to use, 'is now in the facility in Inverness.'

Julien didn't seem too interested in the answer, looking at his watch. 'I had better call his mother,' he said, 'before it gets too late. Then I need to get to the distillery.'

'The distillery?' McClatchie looked surprised. 'Do you need me to organise you a car?'

'I'll take his,' he quipped. 'He's not going to need it, is he?'

'I'm afraid that won't be possible. It is being checked for evidence.' He decided to meet the man's attitude with some of his own. 'This is a murder enquiry, Mister de Runcy. I'm sorry for your loss.' He stood up, eyeing the Frenchman.

'Don't worry, I'll call the chopper back then.'

'Chopper?'

'Do you always repeat everything people say?' De Runcy's tone had become more aggressive. 'Yes, the helicopter that brought me up here from the airport. Only way to travel round here anyway. Your damn roads are so shit.' The way he pronounced shit included a few flecks of spittle, as though he was genuinely disgusted. 'I'll be in Kilchrenan when you have some more information for me.'

Andrew McClatchie watched him go without adding that they would need to interview him properly the next day. He then considered how a helicopter would be handy to get him back home to Inverness and some civilisation. Heather came in through the door he had left open and asked, 'How did that go, Sir?'

'I've had worse grieving relatives, I can say that.' He scribbled a few notes in his note pad, including the word helicopter. 'But I don't doubt he'll be pushing us for a culprit sooner rather than later.' He closed his pad and stood up. 'And so will I, officer. And so will the Chief.'

'Can we get the divers back tomorrow, in the daylight? To look in the harbour, Sir?'

'Look?' he replied. 'Look for what?'

'The gun, Sir. Forensics have sent us a report already.' She had a sheet of paper in her hand and glanced down at it before handing it over. 'Glock. 9mm. Single shot through the heart from fairly close range.'

He looked at the print-out. 'Shooter knew what he was doing, then?' Heather nodded. For all it sounded easy, you didn't just fire a gun straight into someone's heart and kill them instantly without some serious practice, even from close range. In fact there weren't many on the whole force that could do that. 'Contract killing?' suggested McClatchie.

'Can't rule it out, sir. Certainly someone with training.'

'From my experience, professional killers don't just lob their weapon away.' He raised an inquisitive eye at her. 'Especially not at the scene of the crime?'

'We need to look at all angles, Sir,' she said defensively. 'Sometimes the clues are in front of you.'

'Well, I hope they are.' He sighed. 'If only life was that easy. Alright, bring them back tomorrow.'

'Thank you, Sir.'

'What about the boat? Any clues there?'

'Crime scene are still working on it. Sandy's still up there as well. Says he'll join you later, Sir.'

'Well, I'll get going. Call me a taxi, would you please?' He started to pack up his papers into a shiny black briefcase that had his initials monogrammed on it in gold leaf. 'I'm sure DI Lawson will let me know if he finds anything.' He snapped the lock shut. 'I'll see you back in here at eight-thirty, once I've spoken to the Chief Constable.'

As he stepped outside, Julien de Runcy was standing on the street, his back to the wind with his jacket pulled tight around him, speaking on the telephone in French. He stood awkwardly next to the man, barely making out any of the words until a taxi pulled up to the kerb a full minute later. Before he could climb in the Frenchman shouldered him out of the way, still jabbering away, and climbed in the back, not even acknowledging the senior officer. 'Cheeky wee bastard,' he cursed.

It was full 10 minutes later when he eventually got another one, sitting in the back and looking out at the dreary streets of Oban. It's not that the town wasn't pretty, just some of the buildings looked tired when you saw past the tourists, and quite rightly so. A constant lashing from the Irish Sea would make anything look haggard eventually, especially the properties down on the front. He glanced up at McCaig's tower looming in the night sky, a massive circular stone structure dominating the skyline, its arches lit up with coloured spotlights as it held court over the town that had sprung up around it over the last hundred or so years. McCaig, a Glasgow banker, had built it over a span of 10 years, providing work for the local stonemasons in winter. His plans to complete it with an art gallery and museum never came to fruition when he died of a heart attack, and since then it just served as somewhere for the day-trippers to take their picnics, a bench with a view. The taxi peeped his horn at a couple who were taking photographs of the waves lashing up over the balustrade on the seafront, stepping backwards to get a wider view, oblivious to the fact this was a main thoroughfare. They wound their way around the bay, the road rising slightly, until the taxi swung into

143

the sprawling Alexandra Hotel and pulled up at the door. The Deputy Chief Constable paid the driver and stepped out onto a red carpet that led to a revolving door, just as his phone started to vibrate in his pocket. He left it for half a dozen rings so he could make it inside out of the cold blow that was rattling a row of flagpoles.

'Yes, Sandy,' he said, picking an empty seat by the vast window that offered spectacular views into the darkness outside. 'What news?'

'Unfortunately, none at all, Sir. Boat is clean except for the prints from the deceased.'

McClatchie sighed, audibly, eyeing up a tray of drinks that was being carried through from the bar on a silver tray by a waiter who certainly wouldn't be old enough to drink them. 'Why doesn't that surprised me,' he replied.

'There is one thing though, might be helpful. The owner saw a car leaving. He didn't get a make or registration but we may be able to pick something up from a traffic camera, depending which direction it headed. Of course, it may be a complete coincidence, but it's about all we have just now.'

Sandy ended the call saying he would be back at the hotel in 30 minutes, if he could hang on for dinner.

Back in Kilchrenan Scott was seeing to a hungry dog who was reminding him of his mistake in making her wait for her dinner, as she danced and barked around the kitchen. On the way back he had sent a text to Jess, cancelling the table he had booked. Then he sent a second one, saying cancel the cancellation and would she join him for dinner. So far there had been no reply to either text.

It had been a troubling day. Just when he had rounded up a list of suspects in one place, they were all out and about again. Apart from having a reasonable alibi for not killing Jean-Luc and, depending on the time of death, ruling them out of that enquiry, he was pretty sure they were collectively up to something, and more or less sure it had to do with the death of Charlie Edis. Rather than chase them around, he decided he would go to the hotel anyway, and get a couple of beers. If Dougie or John were there, they could have an informal chat. Maybe a beer or two might loosen the information a wee bit. Once he had got the fire lit, he sat with his feet on the hearth, warming his toes until steam started to rise from them. Two murders within a week. One victim being the main suspect in the other case. One murder that could have either been an accident or easily made to look like one, the other a pretty blatant and brutal killing. And what had Jean-Luc been going to tell him that night? Why had he hidden away from them for 24 hours? Maybe he wasn't on the run? Maybe he had information that someone else wanted, and was hiding from them? That didn't really make sense, as he could have just turned himself in at Oban nick.

Then there was this business of siphoning off the good whisky into new barrels. He had no proof if Jean-Luc was in on it, and even less chance of that now the man was dead. Logic suggested that they had been tapping the vintage barrels and passing it off as the newly made stuff. He was pretty sure Customs and Excise would have something to say about that but it wasn't really a crime the force would be too interested in. What had happened on that Sunday night that would have ended the life of the master distiller?

# Chapter Twenty-Two

Sharing a meal with a dead man was something Scott had never done before. Sharing it with his father was equally bizarre. Sometimes situations just happen that way. When Jess hadn't replied to his request Scott decided to head down to the hotel anyway, maybe she would be behind the bar and cheer him up. When he arrived, not only was she not there but none of the other regulars were either. With his chance of getting a chat with Dougie or Mac scuppered for the night, he was just perusing the menu, to see if anything tempted him that he could afford when Julien de Runcy walked through the main door, overnight bag in hand.

The man had a solemn look on his face but he raised an eyebrow in recognition of Scott. Maybe he had seen him at the station in Oban or perhaps he was just aware of who folks were around these parts. Or possibly it was just a friendly gesture that he did with most of the locals. Scott decided to act.

'Mister de Runcy, I am sorry for your loss, sir.' He held out a hand to shake. 'Scott Donald, local police force.'

Surprisingly, the man took his hand and raised a wry smile. 'Bobby.' He said, his accent extraordinarily good for a foreigner. 'Isn't that what they call local coppers? Bobbies?'

It was Scott's turn to smile. 'I've been called a lot worse!'

The Frenchman had already turned his attention to the bar maid, a slim young girl in her late teens who generally worked cleaning the rooms but doubled up as a waitress some evenings and stood in when the bar needed tending. De Runcy handed her his overnight bag through the hatch at the side of the bar. 'You have a room for me, I believe?'

She winced at the surprising weight of the bag, putting it on the floor and straightening her skirt for a second before picking it up again with her other hand, whilst checking in an open ledger on the counter. 'Room 3,' she said, her accent Glaswegian, with an attitude to match. It was fairly obvious De Runcy was used to having his bags carried, and all three of them could see that, but the girl stood her ground for a little longer than necessary, showing her annoyance of having to add 'porter' to her already long list of duties. She had reached the foot of the wide staircase by the time De Runcy spoke again. 'Could a man get a drink, first?' If there had been a bell he would have rung it, just to add to the tepid atmosphere. Scott winced, expecting a line of abuse from the girl but none came. 'And a table for dinner.. for two!'

So here they were, sitting opposite each other in the opulent dining room, sharing a bottle of Pommerol that possibly cost more than the young waitress earned in whole week of her collection of jobs in the place. Scott was more of a white wine man but he hadn't really had much choice in the matter when De Runcy had asked for two glasses and indicted towards the dining room. Still he chose the cheapest meal on the menu, shepherd's pie with a side of peas that he hoped would not conflict with a 60 quid bottle of French delight. De Runcy had ordered a steak, rare, with chips and French mustard.

After a few pleasantries and an acknowledgement that the wine was acceptable, even to a French connoisseur, De Runcy had headed off to the toilet once they had placed their order, leaving Scott pondering the situation in silence, and wondering if he was picking up the bill. When the Frenchman had returned they had eaten in silence for most of the course, Scott feeling a little uneasy about the air of authority the man seemed to be enveloped in.

Eventually the silence was broken and Scott almost

wished it hadn't been. 'So,' said Julien de Runcy, 'who killed my son?'

The policeman chased a pea around his side plate for as long as he dared before answering. 'Oh, I'm just a local bobby. It's not up to me to speculate on murder. There are officers far more qualified to make those assumptions.' As he looked, De Runcy was staring him in the eye, fixing his gaze like a magnet pointing north. The smile had long disappeared, as had the pleasant demeanour, which was replaced with a look of steel that demanded a better answer than the excuse for one he had just given. A lesser man would have repeated the question but De Runcy just stayed silent behind the stare.

Scott had hoped that the dinner may have turned into some sort of interview around the case, himself gleaning some information and perhaps scoring a few brownie points against the Inverness brigade who were trampling on his patch. Instead, it was him being grilled and he knew whatever he said next would eventually be repeated, either at the nick or, worse still, in court. What did the man know already? What had McClatchie told him? Had there been mention of a car leaving the scene? Or the fact that the weapon used was similar to those used by professionals? One thing was for certain, if Scott leaked any of this potential evidence to the man, suspect or otherwise, he would be in hot water with the Super, as well as ridiculed by Sandy bloody Lawson. Should he mention he was supposed to be dining with the man's dead son instead of him that evening? Scott took a deep breath. 'For what it's worth, I don't think it was anyone local,' he finally blurted out, hoping that would suffice. It didn't.

'What makes you say that?' came the question.

Back in Oban's Regency hotel, Sandy Lawson was also being asked the same question, only his answer wasn't quite so guarded.

'Plenty of hit-men in North Scotland, if you know where to look,' he said, without looking up from his plate of soup. 'But my hunch would say the killer came from down the road?'

'Down the road,' McClatchie momentarily glanced at a passing waiter. 'You mean Glasgow?'

'As I said, just a hunch.' Sandy picked up a chunk of bread and was mopping the plate clean. 'If you are from out of town, and looking for a one-off job, Glasgow would be easier to find a man, and keep the questions quiet.'

McClatchie sighed. 'Is it really that easy? I mean, to ask around, find a killer, get the job done. What do they use, the Yellow Pages?'

'Showing your age, guv,' Sandy replied, a little too cheekily. 'The internet, that's where it's at these days. Use a VPN, cyber cafe, not tracing your URL.' Sandy glanced up again, checking that his boss was keeping up. 'Social media, forum's, chat rooms, that sort of thing.'

'And do we monitor these things? I mean put in trip-wires or something?'

'What, the whole internet?' Sandy almost scoffed. 'As much as we can do to monitor the traffic offences, let alone a whole underworld who moves house faster than a premiership footballer!'

'We must have undercover, though? Right?'

'Aye, we got plants, of course. But most of that is based around the drug trade, not one-off hits.'

McClatchie thought for a minute, as the young waiter cleared away his soup plate, including the basket of bread which his colleague was still eating. Eventually he asked, 'could this be drug related?'

Sandy wanted to say, 'That's the first decent question you have asked me all evening,' but instead opted for, 'Possibly. Definitely money related, anyway.'

'What makes you say that?'

'Because a hit like that, it doesn't come cheap, that's for sure.' A plate of gammon and egg arrived for both of them and he waited until they were out of earshot again. 'Whisky business may be swilling with a bit of cash, but you don't hire contract killer out of back pocket change!'

A bit of commotion in the reception took the boss's attention for a few minutes, a couple and their two children checking in at the desk and speaking far too loudly. The accent was strong but not local, as the woman demanded a bath and not a shower in their room. The whole crowd looked stressed but the man behind the desk stayed cool, checking the register and maintaining a smile throughout. Eventually McClatchie recognised the accent.

'What about the Irish?' he said, quietly, as if not to offend anyone.

Sandy was trying to make a piece of fried egg stay on his fork. He stopped when it fell off. 'Could be. Para activity has been quiet these last few years but there's still plenty of buggers know how to use a weapon. From both sides. Especially for cash.'

'Maybe it wasn't a hit. Maybe just revenge? Who knows? Borrowed some money from the IRA, perhaps? Or just generally pissed them off. Those guys would shoot you for a hymn book.'

Nodding slowly, the junior detective considered the question. 'Feasible, I guess. From what plod tell us, the boy was a bit of a player. Into cars and women. Drugs and gambling aren't usually far away, in my experience.'

'Worth a look then. In the morning...'

Sandy audibly sighed. 'A look? A look where?'

For the second time that evening, the Chief shifted uneasily in his seat, mildly annoyed at the other man's tone. 'We have some avenues, take a look down them. Kick some tyres, rattle some locks.' His voice rose a little too high, as he thought back to the days when he was on plain clothes. 'Good god, man. You're the detective. Look in the right places!'

Staying cool, Sandy placed his knife and fork back on his plate, which was empty except for a chunk of pineapple. His tone was professional, genuine almost. 'Would that be in Glasgow, or Ireland?'

# Chapter Twenty-Three

A tiny glow of orange light did its best to hide itself behind the curtains, like a stage-hand with a torch before the show begins. Scott saw it through one eye as he swung himself out of bed and shuffled his bare feet into a pair of slippers that had seen too many Christmases.

Red sky in the morning? A warning, not just to shepherds, but to anyone looking to spend the afternoon outdoors, unprepared. As he trudged through to the kitchen, Beth was already waiting for him, her enthusiasm far out-weighing his own for the day ahead. He thought about the last whisky he had had, the night before, the one he could have done without. As often happens with that place, what had set out to be a quick dram, had extended into a 'one too many' evening.

Scott flicked on the kettle and headed off to the bathroom, considering how the night had gone. The fact that his dinner partner had just lost his son wouldn't generally make for an entertaining situation, and he definitely hadn't expected to get close enough to De Runcy to hear his life story. After sighing with open palms, he had openly admitted that although he had a hunch about Charlie's killer he hadn't the foggiest idea of who had murdered Jean-Luc. The old man seemed satisfied with that, for now, and the mood had moved on.

De Runcy had mentioned the son's childhood and how he had been too busy making his own fortune to be there for the boy growing up. There had been an older sister, Mathilde, who, at the times when he was at home, would get the lion's share of the old man's attention. She had drifted away, along with his wife, who eventually got bored of being second best in the household. After the separation, the three of them had moved to an apartment in Paris which he had part paid for. From then, for the next decade, the parental relationship was fractious, a tension in the air at dinner dates he would organise, a reluctance for them to visit his own home in the west, often with Jean-Luc pulling out last minute with an excuse. As the boy grew into his late teens, he suspected he had problems, and was living a high life in Paris with girls and substances he neither knew, nor cared, anything about. It wasn't really until he had sold his electronics business which, Scott deduced, made solenoids and switches for the boating industry, that he sat down one day and re-thought his priorities in life.

By the time they had got this far, the hotel dining room had been exchanged for two comfortable chairs by the open fire and the wine glasses for whisky tumblers. Despite making the amber nectar in his own distillery in the west, it turned out that the Frenchman preferred the softness and lighter aromas of Speyside. When the waitress, who's name turned out to be Olivia, had brought a half full bottle of Macallan to pour them both a shot, he put his hand on her arm and then just pointed to the low table, indicating for her to leave it behind. The last Scott remembered of the meeting was seeing it sitting there, quite empty.

The buying of a distillery had actually been his ex-wife's idea, when he had agreed to meet her for a drink in Le Mans. By then she had re-married and he had a mistress, but there was still a friendship and perhaps a tiny spark of love left between them. She had been concerned for her son, who was drifting without a real purpose in life. He had enough money to be flash and flamboyant, a real man-about-town in Paris circles, but not enough to do anything positive with it, such as start or invest in a business. She hadn't exactly mentioned buying a place in Scotland, just something in the west that he could maybe get a passion for and produce a product he could be proud of rather than living in his father's shadow. A few months later he sat down with the lad and discussed his future and, beneath all the son-to-father hatred and bravado, Julien had seen glimpses of what the boy's mother was intimating at. They had visited a distillery together in west Brittany, one that was just finding its feet in new world whisky and, despite some hefty investment in infrastructure, had projections of healthy profits in five to ten years' time. Doing his best to enthuse his son in the business, the attraction of such a venture also suited his own situation, where he would soon be due exorbitant amounts of money to the government in taxes on the recent sale of his own business, something that a new investment and good accountancy might just avoid.

Scott had listened to this but, on the odd occasion he had asked questions, the commentary had dried up, as though the older man was telling his story, his way, without interruption. When the tale got nearer to the purchase of Glenlachan, De Runcy had started to wane a little, as though the loss of the very reason he bought it was starting to sink in. The Frenchman had drunk most of the whisky, probably at a rate of two-to-one to Scott's efforts but he wasn't drunk, not by any means. Scott was hoping that the subject of the old building would come up, where perhaps he could put in some real input about his own youthful life there, as well as maybe asking about the unexpected find of a few barrels of whisky. But instead, Julien started talking about the way of the wind in the west, and his own childhood love of sailing, one of the few things he had shared with his son. A midnight chime of the clock, coupled with a hovering waitress and an empty bottle signified this dinner was over. Scott made a show of reaching his wallet from the back pocket of his jeans, only to see Julien de Runcy put out an authoritive palm once more, coupled with a shake of the head.

And a shake of the head was the last thing he required right now, as he dragged a razor across his cheek, and focussed on the day ahead. Thankfully, he hadn't got to rush back to Oban and, if the look of that glowing sky was anything to go by, that might be a road trip best avoided today. Scott had always been a man to work mainly alone, to plan his own day, week, month sometimes. Not that he never had a boss, but more that he always felt the boss was only someone to bother when there were questions to be answered, rather than tell him what to do on a regular basis.

Since last week, and particularly yesterday, that had all changed, for the present anyway. He now had a new boss, and her boss, and possibly his boss, all breathing down on him. He was also part of a team and somehow he felt the team-sheet wasn't equal. His detail today was to continue with what he was doing yesterday morning. Sniffing, investigating and second guessing a bunch of locals, some of whom he had grown up with. Compared to the alternative, such as seeking out gangsters and professional killers, or looking at alibis and traffic camera footage, he concluded he hadn't come out of yesterday's meeting too badly.

At what point did he mention that he had dinner with the victim's father? That probably wouldn't sit too well with an investigation that possibly included the man as a suspect? But he couldn't hide from the fact that they had sat and got drunk together, in a public place. OK there was only really the waitress who had seen them. But she would tell the chef and the odd text would start flying. Only a matter of time before Oban found out. Would they remove him from the case for being too close? After all, the victim himself had arranged the dinner date. Maybe it was meant to be for all three of them. In fact, why had De Runcy invited him to join him in the dining room? And then paid for it all. For all Scott had been grateful for that at the time, could it now be constituted as a bribe? He did a quick count in his head, 40 quid dinner, 60 quid bottle of wine, another 50 for the Macallan. Seventy-five unsolicited pounds, they had arrested coppers for receiving far less. But bribery for what? He hadn't done anything, divulged any information or offered anything favourable at all?

After feeding the animals he checked his notebook and dialled the campsite. This meeting wouldn't be as easy today as it could have been yesterday, when at least three of the folks he needed to interview were all corralled into one space. After four rings the phoned clicked on to an answer-phone message. Scott checked his watch as he listened, 8.22am. 'Thank you for calling Ardnashaig campsite,' purred Liz Mill's voice, 'our main site is closed for the winter. However, we do take special bookings by appointment. Please leave a message or call back during office hours.' He imagined her pulling a false smile at the end of the message, as though directing it personally at the listener! 'It would be helpful if you mentioned when office hours are?' Scott said, rather facetiously. 'This is Scott Donald of the Oban Police force. I would like to speak to you as soon as possible. Please call me back on this number.' He left his mobile number and hung up.

Next he had to search back a few pages until he found the number for Dougie Cairns, at half past eight this man was surely out and about, even in winter. The phone answered on the second ring. 'Yes?' In the background he could hear an engine running, or a motor of some kind.

He raised his voice. 'Dougie, this is Scott Donald, from the police.'

'Ah, yes. Wondered when you would call.' The man was almost expectant. 'How can I help you?'

Scott knew damn well how he could help, by telling him what the hell was going on. Since yesterday morning, they had time to corroborate on a story, and get themselves in line. He said, 'Can I pop over and see you, in half an hour?'

'Can it wait until this afternoon? I'm out on the tractor delivering wood this morning.'

Agitation showed in Scott's tone. 'No, it can't wait, unfortunately. This is urgent police business. Let me know where you are and I'll come and find you?'

'I'm heading down to Ardban woods, to collect a load. Do you know where that is?'

He wasn't sure if the man was being sarcastic or just plain stupid. The thought of going back down to his brother's place caused him to swallow hard for a second, before taking a deep breath. 'Yes, I know where that is.'

'There's a track, runs from the side of the road, opposite the post box.' The phone was starting to lose signal. 'I'll be...'

Knowing the area like a chef in a dark kitchen, he was pretty sure that Dougie would be just dropping down towards the loch, off the road past the fork to Ardnashaig, as that was where the mobile signal faded. When they were younger, his father was offered the chance to put up a mobile phone mask, one that would have covered that area and much of the farm, as well as helped out the village. Despite what seemed like quite a lucrative contract, the old man had declined, more out of awkwardness than anything else. Eventually one had been erected further round the coast, which left that road and the woods in a blind spot. He wouldn't be the first to curse the old bugger for that.

'Come on,' he indicated to Beth, collecting his keys from a hook by the door and stepping out into the cold morning air. The road had been quite slippery on his walk home the night before but at least this morning he was sober. This track didn't see many cars, especially not in winter and he let Beth run on ahead without her lead, as she sniffed around in the hedgerows for any animal that may be braving the morning air. His breathing got deeper as they neared the top of the lane and Scott realised how unfit he had become during the winter months when they didn't get as much chance to walk in the hills. Eventually he reached the pub carpark, his being the only vehicle there.

Beth was in the front seat as soon as he opened the door to the pick-up, her breath steaming up the window from the inside whilst he cleared the ice off the outside with an old scraper that had the faded name of McCarthy written on it in red stencil. That would be his next call, on the way back. The Toyota engine complained for 20 or more seconds as it turned over and over before eventually coughing into life and letting the valley behind it in on its discontent with a billow of white smoke. The road up to the village was slippery this morning, as silver icicles hung from the hedgerows like Christmas decorations. Scott considered the festive season looming just over a month away as he juddered the vehicle into second gear. It wasn't a time of year he enjoyed but he hoped he may have a bit of company this year. Once today's little jaunt was out of the way, he may not be as welcome in the local bar as he had been in the past. At the top of the road the view of Ben Cruachan was enchanting, bathing in the early morning glow like heat from a fire. Anyone local would know that red glow was no more than a red herring, as the day would soon close in around it.

On the road down by the loch he checked his mobile phone for signal. Once he dropped down, any messages would go straight to his answer phone, which he hoped would include one from Liz Mills. As predicted the signal dropped out as he neared the loch side, it too resonating in red with tinges of ice towards the shore. A salmon leapt out of the water towards the centre, causing ripples to spread out like a kaleidoscope of orange across the otherwise still surface. Scott braked gently, slowing down to watch the glorious scene, distracted by its beauty. A loud blast on a horn pulled his eyes back to the road. This time the driver of the tanker had both his hands off the wheel in a shrug as he mouthed out something incomprehensible and probably unrepeatable to Scott from inside his cab. The wheels of the pick-up mounted the icy grass, as if by habit, just in time to let the beast of a lorry past with its load of steaming milk, the back end of it nipping his wing-mirror and turning it inwards. Scott glanced to the left. Another few feet and it would have been him sending ripples out on that golden lake, and he wouldn't have been the first one to do that. He probably wouldn't have been the first vehicle that driver had pushed off the road either. One day he would need to have a word with him, or perhaps a call to his bosses at the dairy.

Scott drove on tentatively, turning right up the track into the wood. The muddy ruts were frozen under his wheels but he could see the marks of a tractor that had been there before him. Above him the trees closed in to each other, sheltering this place to somewhere that rarely saw sunlight the whole year round. A mixture of beech and oak were interspersed with evergreen pines that provided the intensity of an umbrella. As a child this track had been part of his circuit for racing his mountain bike, half a mile or more through the forest before it opened up to grazing fields at the far end and a view back over the farm to the loch. It seemed a shame that some of the trees had since been fallen, to provide firewood to a village that mainly had a good source of oil central heating. Scott preferred peat on his fire rather than wood. There was something in the smell of it that reminded him of the hills and the summer days he spent up above the clouds.

Ahead he could make out the shape of an old Massey Ferguson, its engine still ticking over, occasionally popping up wisps of white smoke to prove it was still breathing. To say the machine had a cab was a slight overstatement, which was more of a canvas cover over a wire frame and flimsy doors that just about kept out the flies in summer but would be useless against the cold on a day like this. Behind it was attached an old wooden trailer, its two back tyres perished with cracks around the edges.

The low wooden sides rattled in time to the motion of the tractor's engine, and a mudguard joined in, as though they were all singing the same song. Scott stilled the pick-up a few hundred yards away, pulling on the handbrake, and sitting watching for a few minutes while he rolled a cigarette. There was no sign of activity near the stack of logs, and the trailer stood empty. He tapped his finger on the steering wheel, waiting for some movement or at least a sight of his man before stepping out into the cold. Even with the window open, the only sound was the ping-ping cooling of his engine, the old tractor chugging and Beth breathing heavily, watching the scene from the passenger's seat. 'Go on then,' he said eventually, pulling on the door handle. Beth hit the solid ground running, all fours already engaged and soon headed off into the undergrowth at youthful speed. Scott's boots made a crunching sound on the leaves and dead bracken, as he walked to the log pile. 'Dougie,' he said, loud enough to scatter a few crows from the higher branches of the trees overhead. It was a good five minutes later, while Scott had been warming his hands on the Fergie's engine cowling when he heard voices further up the track. Not just voices, but a low hum of an engine. As they drew nearer the talking stopped and soon the engine noise was fading away again but Scott recognised it as that of a quad bike, the one he had seen a couple of days before.

'Nice morning,' called Dougie, emerging from the shadows like an actor stepping into the stage lights.

'Aye, if you're a polar bear,' Scott quipped. 'That my brother, over there?'

'He was just passing. Stopped for a chat.'

Scott considered that he was hardly passing this spot on his morning duties, the track being well away from the ones where the cows ambled back and forth to their field. And, anyway, he suspected the cows would be inside now, lying comfortably in the courts. 'Bored, was he?' he muttered.

Dougie didn't reply, as he strode up to Scott, removing a leather glove and holding out a hand to shake. 'What can I do for you, today?'

Scott looked down at the bare hand for a second then decided to shake it, if only to put the man at ease before the real questions started. Dougie put his glove back on and walked back to the pile of firewood, all stacked neatly some months earlier, and covered with a tarpaulin. Scott had hoped they could have sat in the front of his pick-up for this interview but felt that it would appear nash of him if he suggested it, while the man worked.

'You could start by telling me what yesterday's little rendezvous was all about, if you like?' he eventually said, his breath as thick as the smoke he had just extinguished.

'Just having a coffee morning, nice to catch up with folks, eh?'

It was the sort of guarded remark Scott was expecting. Of the four of them, this man would be the hardest to get a straight answer from. 'I think you folks see a lot more of each other than most people see their wives?' Dougie started loading the first of the logs on the trailer, the boards of the floor of it rattling with each thud. Scott had to raise his voice. 'I guess you heard about the Frenchman?' He was pretty certain everyone in Argyll would have heard about the murder by now, despite the police not announcing anything.

'Nasty business.' Dougie replied, not breaking stride with his work. 'Shot, eh? That'll get you boys scratching you heads then. Did his dad tell you who did it, on your dinner date?'

Scott felt himself bristle but chose to ignore the remark.

'I guess that means a change of the guard up at the distillery?' Dougie continued, matter of factly. 'I mean, first the stiller, now the boss. Can't see young Davie running the place, can you?'

'It's the distillery I want to talk to you about.' He thrust his hands deep in his jacket pockets for warmth. 'I know there is something going on up there. Whisky getting moved around, barrels getting moved around. Bodies...' He trailed off and took a deep breath. 'Lies getting moved around.' He stepped nearer to the old tractor again, feeling the faint heat of its engine blowing back from the cooling fan. 'And I know there are at least four of you in on this.

Dougie stopped, batting his own hands together to keep the circulation going. 'Sounds like you know quite a lot, then, pal? But I reckon the man you want to speak to is too dead to answer?'

The speed with which Scott jumped up onto the trailer took the other man by surprise, as he grabbed Dougie's left hand and banged it against the sideboard, holding it there in a vice-like grip. His eyes stared into the man below him, teeth bared for a second. 'No. Pal,' he growled. 'The man I want to speak to is right here, right now.' He clenched the fist on his other hand. 'And if he doesn't tell me what the fuck's going on, he'll be unable to say anything to anyone until he gets some new fucking teeth!'

Dougie tried to pull his arm free but the policeman had it held too firmly. 'Alright, alright!' He yelled, his breath gushing from him in a white cloud.

Still holding his hand, Scott jumped down from the trailer, then pushing the man's arm up behind his back he marched him to his pick-up. 'OK, let's sit in here, in the warm, while you spill some of those Heinz beans.' Dougie still looked a little shocked at the show of violence, as he climbed in the passenger's door, glancing out through the window to his left into the undergrowth.

'OK, let's start with yesterday,' Scott began, quietly. 'You and Davie were siphoning whisky from a very expensive barrel, into an unmarked one. Davie, or one of you, didn't want me to see that, and knocked me out. There's an offence right there.'

'Am I under arrest?' Dougie tone was smug once more.

Scott snarled at him again, refusing to answer that one. 'When I woke up, the barrels had been moved around and you had done your best to cover your little racket. Yesterday Davie showed me the plumbing you had set up down there, all very intricate, even sophisticated. Was that a bit of your doing?'

'Me. Nah. Woodwork, that's all I do. Don't touch anything metal. Leave that to the specialists.'

'Like who?'

'You work it out?' again Dougie looked out of the side window, as if watching for something.

Scott had already worked out who. A man in the village who was good with metal, and motors. He dropped the subject and moved on.

'You make barrels, right?'

'Has been known.'

'Did you make the empty barrel that you siphoned the expensive whisky into?' Scott watched the man's reaction, waiting for a lie.

'As as matter of fact, I did.' Some truth at last.

'And the letters D and C, chiselled into the lid?' Scott pulled out his pack of tobacco again, starting to roll. 'Let me guess? Charlie...and Dougie?'

'Fuckin hell, man. Aren't you a right Sherlock.' Dougie even chuckled' Except you are way off the mark there buddy. As cold as a dead fish!'

'You care to tell me the real meaning of that then?'

'Sure. No skin off my nose. Barrels are numbered alphabetically, ya ken.'

'What, all of them?'

'Nah. Just he big ones. The ones out front.'

'So C and D means the small barrel is filled with spirit from barrels number C and D.'

'Christ, you are quick. Quicker than you brother said you are, anyway.'

With that, a face appeared at the side window, giving them both a shock. It was a man, with an animal in his arms...

# Chapter Twenty-Four

Julien de Runcy pressed the end button on his phone, furiously. 'Fuck you too!'

Within seconds he had selected another number and dialled. 'Jacques, mon ami!' The call continued in French until again he ended it inside of one minute, this time throwing the phone across the room. 'Bastards!' Just as he was heading to the bathroom, it rang again, the vibration announcing its location under a chair near the window. Julien crouched down and retrieved it. 'Oui, allo?'

'Mister de Runcy?'

'Yes.'

'We need you at Oban police station by ten o'clock, today, Sir.'

The message sounded like an order and he was not accustomed to taking orders from anyone, especially not today. 'I have no transport. No taxis in this rural place?'

'That has all been arranged, Sir.' The woman on the end of the phone didn't sound like she was used to being argued with either. 'A car will pick you up in half an hour.'

Within an hour, he found himself sitting in an interview room at the station, something that was masquerading as coffee in a styrofoam cup in front of him. He sniffed it, put it down and picked up his phone, checking again for messages.

In a room at the other end of the station, Sandy Lawson was standing in front of a white-board addressing six officers.

'So, in summary. Prints from De Runcy senior were found on the boat. We now know he was in the country in the days prior to the murder. We haven't found anything in the victim's car, but forensics are still checking for DNA.' Sandy straightened up and looked forward to the crowd, taking a deep breath. 'It also seems there was very little love lost between father and son. Although none of these actually lead us to an arrest, they do give us good reason to officially interview the man so we can at least rule him out as a suspect.'

Heather raised her hand. 'Anything else we should know?'

'There were traces of cocaine on the boat, in the toilet and living area, but also up on deck. There is also a footprint which doesn't match the victim as far as we can tell.'

Jim muttered under his breath, 'Why don't I find that surprising?' The others looked at him questioningly. 'What?' he even pulled faint grin, before adding, 'playboy like that, stands to reason he blow's his nose, surely?'

Sandy dismissed the comment. 'I would like to lead the interview, Ma'am, if that's OK?'

'I think I had better sit in on this one as well, though, eh?' She stood up, straightening her skirt. 'A woman's touch, and all that?'

Jim inwardly winced, a touch from that woman would be a lot more than gentle caress!


'Interview started, 10.23am, Thursday 24th November,' Detective Inspector Alasdair Lawson and DCI Heather Downs in attendance. Sir, could you state your name please, for the record?'

De Runcy stayed seated, eyeballing the officer in front of him. 'Are you accusing me of something, officer?'

Sandy stayed calm, casually holding his eye contact. 'Sir, for the record, could you please state your name.'

'Julien de Runcy!'

'Can you tell us when you first arrived in Britain?'

Julien pulled a half grin. 'About 30 years ago. It was raining!'

Sandy refrained from showing any expression to the remark. 'Sir, when did you last arrive in Britain?'

'In Britain? Or in Scotland?' he smiled this time. 'Or are they still the same country?'

Sandy put the palm of his hand flat on the table, the only sign of frustration he offered. 'Let's try again, when did you arrive in Britain.'

'Last Friday.'

Sandy turned towards the digital recorder which sat against the wall on the table. 'For the record, that would be Friday the 18th of November?'

'If you say so.'

'And where was this?'

'I was in London seeing some friends. What has this to do with anything?' De Runcy's temper was starting to rise. 'What has this to do with the death of my son?'

Sandy looked him the eye calmly across the table. 'And when did you arrive in Scotland, Mister de Runcy?'

The Frenchman made a show of considering the fact, 'er, yesterday. I got a phone call from..' he looked across to Heather, 'you, was it? To tell me my son was dead. My only son.' He dropped his eyes to the table. 'And now you interview me? Suspect that I killed him?' His fist slammed down on the table, skin tightening across his temples. 'What sort of a man do you take me for? I bring business to this desert. I bring money to your people. I bring whisky to your bosses. My son grafts to make this business run smoothly.' He stood to his feet, looking down at Sandy and then up to the window that ran the length of the room. 'And this is how you repay me? My son gets murdered. I arrive too late to see him. And now you blame me for the killing.' He went to walk towards the door.

'Fuck you!'

'Sir, please calm down. And please sit down.' It was Heather using her authority now. 'Nobody is accusing you of anything. We just need you to answer a few questions to help us piece together...' she trailed off.

'We are looking for your son's killer, Mister de Runcy.' Sandy added.

Julien calmed down and sat as he was instructed and muttered. 'Allez zee..'

'When you arrived yesterday. How did you get to Oban?'

'I hired a helicopter. It's the only way to travel round here!'

'Whom did you hire it from?'

'I know people. It belongs to a friend.'

'And that friend flew you all the way from London?'

'No. I was already heading North, by car.'

Sandy considered this, as did Jim and McClatchie behind the smoked glass two-way mirror. 'You were heading North by car? Where to?'

'I was coming to Scotland to see my son. He said there had been some trouble and I wanted to talk to him about it. To stand by him. One of our main men had died, and he said the police had been looking into it. He thought you were going to shut the place down. As I said. I was too late...'

Heather picked up on the questioning. 'So, when I phoned you. Where were you?'

'I had just arrived, in Glasgow.'

'Just arrived?'

Julien sighed, 'are we back to repeating everything I say? Yes, I just arrived.'

'Who did the car belong to, Mister de Runcy?' Sandy

spoke this time.

'A friend, also.'

'The same friend?'

'No. A different one.' He stood up again. 'Look, can we get on with this please. I have arrangements to make, business to deal with!'

Sandy stopped this line of questioning for now. They could check all these details out later, if they needed to. 'Mister de Runcy, did you know your son owned a boat. Moored at Dunlaridge Marina?'

'Yes, of course I do. I paid for the bloody thing, didn't I?'

Sandy was quite impressed with the man's grasp of the English language and particularly his use of swear words. 'So, it was your boat?'

'It is our boat. It belongs to the business.' He sat down again. 'And I would like it back, once you have finished playing with it.'

'Of course,' chipped in Heather before Sandy could wind the man up again by telling him anything they didn't yet want him to hear.

'Did you use the boat, yourself, Mister de Runcy?'

'Yes, of course I did. I like the sea. One of the greatest things about your damn climate over here, the winds up the lochs are a test for any seasoned sailor.'

'When were you last on it?'

'I don't know.'

Sandy shuffled his papers again. 'And a car. Your son had a Porsche..' he checked the document. 'Cayenne S, four-wheel drive.' Looking up at the man, he asked, 'Did you buy that too?'

'I guess so. He chose it. I think to combat these fucking roads of yours. I don't get involved with that stuff. Jean-Luc ran the business, not me. I am sure it would have been put against tax. Is that a crime?'

'I don't think so,' Sandy couldn't resist a dig. 'But would you like me to check with our guys at Her Majesty's Revenue office?'

'I would like the car and the boat back, today. You have had 24 hours to do your looking.' De Runcy stood up. 'If you want to continue with your questions, I think my lawyer might like to hear them also.'

Heather stood up too, stepping in front of the man who was making for the door again. 'Sir. We need to check these things, to help find your son's killer. Don't you want us to find him? You certainly don't seem that keen on helping us catch the murderer?' For a small woman she was intimidating, far more effective than Sandy's teasing.

De Runcy squared up to her. 'That is your job, Madame. Surely you can manage to do your job without my help?' His eyes narrowed. 'Or would you like me to ask some of my friends to come and help too?'

As he went to close the door behind him, he turned. 'And while you are doing your job, can I get back to work in my distillery, or do you still suspect that the death of my distiller was not an accident also?'

Heather let him go and Sandy informed the recorder that he had left the room.

She spoke first. 'Well, that went well? Do you have to be such a blunt instrument?'

'Oh, I think we gathered enough from him, for now.'

'At least we know he has some interesting friends, eh. Probably pals with the Chief Constable!'

# Chapter Twenty-Five

Once Fraser laid the dog down on the tailboard of the pick-up, Scott inspected a wound on her rump and felt his temper rising. 'You shot her? You bastard, you shot my dog!' Fraser was just about to speak when a solid fist hit him squarely on the jaw, with enough force to send him backwards to the ground, getting tangled in a bush full of brambles. Ignoring his protestations he turned back to the dog, whose eyes were open, and was attempting to stand up.

'She was on my land, perhaps chasing my sheep. I am entitled to shoot predators!' Dougie was helping Fraser to his feet, as Scott gathered up Beth and carried her to the front seat of the truck, pulling out an old coat and wrapping her up in it.

Scott closed the door and went around to the driver's side, shouldering his brother out of the way. 'You really are a low life twat, Fraser!' he snarled, firing up the engine and spinning the vehicle round, narrowly missing Dougie Cairns who jumped out of the way. The nearest veterinary clinic was in Taynuilt, and Scott fumbled with his phone whilst driving flat out down the track and onto the narrow road, the open tail gate of the pick-up bouncing up and down behind him. The road was still icy and the vehicle fish-tailed as he rounded the corner heading up the hill. By the time he found the number for the vet, the phone was just coming into reception and he hit the dial button. A receptionist answered and he garbled a message to her, saying he was on his way. She told him the vet was still out on her rounds, but she would try and call her and get her back to the surgery by the time he got there.

As he was speaking a beeping sound told him he had a voice message waiting to be listened to. He ignored it for now, concentrating on the tricky surface of the road, particularly as he climbed the hill past the distillery where snow lay an inch deep. Stuffing the phone in his pocket, he ran his hand over Beth who was breathing hard and scrabbling with her back leg. 'You'll be fine girl. You'll be okay. Hang on in there. Soon be there to see then nice vet.' As he pulled his hand away, it was covered in blood and he pressed his foot a little harder on the accelerator. Thankfully once he was down the hill, sliding some of the way and bouncing off the high bank at the side, the main road had been cleared, making the last five or six miles a bit easier to navigate. Traffic was reasonably quiet this time of day in winter and he spent most of the journey above the speed limit, before swinging into the small car park of a single-story building. Pulling the vehicle to a sharp stop that skidded up the gravel stones, Scott was out and gathering up the dog when a dirty estate car pulled in behind him and a woman in her early thirties jumped out.

'What happened?' she said, her Irish accent shrill and concerned.

'She's been shot, and losing a lot of blood!' the desperation showing in his voice, as he shouldered open the door to the surgery. A girl at the desk pointed towards an open door into a room that smelled heavily of disinfectant. Scott laid Beth down on a large stainless-steel table in the centre of the room while the young vet washed her hands, pulling on a green gown. The dog whined as he pulled the coat from around her, which was heavily stained with blood, and then stood back silently to let the vet take a look.

A full two minutes passed with only the clock on the wall and the dogs breathing breaking the silence. At least she was breathing, that was something. Eventually the woman looked up at him, her green eyes, surrounded by a blonde mess of frizzy hair that was half tied back. 'I'll get her some painkillers and clean this up. There is quite a lot of lead in there, but no broken bones that I can feel.' She put her hand on his arm and rallied a smile. 'I think she'll be OK.'

Scott could have kissed her. In fact, for the first time, he noticed how beautiful she was, all five foot five of her, in her green gown and white wellington boots. Already she had a syringe in her hand and was drawing clear liquid from a bottle. He went to speak but found himself tongue tied for words. Thankfully, his mobile phone rang in his pocket, and the vet glanced across at him, as he stared at her uncomfortably, raising an eyebrow at the pathetic ringtone of some 90s disco music. 'You going to get that?' The smile morphed into a grin that melted something inside him. 'I'm Megan, by the way.' With that she stuck the needle gently into Beth, who winced a little, and then went about her routine business of repairing sick animals.

'Scott,' he mumbled, taking out the phone and wandering out through the door, where the cold wind slapped the embarrassment from his face. Pressing the answer button, for the first time he noticed his knuckles were bleeding and he felt a tiny pang of satisfaction for laying his bullying brother down with one swing. 'Yes, Jim. What you got to tell me?'

Wedging the phone between his shoulder and ear, he opened the pick-up door, pulled out his packet of tobacco and rolled a thin cigarette, while Jim brought him up to speed on proceedings. 'Did he mention I had dinner with him last night?' Scott eventually asked when Jim had given him the bones of the interview. He hadn't, but Jim sounded quite concerned about the fact. 'Not to worry, I'll tell the boss in a bit.' He drew on the cigarette, exhaling a white cloud, and glancing at the window to the surgery where Megan was concentrating on his dog, her assistant handing her some white towels. 'In a bit of a pickle here just now, Jim. My fucking brother shot my dog!'

Over the next ten minutes, Scott was glad of a chat with his fellow officer, as he paced the car-park telling him about what he had learned or, more accurately, hadn't learned from Cairns. 'One thing, though, he more or less admitted they were in this together. Not that that's any surprise. I'm pretty sure he was there when Edis died, but he didn't admit that. Not that I really had time to finish the interview.' He was just about to roll another cigarette when Megan appeared at the doorway, now out of her green overall, instead in a loose jumper over figure hugging jeans and sneakers. Her wayward hair was now under control via a clip at the back, and her smile beamed at him from under it.

'You owe me lunch, big fella.'

This time Scott didn't resist the urge he had earlier and stepped forward and kissed her on the cheek.

'Woah there, paddywack!' Her eyes flared up at him. 'I said lunch, not full-on intercourse!'

Again his embarrassment rose and he was about to apologise when she burst out laughing, turning on her heel. 'Your dog will be fine in a day or two.' Scott joined in the infectious laughter. 'But you make sure you keep her on a lead. There are some bad bastards out there, Scott.'

She was still chuckling when he saw Beth, who certainly didn't look fine, wrapped in half a roll of sticky bandage and her eyes barely open. 'I knocked her out, and I think we'd better keep her in until she fully comes round.' Scott stroked the dog's head, ruffling her ears between his finger and thumb, as he leaned his face down close to hers. 'Good girl, Beth, well done, ya dafty.'

Within a few minutes he was heading back to his pick-up as Megan called after him. 'This evening?'

'I thought you said lunch?' The question was genuine.

'For the dog. Collect her around six?' again the vet was smiling as the sun flashed through her hair, and he wondered how such a wonderful person could do such a heart wrenching job.

On the way back to Kilchrenan he listened to the voicemails, one from Jim from earlier saying to give him a call. The other was from Liz Mills, her smooth voice teasing him with a message saying he could come and see her any time he liked. He considered the woman and her relationship with the dead man with whom she had been having a love affair. She certainly hadn't seemed to be mourning him. In fact, nobody, apart from his wife, seemed to be grieving Charlie's death at all. John McCarthy definitely hadn't, although Jess had said he was acting somewhat strange and Scott was pretty sure that would have something to do with all that intricate plumbing under the big whisky barrels. That got him to thinking about Jess, and about how she had him wrapped round her little finger, knowing he was never quite over his love for her, something that had been with him all his days. Then he considered Megan, and how she was flirting with him. Was that all it was, just a bit of harmless teasing? Did she do that with all the boys, or was she genuinely interested in him? She really was exceptionally pretty; he couldn't deny that. Who knew, when it came to women! Their complicated emotions always had him in knots of confusion.

Big John's Discovery was parked outside his workshop as he passed through the village and Scott wondered if he should just call in on him right now, unannounced. But then he considered he might get more information out of Mills and her husband, especially if he played her at her own game of cat and mouse. Glancing at his watch he saw it was still barely after ten and he was already shattered from his eventful morning, and maybe a leave-over from the night before. Driving much steadier now he took the left fork along the loch towards the campsite, steeling himself for round two. Or was that three? Or four, even.

As he arrived, Liz Mills was standing outside of the office door, dressed in tight pink leather trousers and a low-cut top, pulling out a pack of cigarettes.

'Aha, our ever-caring local bobby,' she purred. Scott resented being called a local bobby, a derogative term he thought, referencing Robert Peel's hard-handed policing of yesteryear. He declined a cigarette she was offering, instead rolling one of his own. Liz fixed him with a gaze. 'Lovely view?'

Already starting to squirm, Scott reminded himself of his tactic here, to play her on the same playing field. Staring back into her eyes he said, 'Definitely is from where I am standing!' Then he broke away and glanced over the loch, to the hotel on the other side in the distance. 'I always enjoy a nice view.'

Liz stubbed her cigarette under the sole of a high heeled shoe. 'So, mister polis man, how can I help you?'

Scott squirmed again. Some of the local expressions were meaningless, almost pathetic when spoken by English people. When a Glaswegian said the word polis, it was sent with venom and contempt that had been inbred for generations. When a middle-aged English woman tried to imitate it, it just sounded plain stupid, in the same way that if he said the word Hertfordshire or Chipping Norton in a BBC voice, it would just come out wrong in every way. 'I think you know what I am looking for,' he said quietly.

She actually put her soft hand on his shoulder, bringing her face close to his ear so he could inhale her cheap perfume. 'I'd eat you alive, Bobby. Right down to your shoe-laces!'

Scott walked away, now the trap was set, flicking the end of his roll-up into the bushes. He could see how Charlie Edis had fallen for this woman, even if she wasn't Scott's type. Did that make him a womaniser? He wasn't so sure. Most men would fall for that advance, maybe even himself if he was ten years older and lonely. And desperate! Who else did this woman have on her books in this village, or any of the other villages around? Did Harry mind, that she had been sleeping around? Scott suspected that he would definitely know. She was so transparent he surely could have seen that when they first met. Perhaps he enjoyed it, sharing his wife about. Maybe even got off on it. What was it they had called those type of men when he had been on a 'Sexual harassment' course in Snecky? Cuckold. That was it.

'That how it was for Charlie?' he asked the question as conversationally as he could, expecting to catch her off guard.

It didn't. 'Charlie, was Charlie. Hardly a difficult one to catch, was he?' As she swung her head, her dangling earrings rattled. 'Not like you, honey.'

The word 'honey' as a term of affection again just sounded wrong in Scott's brain. Did people even say honey anymore? If you called a woman that, you'd be up for harassment faster than flag up a greasy pole.

Scott kept his back to her. 'So why did you catch him then?'

'Why not?' He could hear her feet approaching on the gravel drive. 'A woman has to have some pleasures in life.' He felt her hand slip round his middle as her breath tinged his ear. Was she really making sexual advances to an on-duty police officer, in broad daylight? And probably, with her husband watching. Scott pulled forward, just enough to break the contact, as he considered maybe the man was filming him from somewhere. Didn't she call him honey? Was that what this charade was, a honey trap? More to the point, was that what she had done with Charlie? Had he been the victim in this operation all along?

He lowered his voice, still looking across the water. 'What's the currency?'

'For you?' the sexy voice was back. 'Ooo, I like this game. You'd definitely qualify for a discount, Bobby. What is your offer?'

Scott felt his phone in his pocket, the voice recorder hopefully still running. 'What did Charlie pay?'

'Oh Charlie. Poor Charlie. He had his uses.' She was lighting another cigarette, blowing the smoke in his direction. 'But he was a greedy man, Bobby.' Her hand was back, by his waist this time. 'Are you a greedy boy too?' He felt her fingers caress his groin. 'Do you like to take more than you give?'

'Is that what he did?' Scott turned to face her. 'And paid the ultimate price?' He raised his eyebrows and leaned forward as if to kiss her. 'I think that's a bit too expensive for me?'

'I did offer you a discount, Bobby boy!' But Scott had already pulled back and was heading for the office door.

'A bit cold out here, to be honest. Let's get in the warm?' He shouldered the door open, to see Harry Mills sitting at his desk. The man was looking into a computer screen but as he was not touching the keyboard Scott suspected it was just a cover. On the desk next to the keyboard was a mobile phone. 'Morning, Harry,' Scott said, cheerfully, before snatching the phone and opening the cover.

'Hey. Give that back!' Harry stood up, pushing back his chair as Liz came in through the door. Scott had his back to the pair of them, already swiping up the screen. Thankfully, there was no password required, maybe because this man was too dumb or laid back to use one, or possibly because the phone had not had long enough to lock itself since its last use. The camera app was open, again as Scott had suspected. He hit the play button, and a video appeared on the screen, of Liz standing outside, lighting a cigarette and Scott arriving in his Toyota pick-up.

'Like to do a bit of filming, do we Harry?' Scott was the one doing the teasing now, as Harry still tried to take the phone off him. 'I bet if I went through this, I would find a few juicy videos, eh?' He grinned firstly at Harry, and then at Liz. 'Some really juicy ones?' Scott clicked on the video on the screen and then the menu, deleting the file. 'Perhaps I should borrow this?'

'You can't do that!' Harry was almost pleading. 'That's personal property, you can't just take it... not without a warrant or something?'

Liz stood by the door, cool as ever. 'Let him take it, if he wants. He might enjoy the show.'

Scott considered this, not particularly keen on watching this woman in the act of love-making, although it probably would unveil a few secrets of her local conquests. He suspected Jim at the station might enjoy a look at it though. 'Don't flatter yourself, Mrs Mills, voyeurism is not really my style. Not like your husband here.' He made to give it back, but then snatched it away again. 'All I need to know is why you were blackmailing Charlie Edis! You tell me that, and Harry gets away without arrest for harbouring indecent material, and your tits don't get splashed all over the Sunday papers!'

# Chapter Twenty-Six

The thing about the Whisky Society was that it was self-regulating, meaning it was regulated from within. Experts inside its interior all have experience and many of them have their own involvement in specific distilleries. When it comes to the whisky awards, these experts were whittled down to a panel of around 30. It has to be remembered that whisky is a commodity and as such is traded, often on speculation of future worth. A barrel purchased today for under £10,000 could easily treble its worth in the next decade, without out the investor needing to do anything else, apart from perhaps paying insurance on it. However, the investor rarely gets chance to actually taste what is inside each barrel and, in many cases, has no intention of doing so or may not even like whisky at all. In a volatile market where stocks and shares rise and fall based on world economies, and house prices fluctuate for any manner of reasons, the whisky investment market has been pretty stable over the last few decades and was attracting a growing number of investors. Coupled with the fact that quality whisky was now being well marketed and enjoyed by a younger generation, and the whisky industry generally seemed to be on the up.

This was all information that Jim had found in his research into the business. Although a man who would have a flutter on the odd horse, and who enjoyed a tipple, Jim didn't think he would feel comfortable spending upwards of 10K on something when he had no real idea what was in it. Perhaps it was his years in the force that ingrained him to be suspicious of most things he didn't fully understand but he felt, somewhere along the line, the business was based too much on trust, and when trust is a commanding factor, it is generally open to corruption. Of course, much of the industry was now in the hands of the big conglomerates who had gradually bought up the defunct distilleries and any barrels that had been left in bond where the owners couldn't afford to pay the duty to get them released, which they bottled and sold on for handsome profits.

Both Bill and Sandy were listening as Jim extended his theory.

'So, I am saying that the whisky in the barrel may not always be what they say it is.' Jim puffed his chest slightly, as though he had just found the whereabouts of Shergar.

'Yes, we get that, Jim,' Sandy was probably slightly quicker off the mark than his fellow officer. 'But who seals the barrel and stands to be accountable for what is in it?'

'That would be the master distiller,' his eyes lit up as though a light had come on somewhere. 'In this case, Charlie Edis.'

Sandy scratched his head, thinking. 'Are we allowed to re-open the barrels, to check the contents?'

'Not once they have gone into bond. Not without a bloody good reason!'

'Is murder a good enough reason?'

'A good enough reason for what?' Heather Downs was standing in the doorway.

'To get stuck into some decent whisky, Ma'am!' Jim said, cheekily. He then explained the situation again, suggesting that, only on a hunch, some of the barrels of Glenlachan whisky may have been sold to investors, and perhaps someone had found out that what was inside them wasn't as it should be.

'Can we get access to the company accounts?' she asked.

'I'm sure we can, by pulling a few strings from above,' Jim added, 'if we are to believe the figures in them?'

'How far did you get on checking out the victim's phone records, etc?' Jim's boss was asking.

'I'm getting there, but waiting on report back from the phone towers to confirm locations. Seems like he has been on the boat quite a lot, but no record of him coming back to the distillery on Sunday evening, as yet. Picture on the traffic cam is unclear. Definitely him driving, but no certainty that it is Shauna Edis in the passenger's seat.' He glanced up as Bill Young entered the room, carrying a folder of documents. 'Should have more later today.'

'Ah, Bill,' Heather's face was still stern as ever. 'Come to tell us who the murderer is? Or are you as negative as this lot?'

'Nope, sorry. But I have come to tell you who the victim was. The first one, I mean.' He spread the folder on table, lifting out a sheet of paper. 'Our Charlie Edis has a wee bit of form!'

'Good. And at least someone has done what he was supposed to be doing in the last twelve hours.' Heather's face eventually broke into a half smile. 'Let's take a look at where this man has come from, eh?'

Bill mapped out a life of the master distiller who had been born in Aberdeen in 1971, been a bright lad and ended up at James Gordon school. He had applied to join the Royal Highlanders regiment as an officer but had failed the requirements, mainly on physical grounds. According to his school report, he had generally been lazy. A family friend had got him a job at Moray distillery, as a distiller's assistant. The job sounded pretty grand but it was much the same as Davie was doing at Glenlachan, everything from polishing the stills, loading mash and sweeping the floor. Charlie was cautioned a few times, for being lazy and disruptive until he left after just one year. Some say he was fired. Nearly a year working on a farm near Glenlivet, where they bred pedigree cattle, didn't really work out for him either and he left before winter.

Then a stint down south saw him take a factory role, as warehouse manager in a distribution centre in Manchester. It was here where things got a bit more interesting.

'The operation involved handling a lot of household wares. Everything from soft furnishings to tea pots and Hoovers.' Bill continued. 'It was a fair consensus of a few of his co-workers that Charlie wasn't up to the job and some wondered how had even got the appointment. Anyway, long story short, it seems a few of the goods started disappearing. Not just the odd saucepan but things like dishwashers or pallets of crockery. Nobody was really sure how long it had gone on, maybe a few years, but eventually the law got involved. The north east had a ring of small crime through which a lot of things found themselves for sale on eBay, as well as through a few small shops. Serial numbers had been replaced, packaging exchanged and manufacturer's details doctored, but eventually a lot of the fenced goods were traced back to this warehouse, with Charlie and a couple of van drivers in the frame.'

'So, he's done time?' asked Heather.

'Nope. I don't know how, but a rather fancy lawyer managed to wangle him out of it, lacking in evidence and stating that, although he was supposed to be manager, he didn't know what was going on!'

'Bloody hell. Must have some money to afford one of those type of bastards,' Sandy offered.

'He was still fired from the job and headed back north and took another assistant distillers job, this time at Tomintoul. The boss seemed to like him as he courted and eventually married the daughter. Things were fairly straight from then on and he earned his Distillers Certificate and was recognised for having a good nose for the spirit, as well as a taste for it. He then applied for a few head distillers jobs in the area but had a reputation for being too bolshie and a slightly chequered CV. For a while he traded whiskies, picking up bottles here and there, often in auction, and then punting them out to the public.' Bill stopped and took a drink of tea which was now cold.

'Sounds kosher enough, but is there any money in it?'

Jim picked up on that. 'Och aye, if you know what you're doing. Quite a few wheeler dealers in that game, supplying the collectors. Big demand from abroad.'

'I spoke to an auction house in Glasgow who knew him back then. Collectors whisky is all about the label as many of these bottles never get opened. Never will. Unlike wine which might last twenty years, tops, whisky will keep for a 100 or more. And very often, it is the year on the label that makes the difference. For example, a bottle of 1992..' he checked his notes, 'Glen Ord, would be worth seventy quid but a 1982 upwards of twa hundred!'

'And who would know the difference?' Jim puffed. 'Not even an expert!'

'Precisely!'

Heather was getting more interested. 'What does this have to do with our man, Edis?

'Well, the auction house had him under suspicion for a while, more than one of them. Sale results were exchanged between a couple of well-known Glasgow and Edinburgh companies, and Edis's purchases monitored, along with a few others. Even then it was near impossible to see. Trouble was that many of the middle range bottles would get sold on eBay and we all know that that stream of sale is impossible to detect, especially the smart ones.'

'Aren't the internet trading platforms self-regulating?'

'More so now, but not so much back then. Even if a buyer gave you a bad review, you could just open up a new account and start again. And when collectors get greedy, many of them aren't interested in a sellers trading records at all.'

'So, our man was peddling crap. Where did he get the labels from?'

'And there we have it. The real crime is owned by the folks who print the labels. And that is one highly profitable but invisible business!'

'Did they catch him?'

'By the mid-2000s, one or two of the big distillers realised that some of their stuff was getting out to the open market, and there is no way it could have done, so they started buying a few themselves, at their own expense, and checking what was in them. Even then, it was impossible to prosecute the sellers and eBay themselves weren't going to get involved. So it was really down to the auction houses again, to scrutinise the labels more thoroughly. As it happens, it was my source who actually copped our Charlie. I mentioned Glen Ord, 1982? Well, it turned out, Glen Ord didn't produce a whisky in 1982 on account of it being bankrupt and closed down for most of that decade, only to be re-opened when an investor got involved.'

'A bit like Glenlachan?' said Jim, following closely.

'Yep.' Bill jumped up and went to the white board, drawing a big number nine on it. 'All it took was a sharpie and a steady hand.' Then, with a stoke of a pen, he changed it to an eight!

'As well as banning him from trading, they called the Glasgow unit in, but they couldn't make it stick. Weren't particularly interested, according to my man. Customs and Excise had a look too, but didn't have the manpower to pull a case together. So the house just banned him from trading, and word soon got around the other ones who did same and, once again, our Charlie walks.'

Heather clapped her hands together. 'Good work, young Bill. Good work!' She stood and looked at the top of the white board where Edis's photograph was stuck on, next to that of Jean-Luc. Below Charlie were lines leading to a row of suspects and contacts. 'But how does that help us here?' She pointed to the photo of Jean-Luc. 'Anyone spoken to our wonder-boy in the village yet today?'

Jim raised his hand. 'I did, an hour ago. Got a few issues with his dog, but he had interviewed one of the suspects.'

'His dog?' Heather raised an eyebrow, 'He's a policeman not a bloody shepherd!'

'Someone shot it, Ma'am!'

'Shot it? Christ, not another murder to deal with?'

'It's still alive, and going to be OK.'

Heather was inwardly relieved. 'So, who has he seen? Any good news from over that way?'

Jim filled them in on what he had been told, about how Dougie Cairns had been making new barrels and chiselling numbers on the end to denote their contents. And also about the makeshift siphon set up, and perhaps he knew who had fabricated that mechanism. He was off to see the campsite owner who had been having an affair with the deceased. He refrained from mentioning that Scott had shared a dinner table with old man de Runcy.

Sandy was listening closely. 'So, it looks as if our Charlie has been at it again. What was it the boy had said about Charlie. Moving, and mixing?' he thought for a moment. 'But where is the crime?'

Andrew McClatchie opened the door and all the officers stood up. 'Carry on, chaps. I'm just looking in on progress.'

Sandy sat and continued 'Where is the crime here, to do with Edis?'

'Apart from being a crook, and drunk and a womaniser, you mean,' said Bill cheekily.

'And getting himself murdered?' McClatchie added

quietly.

'Which is what we should be looking at,' snapped Heather, siding with her boss.

Jim raised his hand.

'Bloody hell, Jim, we're not at school!' She frowned at him. 'Spit it out man,' frustration showing in her voice.

'Scott is convinced they are all in on it?'

'All who?'

'The whole damn village by the sound of it!' he looked to his shoes. 'That Charlie was pulling some sort of scam that they were probably all set to gain from. Maybe he crossed them? Looks to me like any one of *them*,' he pointed to the board, 'could have killed Charlie Edis!'

A young police woman poked her head around the door. 'Phone call, for you sir. It's the press.'

McClatchie stood up. 'That's all I bloody need. Have we anything to tell them?'

This time nobody put their hand up.

# Chapter Twenty-Seven

The fresh air was a relief as Scott stepped outside of the warm office and took a short walk up the gravel track towards the small chalets. He had decided to give Harry his phone back, minus the video he had taken of him and Liz. Yes, he was pretty sure there would have been stuff on there that may have incriminated the both of them, but this was community policing where everyone had their little secrets and just being aware of them was enough to keep the peace. If you started opening up all the cupboards, the skeletons would pile up on the village green like a pyre, each member kicking each other's. That was the whole thing about being part of a small society, the live-and-let-live aspect, only intervening when things got out of hand. And, besides, when you started winding these folks up, plenty would come forward to mention that Scott took the odd drive home after a couple of beers, or spent a day up the mountain with his dog when he should be on duty.

He was pretty certain they were all in on Charlie's death, somehow or other. Just who was at the distillery on Sunday afternoon would be difficult to ascertain, unless one of them broke ranks. The boy, Davie, all innocently told him that he went home at six o'clock and he was pretty sure there would be proof of that, him driving the tractor through the village just after opening time. Not even that boy was dull enough to lie about that bit, particularly since he had found out the lad wasn't quite as dim as he made out. So, the big question was, did Davie go home, and then one or more of the others turn up and eventually kill Charlie? Or was he killed before 6 o'clock which brought the boy back into the frame too. Scott had a hunch it was the former.

He glanced through the windows of the small chalets. The one where Shauna stayed seemed empty and her wee car was gone, just now. She posed another question. Why were they so secretive about staying in Inverness and why had she lied about it? Did she and Jean-Luc go to the distillery and back again, killing her father in the process. He hadn't found out the exact relationship between her and her father but it was mentioned that he hadn't liked her seeing Jean-Luc, and perhaps she had found out about her dad seeing the Mills woman? Still all speculation, but somehow, although possible, that scenario seemed implausible.

As Scott walked back to his car, Liz was looking out of the window and he could feel she was discussing him with her husband. He gave her a little wave. Opening the door to the pick-up he instinctively looked around for Beth, before remembering she was still in the hospital. He hoped she would make a full recovery, so they could head back up the mountains, come spring. Poor bugger, getting a gunshot wound. What sort of a monster had his brother become, that he would shoot another man's dog!

Scott was still considering his brother and his involvement in this local scheme, when he pulled up outside John McCarthy's garage. He knew from the records that Fraser wasn't averse to crossing the line when it came to the law. A prosecution for trading some sheep at Dalmally mart which weren't actually his to sell. He got away with a fine and a caution on that one. And there had been a fight one evening, seemingly over a woman, that had ended with him overnighting in the cells. Both incidents had happened while Scott had been away on the rigs but there were records of them in Oban which he hadn't really dwelled on.

Further up the small street he could see a few cars in the car-park opposite the hotel, and what looked like a large van with a satellite dish on the top. As soon as he stepped out of the vehicle a young man approached him, making casual conversation.

'Can you tell me where I can buy cigarettes in this village?' His accent was Edinburgh and his tone was false.

From the morning he had had, Scott was inclined to tell him to politely fuck off, and not to be so stupid as he must have just walked past the local shop. Instead he said, 'I wondered when you would get here?'

'I'm sorry?' said the man, innocently.

Scott pushed past him, heading to the door to McCarthy's office, before turning back on his heel. 'I've got nothing to say to you. You want a press statement, speak to the governor at Oban nick, OK?' He closed the door behind him and walked through to the garage.

For once Big John was not buried under the bonnet of a car but sitting in a greasy chair next to the oil-fired heater. 'Little weasel came in here earlier, asking questions.' John nodded to Scott. 'I threatened to burn his nuts off with the gas torch!' John chuckled to himself.

'Not going to do the same to me, eh, old fella?'

'Less of the old, ya cheeky wee bastard.' He indicated to the heater. 'Get yer erse over here and get a warm. It's time we had a chat!'

As he neared, John held out a small hip flask, without standing up. Scott accepted it from him, and took a slug, swilling it round his mouth and then feeling it burn the back of his throat as he swallowed. 'That what this is about?' he said, quietly, looking into the fire. Silence filled the air apart from the crackle from the flames. After half a minute, when the liquid had reached his stomach, he took another small swig, and then handed it back to the big man. 'This the real stuff?'

John sighed. 'How the fuck should I know?' He took a swig himself. 'Couldn't believe a word that lying bastard said to us, could we.'

Scott wanted to say, 'We?' but remained silent. John McCarthy had always been careful with his words, particularly to Scott. Maybe it was the whisky loosening his voice, or perhaps just a pang of guilt. One thing was for sure, it was out of character. He considered turning on his voice recorder again, but decided that whatever this man had to say, he would be prepared to repeat it again, if required. He started to roll a cigarette. 'You going to tell me what is going on up there, John?'

'Is?' John held out his hand and Scott finished the roll and gave it to him. 'Was, more like?'

'Before Charlie died?' Scott was rolling himself another, making a mental note to drop in at the shop and get another packet. 'A bit inconvenient of him, eh?'

'Don't be fucking sarcastic, ya wee shite.' John lit the smoke from a lighter in his pocket, and then exhaled. 'You wanna hear this or not?'

Scott smiled inwardly. John may have recently been behaving out of character, but this was definitely him back to his normal self, insults and all. He recalled the time when he grinned at him when he found out he was seeing Jess, wielding a heavy Stillsons wrench at the same time. 'Nobody is going to get hurt, are they, ya week piss pot?' his very words back then.

'Should I be writing it down?' he asked.

'Na, you'll remember.' The old man looked comfortable, as though about to tell a bedtime story. 'Charlie was bragging in the pub, one night, about how great his nose was for good whisky and how he could turn bad whisky in to good better than Jesus Christ himself. I had enough of his patter and suggested he prove it. Our lass was behind the bar and got him what he asked. A couple of glasses and three or four bottles off the top shelf. He began with a double measure, something off the optic, a Whyte and Mackay, I think. Then he started adding from the other bottles, a dash of this, a sniff, then another dash of that. I still thought it was bullshit, so didn't take too much notice of his theatre. At one stage I think he even added a tiny dash of water. All the time, he kept muttering the same phrase.' He tried to recall it. 'What was it now?'

'Moving and mixing?' suggested the copper.

'Aye, that was it. Moving and mixing. I think he fancied himself as some kind of magician, shuffling the glasses around on the bar. In fact, he just fancied himself, full stop.' John let out a deep laugh which morphed into a coughing fit. Scott waited patiently until he had finished and was ready to continue. 'Eventually, after maybe 10 minutes or more, he lifted the glass up to the light, looking at it from all angles like a diamond, then took a real deep sniff. Voila, he shouted, like some bloody Shakespeare actor, and took a sip, before banging the glass back down on the bar. 'I give you Glenlachan, a single malt from the lochs of Argyll!' John lent back in his chair, closing his eyes, now his tale was told.

Scott was a little confused. 'You saying he took ordinary whiskies, mixed them together and made a single malt? That can't be right, can it?'

'Right or wrong, Scottie boy, that's what he did.' John kept his eyes closed. 'Now I'm no expert, but when he produced a half bottle of the proper stuff from his jacket hung by the door, we tried the two, side by side, and I'm damned if I could tell the difference.'

'You say we? Who else was there?'

'What, that night? All the usual regulars, Cairns, Harry and Liz, the young lad. Pub was half full. He even got a round of applause.'

'I can see why he would.' Scott pulled out his notebook, scribbling the names down. 'When was this, John?'

'Couple of weeks ago, maybe three.'

'Can't be more specific?'

'Nah, my memory isn't what it was. Our Jess might remember, though.'

Scott made another note and closed his little book, rubbing his hands together. It was an interesting story and did give a bit more background on Charlie. He was about to leave and phone in to Oban when John, still with his eyes closed said, 'You want to hear the rest?'

Scott pulled out his pad again, turning back to the fire. 'Aye, go on then.'

'Later that night, Dougie, Liz and me was talking, when Charlie muscles in on the conversation, and by this time he was well pissed. 'You wanna make some money?' His voice was slurred and I noticed him run his hands down Liz's hips, but she didn't seem to mind. 'You wanna make some real money?' John was trying to mimic Charlie's accent but, apart from the slur, he was way off. 'To start with, I wasn't interested. I'd heard these things before, pub talk, someone has something to sell, or steal. But Charlie kept on talking, telling us what good whisky, proper whisky, was really worth. Like, upwards of a thousand quid a bottle! Fucking hell, boy, a thousand quid a bottle? Who pays that kind of money for a drink?' John had his eyes open now, looking at Scott. 'Then he starts quoting stuff that has made a hundred thousand, and one that just made a million. We knew it was bullshit, well we thought we did until Dougie looked it up on Google on his phone. For a minute, nobody said anything as Dougie got the round in. But each of us had clocked what he was getting at. I think it was Liz who eventually asked the question he had been waiting for us to ask. 'Could he really make that stuff? And if so, why wasn't he a millionaire living on a yacht?' He blew her a kiss and then put his finger on his nose. 'I might not be able to make it that good, but I can mix it,' he told us, and then stood there grinning at us like a twat, each one of us in turn. 'But I might need some help!'

John stood up, heading for a grubby door in the far wall. 'Need a piss,' he said, gruffly. When he was out of sight, Scott pulled out his mobile phone opening a WhatsApp text to Jim. 'Getting to the bottom of it now. The paint is starting to crack.' A few seconds after he sent it, a message came back. 'Charlie had form!'

Scott didn't get time to reply before John came back out and started filling the kettle. He moved over to the big man, almost glad to be away from the heat of the oil burner. He braced himself before asking the question he had come here to ask. 'That where you came in, John? Making pipes and siphoning equipment?'

'Aye.' John put two cups on the counter, and a spoon of instant coffee in each one. 'I heard you'd found my wee contraption. Quite pleased with that at short notice.'

'So, you're telling me that Charlie devised a way of bringing highly sought-after whisky out of what appeared to be a sealed barrel. Mixed it with some other stuff and was bottling and selling it, and you all had a cut? That it?'

'Sounds like you had that all worked out for yourself.' He poured the water. 'Except that he wasn't bottling it at all. Just barrelling it. For now, anyway.'

Scott considered this and accepted the coffee. 'So, who killed him?'

'That, young man,' he sighed, 'I can't tell you. But, despite not liking the man, I sure as hell wish they hadn't!'

# Chapter Twenty-Eight

'That was a bit harsh, eh?' Dougie leant on a farmyard gate, his tractor chugging away in the background.

'Serves the little fucker right. Poking his nose in round here as if he owns the place,' Fraser Donald pushed his tweed cap back off his head. 'I only winged the dog, anyway. Bloody thing, having the freedom of the place.' He spat on the ground out of disgust.

Dougie glanced across to where two dogs, a Collie and an Alsatian, were boxed into a kennel, a long rusty chain attached to each of their collars. The fact they were living out in all weathers made him shudder. Evidently even the resident dogs didn't get the freedom of the place. 'How they looking?' he said, changing the subject, 'Can I take a shufty?'

Fraser eyed him, almost suspiciously. 'Aye, sure. But you'll no see much.' Dougie followed Fraser across the muddy farmyard and in through a rustic wooden door into an old stone out-building. The place was full of dust and smelled of rats, an ancient wooden hayrack fastened on one wall the whole length of the shed.

Dougie admired the turned spindles, each about 70mm thick and a metre long, maybe thirty of them. 'Don't fancy selling that, do you?' Fraser ignored him, making his way to the far end and another door, this one with a keyhole about 50mm across. He reached up onto a beam above the hayrack, and pulled an old rusty key down, easily 200mm long. Although the lock turned with ease, the door sounded like it hadn't been opened in half a century as he pushed it back on rusty hinges. Above them, a pigeon fluttered its wings, as though the noise had disturbed its otherwise peaceful winter hibernation. Fraser closed the door behind them, turning on a cankered old switch that operated a row of single overhead bulbs, each starting out dark yellow as they yawned into life, bringing enough meagre illumination to show-up a cradle of cobwebs in the rafters. Of similar size to the first one, this room was layered with dust, and a channel along the floor indicated that it had once been a cow byre, when cows would stand on its raised side platform and, by the looks of the stalls, be chained up for the winter. The channel had been swept clean, as the two of them made their way to the far end again. The room smelt musty, as though the outside didn't find its way in here often, but was accompanied by a sweeter aroma. Against the far wall was a stack of turnips, maybe a metre high, covered with a thin layer of yellow straw to keep the frost away.

Dougie started to glance around, his suspicion rising when he realised that was all that was in the building, which this local farmer had led him into. It certainly wasn't where he expected to go.

'Nothing to see here!' Fraser said, almost excitedly, as he could sense the concern in his colleague's eyes in the dim light. 'Unless you know what you're looking for!' He knelt down at the foot of the pile of roots, moving a few of them to one side.

'I know what I'm looking for,' exclaimed Dougie Cairns, refusing to be intimidated, 'and I'm not seeing it?'

'That's where your wrang, pal' The farmer pulled away a few more neeps and exposed a tarpaulin underneath them. 'You're seeing it alright, you just dunnea ken you are?'

'Under there?'

'Surely.'

As he scraped away some more, he lifted the tarp sheet, just enough to expose the bottom half of a wooden barrel. Dougie knelt down to look, as the sweet smell of whisky drifted out from it.

'Warm, and moist, and outta sight. That's what I was told. And that's what I done.'

'Are you sure they'll be OK, under that lot?'

Fraser snarled. 'What? You the fucking expert now? Now the other wanker is out the way?' He let the sheet drop, kicking the turnips back into place.

'I only know what he told us, that these things have to breathe?'

'Well.' Fraser looked him in the eye. 'He's no breathing any more, is he? That's stopped his fucking cheating?'

'Mind if I take a photo, to show the others?' Cairns was pulling out his phone.

'You do that, and you'll be the one no breathing next!' He pulled some slime from his nose, shaking it from his fingers. 'Anyone see's that, wouldn't take em long to place it?'

Dougie nodded.

'No, son.' Fraser was already heading to the door. 'I'm keeping my side of the bargain, and you all best take me at my word.'

It was a long cold half an hour as Dougie's ancient Massey chugged up the hill past the loch, towing his heavy load and coughing out black smoke in protest. At the top he continued straight on instead of turning up for the village, following the water down towards the campsite.

Harry and Liz Mills lived in a white period house, a few hundred metres before the site, with a tarmac drive that curled in behind a high hedge. The house had been built by some swank at the turn of the twentieth century, with uninterrupted views over the loch. Since then, the box hedge had been allowed to get out of control, obscuring the view from all but the second story windows. He had sent a text to forewarn Harry that he was on his way and the man met him on the drive as he swung the tractor in through the gap where the trailer brushed the thick hedge.

Dougie had been inside the house once, to a party they had held, not long after they first arrived. He remembered its wooden panelled walls and just how cold it was inside. That was confirmed by the fact that this was the second load of logs he had delivered this year, and it was still only November. Harry gave a wave and pointed around the back, to where he had delivered last time. 'You going to stack them for us this time?' he shouted above the noise of the engine.

'Fat fucking chance,' Dougie muttered, his words drowned out as he pulled the throttle open, after clicking into reverse gear. With that the bed of the trailer slowly started to creak and rise, canvassing a few shouts of abuse from Harry that he couldn't just dump it on the drive! Harry pulled his head close enough so he could hear Dougie's words.

'Just lifting it so I can see?' he shouted. It was quite a common thing with older, smaller trailers where the driver would raise the trailer bed on its hydraulics, so he could get a view of the wheels and the ground behind it. Dougie wasn't long, skilfully reversing the machine around the side of the house to where a near empty cash of firewood was stacked neatly against the house wall. He jumped off, went around the back and bashed a handle open with his boot, allowing the contents to spill out on the gravel. Back in the seat, he lifted the hydraulic lever again, pulling forward slightly so all the contents could find its way to the floor.

Harry shook his head, knowing it would be him stacking the wood again, as the groundsman from the campsite was off this time of year. 'Boss wants a word!' he said, now the engine had died back down to its usual tick-over. 'She's in the office.'

Pulling the tractor and empty trailer out on to the

road, again he left the engine idling, as the old Fergie sometimes didn't like to start again on these cold mornings. 'Morning madam,' he said, giving her a kiss on both cheeks.

'What did you tell him?' her face was stern, eyes narrowing. 'The copper, what did you say to him?'

'Woah, wait a minute? I never spilled any beans.' He still held a smile. 'Nothing past these lips. Nothing he didn't know already.'

She leaned back against the desk, thighs stretching the fabric of her pink trousers. 'And what does he know?'

Dougie pulled up a chair. 'Any chance of a cuppa?'

'No there fucking isn't!' she stood up again. 'What does he know?'

'Well, he knows about piping the whisky, and I told him I made a few barrels, not that he couldn't work that out. And I'm pretty sure he knew who made the pump.' Cairns thought for a few seconds. 'Beyond that, I couldn't say, but not a lot more, I reckon.'

'He was here too.' She mellowed a bit. 'I tried to tame him but it didn't quite go to plan. He was asking some awkward questions, and I'm guessing he might have a few bartering chips to play with now.'

'Fucking hell!' he started laughing, 'You didn't shag the copper did you?'

Liz stamped her foot. 'No, I did not!' She pulled out a cigarette and headed for the door. 'But he's getting a bit too close. Maybe time we did something about it?'

Dougie look a little stunned. 'What get rid of him, you mean?' shaking his head. 'I'm not sure I signed up for that.' He stood up, looking out over the loch. 'What had you in mind?'

'Oh, I dunno. Fix his brakes, blow his car up. Run the bastard over with that tractor?'

'Christ, woman! Have you lost your shit?'

'My shit?' she shouted. Then calmed down again, coming back inside, sitting back on the desk and crossing her legs. 'You got us into this, Douglas. We have a lot at stake here. All of us!'

The room was silent for half a minute or more, until he answered. 'Nah. I'm not getting involved in that one. Get someone else to do it.' It was his turn to head for the door. 'Oh, and by the way, I just seen the goods. All nicely tucked up in bed, out of sight, out of mind!'

'Just keep your trap shut,' Liz offered as a parting word, as the man headed to his tractor.


Further up the road, Scott closed the door on the garage, checking around for the reporter who was nowhere to be seen. He walked the 200 metres up to the post office, its little bell chiming his arrival as he opened the door. 'Morning Jeanie, looks a bit busy about the place? Might be good for trade, eh?'

'Scootie.' The woman was already reaching behind her and opening a sliding door. 'The usual, is it?'

'Aye, but with extra gossip, please?' He chuckled, 'Don't spare the detail!'

Jeanie didn't need asking twice. 'Well, we got The Herald and the Record, so far. James. That's him from the Daily Record, thinks the van out there belongs to STV, but I haven't seen anyone yet.'

'But, you have spoken to this 'James'?'

'Just pleasantries, you know, chatting the time of day?' Jeanie looked out the window, as though he might be looking in. 'Quite a nice young man, as it happens.'

Scott sighed, pulling out his debit card to pay for the tobacco. 'What did you tell him?'

Jeanie went about her business in an everyday fashion,

tapping the amount into a card machine. 'Oh, you know, about Charlie and that. And he was asking after you?'

'Me? Personally?'

'Aye. Said he knew the man in charge, and were you around? I told him you were always popping up somewhere, and drove a grey pick-up, along with your dog. Lived in a cottage. And had the hots for Jess McCarthy. Liked the mountains.'

'Bloody hell, Jeanie. How many times have I told you not to gossip to strangers?'

'Well, it's not exactly secrets, is it? And he had such nice manners!'

'Aye, until he comes to putting you on the headlines as his primary source of information, a loose-lipped old woman who's never been out of Argyll!'

'No need to be rude,' she snapped. 'I was just doing my bit for the community!'

He sighed again, louder this time. 'I guess he's staying at the hotel?'

'Yes, I suggested it to him. Told him the rooms aren't quite so clean since the new lass started there, but as long as you ignore the state of the carpets, and checked the tea-cups were clean, he'd be fine!'

'You're something else, you are!' Scott shook his head, picking up a ham and cheese roll from the counter, looking for the sale date and raising an eyebrow.

'Aye,' she grinned at him. 'On you go,'

He stuffed the bread in his pocket and stepped back out onto the street. A man was putting a piece of wood under one of the wheels of the TV van to level it up, as he passed. 'Bloody press. Vultures, all of them!'

# Chapter Twenty-Nine

Pulling into the entrance to Glenlachan distillery, Scott switched off the engine and sat staring through the window down the valley. He needed time to think before he phoned in his findings to the station in Oban. Although it had been a long morning, when he pulled out his notebook he was quite surprised how little he had written down. He folded it open on a new page and started scribbling, recalling Dougie's words about the letters on the barrels, and Liz saying Charlie was a greedy man and took more than he gave. And then all the information John had volunteered as though he knew he was in the mire but wanting to distance himself from Charlie and his murder. That got him to thinking about the barrel that was intended to be bottled. What had he said 'Not is, was!' Who was going to pick up the mantle now the distiller was gone. And where was this barrel. Or barrels?

Halfway through a conversation with Jim, a car horn distracted him and he glanced in his mirror to see a grey taxi behind, the man gesticulating to get past. Scott ended the call asking him to send more information and dropped the phone, starting the engine and heading up the drive to the yard by the main door. He considered that frosty morning when he had arrived here just a few days ago, after a call from Davie. Since then, two murders and a lot of skulduggery! The taxi pulled up beside him and Julien de Runcy stepped out, a heavy coat pulled tight around his shoulders. He looked across at Scott.

'Are you still following me around? Shouldn't you be doing police work?' The greeting didn't seem as friendly as the one the night before and Scott thought twice before responding. In the finish, he decided that this man may have a lot more answers that he was prepared to offer over the dinner table in a hotel restaurant.

'I just came to thank you for dinner.' He stepped out of the pick-up and followed the French man inside, pulling out his wallet as he passed under the heaters into the warm foyer. 'And come to pay for my half!' He proffered two twenty-pound notes towards the man who was already taking off his coat and sitting down at a desk in front of a computer terminal.

'Bullshit,' he said, grumpily. 'I can easily afford to pay for your dinner.'

'So can I!' Scott folded the two notes and chucked them down on the desk. 'But I'll let you pay for the whisky!' He smiled. 'I certainly did, this morning!' Pulling up a chair in front of the desk he sat down, facing the man.

'Look,' sighed De Runcy, 'I've had enough talking to you lot this morning. I need to deal with some stuff here, if you don't mind?'

Scott waited for him to log on to the screen, eventually entering the correct password, before asking the question. 'Why did you employ Charlie Edis?' He made a point of watching the man's eyes as he answered.

'You would need to ask my son that.' He said, just a bit too slowly. 'Except you cannot, can you?' He was already typing into the computer.

Scott decided to press the matter. 'But you are the boss. You built this place? You wouldn't let your son, who knew nothing of this business, choose who would run it for him?'

De Runcy looked up at him, eyes narrowing. 'Jean-Luc ran this business, hands-on, every day, OK. Edis was just an employee, like the others.'

Scott stood his ground. 'I still say you must have had a part in choosing who would distil your wonderful product?' He returned the man's stare, inquisitively.

The Frenchman gave a shrug. 'Yes, I saw the list of

potential distillers, and we had a brief discussion about it. OK?'

'How brief?' He glanced up at the rows of bottles on the racks. 'I mean, did you see his CV? Interview him? Or know anything about his past?'

'Look. Can this wait?' De Runcy was looking stressed.

'It's just a routine question, asking an employer about a man who has been killed in his factory.'

'You could have asked me that last night?'

'Off duty,' Scott pushed the two bank notes towards him. 'Besides, I didn't know then what I know now.'

'Which is?'

'Edis had a record of crime.' Again, he watched De Runcy closely, to gauge his surprise.

'No criminal record, not that I saw.'

'So, you did see his records, then?' Scott pulled out his phone. 'Seems to me like Charlie had a list of wrong doings?' He scrolled down a WhatsApp message. 'Sacked from one distillery, banned from trading at auction houses.' He looked up again, raising an eyebrow. 'Should I go on?'

'I didn't know about any of that shit. He had a good nose, and that's why we hired him.'

'So you did hire Charlie Edis, then?' Scott raised a teasing grin.

'Fuck off!'

'You hired a known criminal, with a great nose for all sorts of whisky, and a record of selling things that were not exactly what they were supposed to be.' Scott teased again. 'How did that work out for you?'

'The man might have been a loud mouth and a drunkard, be he won us an award, didn't he?' He corrected himself. 'We won an award, for our whisky.'

Scott dropped the subject, scrolling through the text

again. He took a deep breath as Julien returned to his work. 'Whisky is a slow return on investment, isn't it?' he asked, conversationally.

De Runcy ignored him completely, focussing on his screen.

'Must take a lot of cash flow?' he glanced back behind him, to the store of barrels, 'to keep this lot for three years?'

'It was all in a plan, before we started,' he followed Scott's gaze. 'A three-year plan with no payback. It's not uncommon.'

'You must have some very understanding investors, Julien.' Scott looked back to the man again. 'You don't mind me calling you Julien? We have had a dinner date, after all!' De Runcy showed no emotion, as if he knew what was coming next. 'I bet they are getting twitchy now, though?'

'I can handle them. We just won an award, didn't we? That should suffice.' It was almost as though Julien was asking a question. 'We won an award and have a lot of it in storage. They will stay with it.'

Scott looked at the reflection of Julien's computer screen in the window behind him, trying to make out the name and logo in big red letters. Was that what his urgency was, to pacify the investors now he had no helmsman and no manager, both murdered? It would be a big ask. He led with his next question. 'Do you sell some of your whisky by the barrel, Julien? Forward buying, do you call it?'

It was fairly evident that De Runcy was finding this tedious, and Scott had half expected to be shown the door by now, but the man fell into line. 'Yes, sometimes we do.'

'You would be selling to investors. Would these be the same investors that already have a share in the business?'

'Occasionally my people will bring an investor in, but

often these are outsiders. Professional whisky investors, who buy and sell all the time.'

'And winning an award would bring lots of publicity to you, and buyers with it?'

De Runcy just nodded at the obvious question.

'Do you have a list of all those sales?' Scott knew this one was pushing it, but it was on Jim's list that Heather had requested it.

'Not for your eyes, no!' he sniffed. 'First rule of investment, is that nobody knows who is buying, else it would become, err, what is your word? Corrupt?'

'Seems to me that it already is?'

'Is that an accusation, Scott?' De Runcy's eyes narrowed again. 'You don't mind if I call you Scott, do you?' He did a commendable job of mimicking Scott's accent. 'After all, we did...'

'No, on both counts. I didn't say your business was corrupt. Just that the whole system seems to have an element of secrecy around it that could, how should I put this, be misused?'

'I am a businessman.' he pointed at the screen in front of him. 'Always have been. I let others sort out the detail, while I see the bigger picture. If we have small time investors buying the odd barrel, yes that helps to pay a few bills, but the long term is secure.' He shrugged again, something the French were particularly good at. 'Now, if you don't mind, that business needs my attention.'

Scott took this as his cue to stand up, again making sure De Runcy was aware of the forty quid lying on his desk. 'Thank you for your time, Mister de Runcy.' He held out his hand to shake and De Runcy took it.'

'I'm glad we understand each other,' he said. 'Now please go and find out who killed my son.'

Outside in the car park, the skies had darkened and Ben Cruachan was already almost out of sight. Scott checked the weather on his phone and shuddered at the sight of a line of snowflakes for the rest of the day, re-considering his trip to Oban to meet with the team. Glancing at the empty passenger's seat brought Beth to mind, lying there in the surgery. He opened WhatsApp again and entered Megan's number into it from a card she had given him.

'How's she doing?' he typed.

Next another message, this time to Jim. 'Weather closing in here, what like there?' Then he re-considered that. Oban was right on the sea, so snow would hardly ever be a problem there, so he deleted half the sentence, and sent it.

A message came back, from Megan. 'Everyone is fine. Who is this?' Scott laughed out loud. Either she was teasing him for not including his name on the message or she hadn't yet put his number into her phone. Both of these would have different consequences and his heart hoped it was the former.

He wrote, 'Police dog urgently required, to sniff out the bad guys!' with a big grin on his face. Starting the engine, he felt the cold air of the heater fan blow on his face and decided to step back outside and have a smoke whilst it warmed up.

The phone pinged again. 'You'd be better with a Husky today?' and then a second message. 'Beth's fine, btw,' with a smiley face emoji next to it.

Scott smiled and was about to reply again when the phone rang. 'You still out chasing sheep?' It was Heather and he wasn't quite sure if she was joking.

He decided she was. 'A profitable day with the flock, I'd say. Something definitely doesn't smell right, but I'm gaining on it.' He stubbed out the cigarette under his boot and got back into the warm. 'What's the news on Jean-Luc? I just met with his father.' The line went silent and he checked to see if he had lost signal.

Eventually the caller said, 'Again?'

Scott felt the back of his neck stiffen. He was about to phone in and tell her about last night but looks like someone had beaten him to it. He hoped it wasn't Jim. 'Yes. Again. Looking for new information.'

'New information? You hadn't revealed the old information yet.' More silence followed by 'What the fuck do you think you're doing, Donald?' It wasn't a question.

Scott's turn to stay silent, let her add some more venom if she had to. She didn't, so he piped up a defence. 'OK, so I met with the man last night, and he joined me for dinner.'

'He joined you?'

'Yes!'

'He's a fucking suspect, Scott. You had dinner with a suspect before we had time to question him! Jesus Christ! Do you know how stupid that was?'

By now he was holding the phone away from his ear, his knuckles whitening under the grip. 'If it's any consolation, I am pretty sure he didn't do it.'

'If it's any consolation, it is only me stopping you losing your job!'

Scott soldiered on. 'Julien didn't kill him. Neither of them.

'On first name terms now? For fucks sake man!' she was still shouting, but then quietened down a bit. 'And you know this how?'

'I'm pretty sure it was a hit, and I have an idea why. Just not a who.'

'Aren't you the Sherlock?'

Scott revved the engine, to warm up the heater, and also flicked on the wiper as the snow began to fall. 'I can read people. And I think he knows who placed the contract.'

'We,' she sighed, 'that is the team of policemen who are working on this case rather than the one running around having dinner with his dog.' She stopped and her voice softened. 'Look, I'm sorry about the dog by the way.'

This was probably the first time he realised she had any heart at all, but it didn't last long.

'We think he ordered the hit.'

Scott swallowed hard, considering the possibility. 'Do you?'

'Where are you now?

'Right outside Glenlachan. I can see De Runcy through the window.' He nearly added 'In the warm,' but thought better of it.

Heather hesitated and then had a garbled conversation with someone that he couldn't quite hear. 'OK,' she said. 'We want you to tail him. Don't let him out of your sight. See where he goes.'

Scott glanced up at the sky, and the flakes coming down heavier now. 'Can't we just track his phone?'

'Just fucking do it, that's an order.'

During the call, the phone pinged another message. He ignored it.

# Chapter Thirty

De Runcy watched Scott through the window, having an animated phone conversation, as the snow fell. His next phone call was to the very same person.

'I need that car, the four by four. Snow is coming down and I need it, so you had better be finished with it, right now. My lawyer will be around to collect it within half an hour.' Heather started to protest but he was not up for negotiation. 'Half an hour,' he repeated and ended the call.

This was followed with a text message. 'Go pick-up the Porsche in Oban and bring it here to the distillery.'

Next, the Frenchman was back on the internet again, pulling up a finance company on Google. As he scrolled through the list of directors, he picked on one and opened the photo of a man to full screen. Scott discretely watched him through the snow, but couldn't make out who the person was. He tried to take a picture with his phone, making sure to turn off the flash so he wasn't noticed. The shot wouldn't be any good, but he forwarded it to Jim anyway, along with a question mark. De Runcy wrote something down on a post-it note and put it in his pocket.

Whilst waiting, Scott pulled his thoughts together on his mornings' work, and considered it for some time, before typing it into his phone. Nobody had admitted being at the scene of Charlie's death, but it was pretty obvious someone was. Had he actually asked them? Time had been so fractious, but the question should have been asked and alibis checked, from at least four suspects. It was time to get tough and see who blinked. But here he was, shadowing a man he didn't believe had anything to do with Charlie's death. Couldn't the detectives at the station do their own dirty work? After the last phone call, he wasn't going to question the order but at least he had time to think through some more. There had been no evidence back from forensics about the fork-lift, other than Davie's prints, but it was winter and the driver could have conceivably worn gloves. There was no clear evidence that Charlie had died from the blow, either. He could well have drowned, either before he was put in the tank, or afterwards. For all he knew, Charlie could have simply fallen and knocked himself out, died even? So why fabricate a story of him falling in the mash tun? No, somebody must have hit him, and at least three people had good reason to. Somewhere, there would be a weapon, then, but that could easily have been cleaned up and put back where it came from rather than hidden. Would Liz have the strength to kill a man? Maybe not, although she may have enough malice to do it. He was pretty sure John hadn't done it, but he would have been the one with the right tools, and he did have a temper. Dougie as much as admitted that they were stealing whisky, and that Charlie was in on that. The distiller's history backed up that theory. Simple scenario, they were expecting something from him, and got something else? Or nothing? Gave him a clout, and then tried to make it look like an accident? Would they have all paid money to Charlie? That could be proved somehow, he was pretty sure. Then there was Davie. Would he have any money to pay into a scheme?

He scratched his ear. If Edis was trying to fence some stolen whisky, how would he go about it? A few hundred bottles of Glenlachan or anything else pricey, hitting the market at the same time, would surely have raised suspicion, amongst this close-nit world? No, he would either shift the barrel on to someone else for a quick buck, or stash it away for a while and then bottle it?

Scott drew a line under each of the four names, and then considered others. Jean-Luc and Shauna had alibis of sorts. The only other one possibly involved in this was his brother Fraser, who had been at the place earlier the same day. That reminded him of Beth again and he checked the message from earlier.

'Pick her up at six, OK?' Megan had added an emoji of a dog wagging its tail. He checked his watch, three-forty-five, and then the weather outside before replying. 'Thanks for your help. I'll do my best.'

The sound of an engine shook him from his thoughts, as Davie pulled into the yard on his quad bike, wrapped in a scarf that was an inch deep in snow. He climbed off, slapping his gloved hands against around his shoulders to bring back some circulation. Scott stepped out and went to speak to him. 'Big boss is inside,' he said, 'thought you would want to know?'

Davie looked quite surprised. 'Thanks.' He pulled off one glove and wiped snow from his eyebrows. 'I just came up to make sure we still had hot water, in case it freezes tonight.' He glanced around the otherwise empty car-park which was now white over. 'What you doing here?'

'You really should get a helmet,' Scott said, following him into the building. Once inside he said 'How much do you earn, Davie?'

'Minimum wage, just now.' His face saddened, 'was hoping for a raise!'

Scott stamped the snow from his boots. 'Charlie promised you a bonus, did he?'

'Something like that.' He was already checking the dials and made a small adjustment to one tap.

'For what in return?' Scott kept his voice down, not wanting to alert the boss in the office. 'A blind eye?'

Davie looked nervous. 'I don't see everything that goes on,' he sniffed.

'Don't see? Or pretend not to see?' He caught the boy's arm. 'Look, you are a suspect in a murder case, Davie.' His voice still quiet but harsh. 'Who pays you to look the other way? Charlie? Or someone else?'

Davie said nothing for a second, looking at the ground and the puddles of water forming out of melted snow. 'I never killed anyone.'

'I'm not saying you did. Just answer the question?'

'It gets left in an envelope,' he glanced to the next building, 'under the grain sacks.'

And you don't know who it comes from?' Scott raised an eyebrow.

'Better that way, eh?'

'How much?'

He looked at the floor again. 'Only a tenner or so!'

The policeman squeezed his arm tighter. 'OK. Fifty. Fifty quid a week!'

Scott was about to press harder when he heard an engine outside. 'Why are you really up here in the snow this afternoon, lad?'

A faint grin came across the boy's face. 'Boss sent me a message.'

With that Scott was out of the door, just in time to see the black Porsche Cayenne heading out down the drive at great speed, its tail lights disappearing behind a shower of white flakes as big as oak leaves. He almost tripped as his boots skidded on the snow, while he raced across the yard and dived for his pick-up, firing up the engine. The vehicle was already out of sight by the time he turned round so he had to make a rapid decision, hoping it was the right one and almost hearing the wrath of the Super. Turning right would just go to the village unless you wanted to go over the mountain route to Oban. The speed that De Runcy left, he doubted he was just out for a tourist drive. Scott swung the pick-up to the left, and headed up the hill, thankful for his four-wheel drive.

Julien was thankful for his, too, as his colleague sat

white knuckled in the passenger's seat, listening to a warning light telling them that they were breaking the speed limit on an ordinary road, let alone one only wide enough for one car with three inches of snow covering! The odd flash in his rear-view mirror warned De Runcy that he was being followed, possibly by a man who knew these roads better than he did, but also someone who didn't have seventy-thousand pounds worth of technology at his feet. The Porsche had already worked out that the outside temperature was low, and had engaged various winter gadgets by itself. Wheels clicked, and spun, depending on the grip they found, as the four-litre engine roared like a bear, easily gaining distance from the copper on his tail.

'Is now the time I ask where we are going?' asked the passenger, his accent course, Glasgow east side.

'All in good time, Alfie,' Julien battled with a corner, 'all in good time!'

'But you've got my money, right?'

'Sure I have. I don't break promises, mon ami, you know you can trust me?'

'I could have just taken this thing and fucked off?' Alfie scoffed. 'Did you think about that?'

'Not your style,' the car skidded forward down the hill, causing Alfie to temporarily close his eyes. 'You're far too old to be stealing cars? And anyway, they know the vehicle, wouldn't have taken them long to catch you.'

'Like the one behind us, eh?' they both saw the headlights light up the sky as the pick-up came over the summit of the hill.

'What local Bobby? He won't get anywhere near us. The man's just a pussy!' With that, Julien switched out the lights, and then swung hard right into a narrow track, just about seeing through the falling snow. The vehicle groaned under that command and took a dent in the side off the stone wall for its troubles. Undeterred, he gunned the engine again, but only for a few hundred yards, where he skidded to a halt in the darkness.

Scott was trying to dial on his phone and keep the pick-up on the road at the same time when his right wheels mounted the grass bank and the vehicle lurched over to near tipping point, sending his phone off the seat and down into the passenger's foot-well. The only way he would retrieve that would be to stop and he knew if that happened, the Porsche would lose him. He would try and retrieve it when he got to the main road junction, at the foot of the hill. The falling snow was mesmerising to drive in and he rubbed his tired eyes with the back of his hand, in between gear changes. These pick-ups were all well and good for extra purchase on a muddy path, but to get any real traction you needed some weight in the back, and he had nothing. Hence the rear-end was all over the place as he sped on as best he could, praying that he would be able to stop at the bottom. Above him the wind was whipping up, picking up already fallen snow and depositing it on the right side of the road in growing drifts and covering the tracks of whatever had passed this way recently. It wouldn't be long before nothing would pass, which got Scott to wondering how the hell he would get home. It also got him to wondering, not for the first time, where the hell De Runcy was heading, in this weather? When he eventually reached the main road, it was pretty deserted. Which way to go now? Left for Oban, or right for Glasgow. Opening the door was tricky as the wind forced it back on him, so he climbed over to the passenger side and retrieved his phone from under the seat.

'Suspect on the move,' he typed, his fingers shaking over the keys. 'Can you pick him up on APR?' The message disappeared after hitting the send button, but then re-appeared seconds later, un-sent. He cursed himself for not stopping at the top of the bank where there had been some signal, and swung left towards Taynuilt.

De Runcy started the engine again. 'A fucking pussy cat!' he said again, heading up towards the quarry. It was quite steep going and the vehicle made good work of it, but not in a great hurry.

'Where are we going?' Alfie asked again.

'Your money,' Julien grunted. 'It's hidden up here. You don't think I would keep cash on me, do you?'

Alfie said nothing, waiting until they reached a plateau strewn with some rusty machinery, lit up by the headlights. The snow had subsided a little now, but the clouds were still low and the sky as black as coal. De Runcy pulled the Porsche to a stop, and looked across at Alfie. Then he reached down into his jacket and pulled out a Beretta, waving it in the man's general direction. 'I want answers,' he snarled.

Alfie barely blinked, as he looked at the weapon, as though he almost suspected this might happen. 'Answers? Ha, you should be the one with the answer. The men who employ me don't do answers, only questions?' He slowly reached into his pocket, and De Runcy waved the gun barrel. 'OK, if I smoke?' Slowly he pulled out a small pack of cigars, the black of his signet ring catching the light.

'No it isn't.' His eyes narrowed further. Silence for a minute, the two of them looking at each other. 'He was just a boy,' De Runcy sighed. 'A boy caught up in big men's games. Out of his depth.' Considering the statement, he thought of his son, floating face down in the harbour, and a tiny tear appeared in the corner of his eye. 'Was it quick?'

Alfie shrugged, saying nothing for a minute, then, 'Look, what the fuck is going on here. You going to shoot me? That it? Some people might not like that.'

De Runcy's turn to say nothing again, until Alfie reached forward and pulled the door handle, pushing it open a fraction. He waved the packet of cigars, and a questioning eyebrow. De Runcy nodded, opening his door as well.

An icy wind directly off Ben Cruachan itself muffled the sound of a single gunshot. A minute later, the Porsche was heading back down the track, turning right for Glasgow on the main road.

# Chapter Thirty-One

Sandy glanced out of the window, and the black threatening skies. The darkness had come down while nobody had really witnessed it as they all trawled away at their screens. 'What like of snow you get round these parts?' he called out to Bill Young opposite.

Bill grinned, always looking for an edge. 'We don't get much more than a couple of feet,' he mused, 'in November! After that it gets a bit more serious. Probably a metre deep on the front by now. I hope you got your wellies?'

'Aye?' he returned the grin. 'Well at least Jim's got the Landy, eh? You'll get me a ride to my bed by nightfall?'

'Take no notice, it may be a few inches up by the tower, but we'll not get anything down here, apart from rain that would take the fillings out your teeth.' Jim glanced outside too. 'Might be a different story from the village. Not heard from him since he sent this photo. Don't think we can make anything of it though.'

'How are we getting on with these friends? Known associates of De Runcy senior?' Sandy asked the room, although the question was aimed at Bill, getting him back for winding him up about the snow.

'I've pulled a directory together on the computer network, and the file is growing rapidly. Including the picture that Scott sent in. The Met have a few interesting photos of him, mixing with some known villains. One or two really bad guys but mainly on the lighter side, mostly gangs we know that fence stolen goods. Nothing too regular though.'

'Who owns the chopper?' Sandy asked. 'Gotta be dodgy, owning one of those things!'

'A bit of a generalisation, Sandy?' Heather looked up from the desk she was using. 'You mean if you won the lottery, you wouldn't get one of those to ferry you around, especially living round here?'

'If I won the lottery, I'd be in Spain, in a heartbeat. Feet up, on the beach, bit of snorkelling.'

'Don't be daft,' chipped in Jim. 'Red hair like that, you'd be more fried than Colonel Sanders!'

Bill stood up, to get himself back into the conversation. 'The machine is leased by Jardin International, a holding firm based in Croydon. That's near London!' he winked at Sandy. 'It's not exactly known what they do, apart from shift property and money around. Apart from a lawsuit by one of its employees a few years back, nothing in the bad books of note. Two of the Directors are brothers. Robert James Matheson, and his younger brother, Alfred.'

'Sound like a couple of toffs?' Jim said.

'Nah, these guys are hard nuts, came up through east end Glasgow.' Bill glanced at Sandy again with a grin. 'One of them lives in Spain. Could be you new neighbour, pal!'

Sandy ignored the remark, especially when he heard the word Glasgow. 'Any form?'

'A few run-ins over the years, but nothing that's stuck. Apart from one of the sons getting busted for coke, recently.' He sniffed. 'That's what they teach you at the Academy, I guess. Serva Fidem, and all that shite!' The reference was to Glasgow Academy, one of Scotland's leading private schools and something Bill had experienced in another life which he now viewed with contempt.

'Doesn't sound like the sort of boy who would share his toys, then?' Jim was taking a disliking to these brothers.

'Aye, you need to be a pretty good friend before

someone would lend you a 200 grand flying machine, and a driver, that's for sure.'

'Or owe them a fair amount of money?' Heather caressed her top lip with the end of a biro. 'We think these guys have been bank-rolling De Runcy?'

'S'a fair chance, I'd say.' Sandy replied. 'You want the Flying Squad to go kick in their door and rough em over?'

'Aye Sandy, that's just how they work down south, eh?'

'It was a joke, Jim.' Sandy took a printout of the two brothers from Bill and pinned them on the whiteboard. 'Anyone else?'

'Young Jean-Luc had a pal that has a wee record. Name of Eddie Horsham. Another Teflon bad guy, been fingered a few times but never convicted. Drugs mainly. And a real-time playboy.'

'Drugs?' Heather asked.

'Possession, dealing, generally never being far away from them.'

'So much for the squeaky-clean French?' Heather wrote down the name. 'Don't tell me, Glasgow boy too?'

'Aye, the Academy.'

'So, not only does the old man know these two villains, but the kids are friends too?' she was thinking again before adding. 'A right happy family. But where does whisky come into it?'

'I think we know the answer to that one, Ma'am. Definitely some trade going on there, in the investment world?'

'OK, Bill, get digging into any known trade deals De Runcy has had with Jardin.' Heather spoke the order firmly. 'Especially in France.' She glanced around at the others. 'Anyone know how much cargo one of those wee helicopter things can carry?' Bill shook his head.

'Sandy, track down this Horsham, and get some dirt on him so we can bring him in.' She looked at Jim, who was awaiting his detail. 'You go and find out where the fuck our shepherd has got to, and, more importantly, where is De Runcy?'

Jim was pulling on his waterproof clothing and collecting the keys to the Land-Rover when the former question got answered for him.

Scott had made the decision to head in the direction of Oban and it had taken him a lot longer than he had expected until he reached Taynuilt and the low building. There were five or six cars in the car-park this time of day, most of them four-wheel drive, as the vets ran evening surgery. He pulled on the handbrake, jumping out into the well-trodden snow and ran to the door. As he burst it open, a couple of women looked up in shock, one with a barking terrier on a lead, the other a grey plastic cat-box on her lap.

'I need to use your phone,' he gasped at the receptionist. The girl looked most defensive, so he added, 'It's a police matter and it's urgent!'

Megan poked her hear round the door, dressed in her green overall again. Seeing the stress in his face, she said, 'everything alright?'

Scott already had the receiver in his hand. 'You don't mind, do you?'

'Doesn't look like I have much choice, does it,' the vet letting her annoyance show through. 'Have you actually come to collect your dog?'

'Can she wait a while?'

'We close at seven,' she moved closer to him, so he could smell a light perfume mixed with bleach. 'Or earlier, if I can get this lot seen to.'

'I was more thinking overnight?' The question didn't get answered as Jim picked up the call on the other end.

Scott moved himself into a small room next to the reception and closed the door. Inside, shelves were stacked with drugs, all with complicated names, making him half wonder what his vet's bill would be for Beth. 'Jim, I lost him!'

Jim made sure nobody could hear him before replying. 'Lost De Runcy? Fucking hell, Scotty, you're having some day?'

'Tell me about it. Can you guys get APR to track the Porsche?'

'Track it? Track it where?'

'South, I'm guessing, back down towards town.' They both understood 'town' as being Glasgow.

Jim kept his voice down. 'Boss ain't going to like this one. How the hell did he slip you?'

'It's a long story, but the short version is that he is a cunning bastard. Get Glasgow traffic in on this.'

'Where are you going?' Jim asked.

'I'm heading to the boat.'

'A bit rough for a fishing trip?' Jim grinned to himself. 'But Glasgow might be a good call. We looked up a couple of his contacts, he sure has some ugly friends.'

Scott took that on board and asked Jim to bat his corner with Heather.

'Again?' sighed the sergeant, as the call ended.

Megan opened the door. 'You're not supposed to be in here, Mister! Copper or not!'

'Confidential police stuff,' he said, a bit too curtly.

'Out!' She stamped her foot, as though telling off a naughty puppy.

Scott obeyed, detecting the flash of anger in her green eyes. 'Shit, sorry!' He pulled a half smile. 'I guess that's two lunches I owe you.'

'Do I look like I have time for two lunches?' she glanced down at her white wellingtons. 'Nope. You just doubled it up, to dinner.' The grin was back. 'Now get the fuck out of my storeroom before I call the cops!'

'He did what?' Heather made no qualms about hiding her anger. 'Why do we employ this numpty?' She took a deep breath. 'Jeez. He had one job to do!' As her fist hit the table, three grown detectives winced.

Sandy had already taken the initiative and phoned Glasgow traffic department. He was giving the registration number of the car, using phonetic letters. 'What time are we looking at?' he called to Jim.

Jim hadn't considered asking the exact time Scott had lost sight of the car so made it up. 'Reckon he would be down the side of Lomond, maybe Glen Luce roundabout around 5ish.'

'And he's sure he went that direction?'

'Shit no. He's in the dark as much as...' Jim tailed off, remembering he was supposed to stick up for the local copper he had been friends with for years. 'There aren't many other places to go, are there?'

'Wouldn't he just go to Snecky? To his son's flat there?' Bill Young asked.

'If he was doing that, he wouldn't have given Scott the slip would he?' Sandy was thinking fast. 'But we could check.'

'Where is Scott now? Is he on the chase?' Heather was still too animated to keep her voice steady. 'Why didn't he phone it in earlier?'

'Snow, Ma'am. Deep snow, no phone reception.'

'So how did he get through to you just now?'

Jim thought again, trying to provide cover but not wanting to get caught up in a deception. He decided honesty would prevail in this answer. 'He was at the vets!'

The intake of breath that Heather took nearly drew the paper cups from the table, before, 'the fucking vets?' If the intake had moved the cups one way, her shout would certainly blast them back again. 'We have two murders, a possible multi-million-pound ring of theft, a couple of top-class villains in the mix, our main suspect on the loose, and he's at the fucking vets?'

'It was the only phone he could think of, Ma'am.'

'And where is this vets?'

Jim looked at his shoes. 'Taynuilt, Ma'am.'

Sandy calmly answered the next question Heather was about to shout. 'Ten miles in the wrong direction, Boss.'

'So where is he now, the pillock?' Jim winced at the selection of names being applied to his pal. 'Don't tell me. In the pub with a pint of ale?'

The level of her voice caused the door to open, with Andrew McClatchie on the other side of it.

Jim knew his next words would definitely not do Scott any favours. 'On a boat!' he blurted.

Heather's reaction was quashed by the Super, asking what in God's name is all this shouting about? 'In my office, Detective, please?' Heather followed him out the room.

'Some fucking pal, you are, Jimbo?' said Bill quietly. 'I'd hate to be your enemy!'

# Chapter Thirty-Two

Scott was still considering the invitation to dinner as he pulled down the slope towards Dunlaridge marina. By now the snow had eased but what was still coming down had turned to the type of sleet that could go through brick walls. He parked the pick-up at the bottom of the ramp, considering the area, and his future. Today hadn't been a great one, by any means. The lack of any sign of a Porsche Cayenne Turbo didn't help it along.

What was it De Runcy had said, he loved the west coast for its challenging winds. It had been playing on his mind. If whisky was being transported illegally, by sea would have been an easy option? He let out a chuckle. Christ, smugglers had been shifting contraband whisky by boat for thousands of years. Funny how things go full circle?

A light was on in the main building, and he could see a cleaner finishing up for the day. There would be records, of every boat that came and went. The young lad running the place seemed organised enough and he guessed all the journeys would be recorded on computer these days. Probably a list that could be emailed, but he thought another chat with him might just be worthwhile. If any cargo went in and out, the lad would surely know about it?

Pulling his windcheater up around his ears, he wished to hell he had dressed for the weather today. In fact, he part wished he had stayed in bed all day.

'Sorry, we're closed,' said a middle-aged woman with a broad west coast accent, mop in hand.

'Ronni around?' Scott enquired.

The woman lent on her mop, possibly glad of the

distraction from such a mundane task. 'Not seen him in a few hours,' she said. 'You want me to phone him?'

'I could do with his phone number, please?' Scott asked, politely.

'And you are?' then she saw the badge in the wallet he was holding out and sighed, 'What's he done now?'

Scott pulled up a plastic chair and sat looking out towards the darkness of the bay. 'Been in trouble before, has he?'

'He's a good lad,' she said, laying the mop down and leaning on a table. 'Heart of gold. But trouble seems to follow him around like a feral dog.'

'What sort of trouble?'

'Oh, you know. Girls. Mischief.' She thought for a second. 'Poor choice of friends!'

'Who owns this place?'

'He does,' she replied. 'Well, him and his old man. But mainly him, I think.'

'Bit young, isn't he?' The woman shrugged and Scott suddenly felt old for asking the question. 'Some of his wealthy friends have boats out there?'

'Now,' she stood up again. 'You're asking too many questions. And to the wrong person.' She picked up the mop again. 'I need to get finished up here, if you don't mind!'

'That phone number, please?'

The woman gave it to him and he was just about to type it into his phone when it rang, the name Jess appearing on the screen.

He took a few seconds to answer, giving the woman a wave and heading for the door. When he got outside and under an overhanging glass cover that kept the rain off, he gathered his thoughts about this woman who had him on a string for a decade and more. 'Hi, how's it going,' he said, trying not to sound too irritated.

'Scott,' she said, hurriedly and without any feeling. 'It's my Dad!'

Scott changed his tone. 'What's up with him?'

'He's in the hospital?'

'Jesus. Heart attack?'

'Fractured skull!'

Scott felt the words sink in. 'Fractured skull?' he repeated.

'Suspected, anyway.' He heard her sigh above the sound of the wind.

'What happened?' Scott recalled the hip flask of whisky they had shared a dram from earlier. 'A fall?'

'Spanner's more my guess,' the line was quiet for a second. 'But you might know more than me?' Scott had the feeling he was in for another scalding from a woman, and he had lost count how many of those he had had recently.

'Where is he?'

'Oban.'

'Where are you?' he checked his watch, 6.22. 'Want me to come pick you up?'

'I sure could do with a drink!'

He considered this, and his evening's potential plans. And the day he'd had. 'Will he be OK?'

'He's sitting up, and cursing! But they'll keep him in until they get fed up with the old bugger.'

'Perfectly normal, then!' he quipped, but then his tone changed. 'I'll need to question him, though! You know that?'

'I guess.'

'Did he say who did it?'

'What do you think?'

227

Scott sighed. 'I'll be there in twenty minutes.'

Before he could end the call, the phone was ringing again and he considered how much longer the battery charge would last. 'Yes, Jim?'

'We got a match, on the Porsche. Your hunch was right, Glasgow.'

Scott felt inwardly relieved. 'You pulled him in?'

'Fraid not. It's the back of the Gorbals. Burnt out like a bbq rib!'

'Any sign of the driver?' Scott knew the answer to this one.

'Aye, Allan McBride, 256, Adelphi Heights, aged 13!' Jim laughed. 'Said, and I quote: "it's a braw motor, wish I had bought it years ago!"'

'For fuck sake.' He pulled his pack of tobacco out, turning his back on the rain to roll one, phone wedged under his ear. 'One step forward, so many steps back, my feet are nearly in the water.'

'Nearly?' Jim raised his voice as he heard the wind whistling. 'Aye, well. At least it will be hot!'

'Fuck off!' Scott was about to end the call. 'Jim?'

'Aye?'

'You all still around? In the office?'

'Oh aye. Trust me pal, I done my best for you, but I cannae push water uphill.'

'Meet me in Oban General in twenty minutes?' he lit the cigarette. 'We got an interview to do.'

Getting back in his pick-up, he decided the young marina manager could wait a while longer and instead sent a message to Megan. 'Might have to stand you up, tonight, sorry.' He added a sad face and sent the message.

The drive into Oban was eerily quiet and a rise in the temperature had cleared most of the snow from the roads before Argyll Council had chance to push the snow plough through it. He suspected that it might be at work on the higher ground, which got him round to thinking about his few animals, out there in the paddock. They were bred for hardiness, that's for sure, both the cow and the few sheep were all of stock breeds native to the area. Gemma, the old Highland cow would have dug the snow away with a hoof and would be sharing a greener patch with the others but he still felt guilty about not delivering them a bite to eat when they needed it most. He thought about Beth, there in the surgery, and that he never even went in to see her when he was there a short while ago. Police business took priority over most things, animals included. What a thankless task it was, running around the countryside at all hours, asking folks questions they won't tell you the answer to. He considered Heather, and the bollocking she was lining up for him. Possibly a reprimand or an official caution. A bridge with her would take a bit of building.

Oban Hospital, or Lorn and Islands, to give its correct name, was on the south side of the city, but thankfully the traffic wasn't too heavy. A sprawling low rise building of only one or two stories that was built in the mid-nineties, formed in a couple of squares and totally out of keeping with other buildings in the area. Scott navigated his way through a series of car-parks until he could get no nearer to the building, noting two red helicopters parked side by side on a raised platform to the south. He also spotted a police Land-Rover parked on yellows near the main door, its engine still running.

Scott found an empty space, not wishing to add 'illegal parking' to the growing list of his misdemeanours Heather already had on him. As he approached the police vehicle the passenger door opened and Jess skipped out, a blue woollen hat pulled well down over her ears. She had him in a bear hug before either of them got chance to speak. Nearly a minute went by, him hearing her faint sobs on his shoulder until Jim got out of the Landy, grinning.

'You stealing my bird?' he laughed. 'I was doing rather well!'

This broke the ice and Jess raised her head, laughing for a second as well. 'Sorry, Jim, but I prefer older men!'

Scott, by far the younger man, feigned a hurt, and then looped his arm into Jess's. 'Come on, let's go and see what the really old bugger has to say.'

'I thought we were off for a drink?' she whispered as they entered the building.

'Maybe later, but for now there is some police business to clear up.'

Jess stopped, her eyes narrowing and the smile disappearing. 'Can't it wait?'

It was the sort of question she had always used against him, when she would prefer to do something different and used her charm to get her own way. 'No, it can't.' They passed reception and she took the long corridor to the right, the far end of it barely visible, as the two policemen tagged along. His phone pinged a message and he pulled it out and checked it immediately, pulling his arm away from Jess for a second. A nurse frowned at him from a doorway and then glanced up at a sign saying 'No mobile phones'. Scott read the message, and then burst out laughing. 'Your dinner is in the dog!'

Jess stopped suddenly, smiled quizzically and looked him in the eye. 'You going to share that?'

He felt the heat rise at the back of his neck and loosened the zip on his jacket. 'Nope,' he said, firmly, putting the phone away in his pocket, and sensing Jim inwardly chuckling at his embarrassment.

The next five or so doors were passed in silence. Then all three of them heard a muffled shouting from one to the left and Jess rolled her eyes. 'Want me to come in with you?' she asked.

At that a short plump woman in a dark blue uniform

appeared from the room, with a face like thunder. She eyed the three of them, recognising Jess. 'No visitors this time of day!' she snorted. Jim stepped out from behind Scott. 'Hello Alice,' he said.

Alice eyed him, for a second. 'What the bloody hell do you want?'

Those were pretty much John McCarthy's words too, when the three of them entered the room. Scott nudged Jim in the ribs, in a "you old dog, you" sort of way, and then turned to the patient, who was sitting up, a bandage wrapped around his skull and a saline drip in his arm.

'Good to see you again, so soon, John.'

'Fuck off!'

'Father, behave!' Jess used the same tone that the used to tame Scott. 'These guys need some answers, and this little charade needs to come to an end.'

'And I need some bloody rest,' he pointed to the bandage, 'see?'

'We can see that,' said Jim. 'So, it's up to you to be as quick as you can. And, the more you tell us, the less chance we will be back at midnight with more questions.'

'Good luck getting past that old monster at midnight,' John grunted, referring to the Matron.

'Who, Alice?' Jim smiled. 'Oh, she's just a pussycat doll.'

Scott let out a light cough at the word. Jim really was a dark horse. He decided to let him take control of the interview, which he promptly did.

Jim placed his mobile phone on the side table and stood over the bed. 'Don't mind if we record this, do you?' His style was much more old school and intimidating than Scott's, which was why he had asked him to come in. And with Jess there as well, it was their best chance of getting some more truth out of the old man.

'OK,' Jim opened, 'Let's start with who hit you?'

# Chapter Thirty Three

'Woa, that's weird!' Sandy looked up from the computer screen. 'Boss, you'd better come and see this.' Both Heather and Bill ambled across to his desk. 'You know someone said about tracking De Runcy's phone?'

'Aye, Scott suggested that hours ago,' Bill said.

'Well, we couldn't see any signal hours ago, maybe due to the snow. But since then, we have been looking in Glasgow. I half expected the kid who took the car to have nicked it.'

Heather rubbed her eyes. 'So, what the hell is it doing there?' She pointed to a flashing beacon on the dark map on the screen. 'Wherever there is?'

Sandy changed the layer of the computer-generated map to *terrain*. 'There, Ma'am,' Sandy was already reaching for his phone, 'is the foot of a mountain known as Ben Cruachan.'

At first Jim ignored the call coming in from Sandy, turning the ringtone off on his phone, when it rung the second time.

Getting information out of John McCarthy had been just as difficult as Scott had suspected, but from earlier that day he knew there was something the old man was hiding. It was the way his eyes glanced a few times at Jess before he spoke that equally concerned him. He had left Jim to the questions as he and John went way back, to the days when they had been in a curling team together.

To start with John had denied knowing who had hit him. In fact, to start with, he had denied being hit at all. But eventually, the truth outed, along with a mild sense of embarrassment. It had been a girl.

When Scott's phone rang for the second time he noted

the low battery signal but took the call out into the corridor. 'You guys on the overtime sheet, then?'

Sandy ignored the reference to the fact he would get an hourly bonus on this job. 'Been trying to reach you idiots. You asleep, or what?'

'Questioning a suspect, if you must know.'

'Mind the fuck he doesn't run and hide, eh?' There was no humour in Sandy's voice

'What you want, Sandy?' Scott checked his screen, 'only my battery is low and I want to save it in case I have someone important to speak to!'

'When you went after De Runcy in the snow, could he have turned off the road?'

'Before he reached the A82, you mean?' Scott considered this. At the time it had been difficult to see your hand in front of a mirror, let alone tracks on the road. 'It's possible, why?'

Sandy told him about the location of the signal. 'Could he have just lobbed it out the window?'

'Not if it's where you say it is. There's an old quarry up there. We used to go up there as kids.'

'How long you plan on being with your current suspect? Can you head up there and take a look?'

Scott would have thrown in a dozen protestations and reasons for not heading into a dark quarry at 7pm, not least because it was winter. Or that he promised to take Jess for a drink. Or that he had a dinner date with a pretty girl who had mended his dog. But mainly because he was extremely tired. 'I'll take a look on my way home,' he sighed.

'Better make that soon, then.' Sandy hissed. 'Boss wanted me to send Jim. Say's you couldn't find your own arse with both hands...'

Scott checked his phone and saw the battery had

finally given up for the day, so he popped his head back into the small room. 'Don't suppose you have a charger in here, do you?' he waved his phone, 'only...'

Jess shook her head while Jim ignored him. 'I gotta go,' he said.

'Go,' said Jim and Jess in unison. 'Go where?'

'Jess, I'm sorry, we'll have to make it another night.' He checked for pain in her eyes and wasn't sure if he saw any. 'Jim, check your phone messages.' Then he looked at the patient. 'And you,' he growled, 'be more careful, OK?'

'Fuck you too,' the old man muttered.

Scott headed back down the long corridor still amazed at the size of the place. In his pick-up he plugged the phone into the cigar lighter and then fired up the engine. Whatever Sandy was saying, when the conversation ended, would have probably been an insult anyway. One thing was for sure, his day hadn't got any better, not when it came to credibility with his boss anyway. Nor his peers for that matter.

Back in the small hospital bedroom, Jim was writing in his notebook. Good old-fashioned policing, he called it, despite the fact that his phone was recording the entire conversation as evidence. 'Shauna Edis,' he scribbled. 'And you are sure of that?'

'How many times you want me to say it.' John rubbed the back of his head. 'She banged on the door. Came in shouting and balling. Called me all sorts of names.' He glanced up at Jess. 'Called her all sorts of names.'

'Can you remember what she actually said, John?' Jim had his pencil poised.

Again, he looked at Jess. 'No.'

'No?'

'No.'

Jim looked at him quizzically. 'No, you can't

remember something that someone said to you an hour ago?'

'Maybe it's the bang on the head. My memory isn't what it was,' he said, feebly.

'John McCarthy, when we were younger, you could quote the whole of Scotland's curling league scores.' Jim grinned. 'Going back a decade, at least.'

'I was younger then.'

Jim sat on the bed, determined to get the best of this situation. 'I've got all night.' He glanced at his watch, 'Might even get paid some overtime.' He placed his hands on the older man's leg, feeling his rugged knees through the flannelette bedspread. 'What did Shauna say to you? And why did she hit you?'

'Yeah, Dad.' Jess spoke up for the first time. 'What did that little wretch say to you?'


Scott squinted through the dark night as he passed the Marina again, slightly quicker this time. He couldn't see any vehicles and the lights were off in the main building. He considered phoning Ronni and lifted his phone, switching it on. Still only up to ten percent, he decided to leave it off for a while longer, in case he might need it later.

Ten minutes further on, he swung the pick-up into the car-park of the veterinary surgery. The lights were off too, but one car remained, frost glinting off its window. It was an estate car that needed a wash. First, he tried the main door which was predictably locked, although he rattled the handle to be sure. On the window was a note giving an out-of-hours emergency phone number which he ignored. In his experience those things put you through to a switchboard in Ness, where nobody knew anyone's name. Trudging round the back of the building, he saw a glow of light from a single bulb, seeping out from behind some roller shutters. Avoiding a few obstacles in the dark, he made it to the window, trying to peep in. A radio was playing softly, some jazz station. Scott tapped on the window-pane.

Inside, a faint scream was followed by a number of dogs barking. He thought he heard some swearing too as another light came on followed by the sound of a door lock being pulled back. 'Who's there?' called a shrill but scary voice. 'Show yourself!' The dogs barked even louder.

'Scott,' he called back.

Megan went quiet for a second so all that could be heard was the sound of her heavy breathing and four or five dogs still unsettled. He recognised the sound of Beth as one of them.

'Ya feckin eejit, scared me half to death.' She stepped through the door to greet him, a smile arriving with her. 'Lucky I didn't set the dog on you.' Beth loomed into sight, still bandaged but her tail wagging. 'Why didn't you phone, ya loony. Instead of creeping around in the dark like a...' she struggled for the right word. 'Like a feckin cat burglar.'

'Do burglar's really steal cats?' he said, straight faced whilst stroking the dog.

"You're the friggin policeman, you tell me.' She managed to fill the doorway with her petite frame. 'Normal folks use the front door!'

Over a cup of coffee Scott explained about his phone battery and that, reluctantly, he wouldn't be able to make it to dinner that evening. Megan fed him a couple of digestive biscuits, genuinely enquiring about his day in a sociable but interested manner. 'I heard there's been a murder,' she continued. 'It was on the car radio. Wasn't the same bloke that shot your dog, was it?' They both looked down at Beth. 'The shite-bag!'

Jim was writing furiously. 'Sounds like a case for assault,' he said, looking up. 'Want to press charges?'

'No.'

He read back his notes. 'She said you were a murdering bastard, and that you would all pay? Sounds a bit dramatic, John?' Jess was looking unconcerned. 'All? John?'

'She was aff her nut. Drugs I expect. You know what that family is like?'

'Well,' Jim wrote 'aff her nut', 'I don't actually. Had she been on the drink as well?'

'The fuck should I know,' again he touched the bandage on his head. 'But something pretty strong to start hitting folks with tools.'

'What else did she say?'

Again, John looked up at his daughter and Jim detected a glimmer of defiance from her, not quite a shake of the head, but the notions of one. 'Said I deserved to get what he got.'

'And she came at you then?'

'Aye, my back was turned. I was going to make the lass a brew, to calm her down.' Again he looked embarrassed. 'Next thing I'm on the floor, in a pool of blood!'

'What he got?' Jim repeated. 'Referring to her father, I guess?' He bided his time before adding: 'Was it you, that hit Charlie Edis, John?' Jim spoke the question slowly, looking him directly in the eye.

'Me!' John exploded. 'Get tae fuck. All of you. Accusing me?'

Jim waited for the outburst to end, again raising an inquisitive eyebrow.

'No. I didn't kill the toe-rag, Charlie Edis. Or anyone else for that matter.'

Jess pulled a half smile. 'Well, I guess that's that over with.'

Jim stood to his feet, stretching out his arms and then checking his watch. 'Interview over, seven fifteen.' Picking up the phone, he switched off the recorder, remembering Scott's parting words. Check your messages.

'Get well soon, John,' his words were genuine. 'And meanwhile we'll see what she has to say.'

'Said I didn't want to press charges, didn't I?'

'You don't,' he shook the man's hand, 'but we might.'

By the time Jim reached the Land-Rover he had noted two missed calls from Sandy and a message saying 'We found De Runcy's phone?' Jim dialled him immediately.

'Tell that twat to get a new phone, will you?' Sandy showed frustration in not being in contact with Scott. 'Or doesn't this nick have enough budget?'

'Where?'

'Up in the mountains, a faint signal.' Sandy yawned. 'Your man is taking a look. And I'm knocking off.'

'Don't you want to hear about this end?'

'Aye, go one then. Just the highlights. Save the detail for your report in the morning.'

'Edis's daughter, the goth.' Jim sighed, recalling the girl and her purple hair.

'What about her?'

'Going round accusing folk of killing her old man. Banjoed old John McCarthy with a wrench.'

'Straight forward report then? You'll have it done in minutes,' Sandy was about to hang up the call. 'G'night.'

'Sandy, wait.'

'What?'

'It's no the girl that worries me. It's the other woman.'

Scott looped the pick-up into the high-sided track up to the quarry. Although most of the snow had melted away recent vehicle tracks were still showing despite the water trickling down the cutting. Pulling out his phone he noted twenty five percent charge now, so he dropped the cable out of the end of it and switched it on. An icon blinked to show there was voicemail but he ignored it for now, scrolling down his list of contacts until he found the one he needed.

As the pick-up reached the end of the track that opened up into a clearing, he swung the headlights around in a slow circle, opened his window, and hit the dial button.

Less than fifty yards away, he saw a lump, half covered with snow. In the distance, a phone's ringtone sung the Marseilles out above the wind. Scott was out of the vehicle in seconds, immediately recognising a body when he saw one. A man in a dark jacket lay face down.

Scott switched off the phone call and fumbled for the torch app on the screen. As the light burst into the scene, he rolled the body over to reveal the unmistakable face, of Julien de Runcy.

# Chapter Thirty-Four

Shauna had her back to the door when she heard the lock click open. Turning round quickly, she grabbed a sharp knife off the sink, and faced the intruder.

'This place is private,' she snarled. 'You have no right to break in here!'

'I might not have a right but I do have a key.' Liz Mills glared at the girl for a few seconds and then sat down on the leather sofa, tucking her heels beneath her. 'What have you been up to, you silly girl?'

Knife still in hand, Shauna pulled at one of her purple braids in a defiant manner. 'Bastards, all of you.' The words were spoken softly but there was no hint of calm in her voice. 'He might have been a shit Dad. But he was my Dad.' Pushing herself forward, the strap of her dungarees fell back into place on her shoulder. 'He didn't deserve to die.'

'I totally agree,' Liz replied. 'But you can't just go around randomly seeking revenge on everyone. We all have a part in this. We all have to stay tight.'

'That's it, though, isn't it? The old man had been spouting off. And now the plug is out on your little venture, the whisky is already running down the drain. You killed him, and now you've lost control.'

'Ah, that's where you're wrong. We didn't kill your Dad. And we do still very much have control!'

Shauna lurched forward, swinging the knife. 'You lying fuck!' she screeched. Liz had anticipated the move, and lurched sideways, toppling over the arm of the sofa and jumping to her feet.

'Calm the fuck down, Shauna.' Her eyes bored into the girls, who was visibly shaking. 'I came to talk to you.'

Frosty silence filled the air until eventually Shauna lowered the weapon. 'Lie to me, you mean?'

'Look, put the kettle on and let's get to the bottom of this like adults, OK?' Liz could throw in patronisation like confetti. 'Why would we want to bite off the hands that feed us, eh? Your father wasn't a strong man but he had his uses. He was going to make us all rich, but he played a dangerous game. He knew the rules and he overstepped the mark. But you know all that.' She pulled out a pack of cigarettes, taking one and then tossing the packet to Shauna.

'What if I do?' Shauna caught the pack and pulled one out as well. 'Yes, I know that, but it won't bring him back.'

'Precisely. And nor will going round hitting people.' Liz pushed the door open a fraction with her foot to let the smoke out, standing by it and facing the girl. 'All that will do is bring the police in closer. Which is why I want to speak to you. They will be here. Maybe tonight, maybe tomorrow. And they'll want answers. Understand?'

Shauna leant back against the sink, her shoulders dropping. 'I won't talk to them,' she said. 'Not about that.'

'No,' Liz hissed, 'you won't! Because if you do, you'll go down with the ship. I can promise you that much.'

'So, you came here to threaten me, is that it. You whore.'

Liz ignored the comment, it wasn't the first time that name had been thrown her way. 'You have your alibi. We all have our alibis. They can't pin your father's death on any of us. And they won't find evidence of our scheme.' She waved the smoke away from her face. 'They'll concentrate on Jean-Luc's death. And that has nothing to do with any of us, does it?' Liz smiled.

'Nothing to do with me, that's for sure. That guy had more enemies than Batman, low-life bastard that he was. Good riddance, I say.'

'So,' Liz continued. 'They'll get to the bottom of that, eventually. He's the big fish, and the headlines will go his way. In a couple of weeks, your poor old Dad will be buried and forgotten, no offence, but his death will just be recorded as misadventure. We stay put, and stay schtum. And eventually everything gets back to normal. OK?'

A tear had formed in Shauna's eye. 'How could you be so callous?'

'Just being practical,' she opened the door, chucking the cigarette butt out into the night. 'Not callous, just practical!' As she stepped outside, the sound of a helicopter thundered overhead causing her to jump back in. 'Bloody hell!' Up on the hillside the glare of blue flashing lights arced across the sky. She pulled out her phone, scrolled down the numbers and hit dial.

'What's going on?' she yelled.

'Search me?' Dougie's voice stayed calm. 'Some activity though? Looks like an air-ambulance on Cruachan. Probably another hiker getting lost. Stupid bastards.'


As the giant machine hovered above the plateau, Scott waved it down towards a clearing in the car-park with practiced hand-signals. This was a job he'd been trained in and done too many times before. Clouds of snow whipped up under the rotors as they whooped their reverbing noise up the hillside. A yellow beam of light under the chopper lit up the scene, mixing with the blue flashing beacon he had placed on the pick-up bonnet to mark the spot. As soon as the wheels touched down, two paramedics were out of a sliding door, green rucksacks in hand.

'Single gunshot, below the rib,' he shouted over the din. 'Lost a lot of blood and consciousness, but he's still alive. Just!'

'Roger that, Scottie.' The man put up a thumb. 'We'll

take it from here!'

Skilfully the two men opened out a stretcher and lifted De Runcy's body carefully on to it. The whole operation was over in less than two minutes before the big red machine took to the skies again. Scott watched it go, before heading to the pick-up and switching off the beacon, returning the scene to darkness. Beth tried to jump out when he opened the door, frightened by the noise, but Scott held her back. This was a crime scene now and a dog paddling through the blood wouldn't do anyone any favours, least of all him. De Runcy's phone lay on the dashboard wrapped in a plastic bag, and it started to vibrate so he glanced at it.

Caller ID, Jess McCarthy.

# Chapter Thirty Five

The mantelpiece clock showed it was past ten o'clock when Scott opened his eyes, the embers of the fire burning down low in front of him. He'd been asleep for thirty-five minutes. Nowhere near enough but it went somewhere towards regeneration after a knackering day. By his side a pasta dish lay empty and licked clean, and he tried to recall if he had finished it earlier. He suspected not, as he gazed at Beth asleep by his feet. Well, she deserved it perhaps. She'd had a hell of a day as well.

Standing up and stretching his arms he went to the back door, and was about to lock it when Beth woke and suggested she needed to go outside. Scott opened it to note the snow had started again. 'Don't be long, it's damn cold.' He looked at her bandage, much of which she had since removed herself, teeth marks showing up tears in the strong material. He tried to recall what Megan had told him to do but it was all a blur. Maybe he should call her, just to check? Beth wasn't for staying out long in this weather and shook herself on the doormat, spraying dampness across the floor. Rubbing his eyes, Scott flicked on the kettle and pulled a chair up to the table where his laptop lay open. He flicked the keyboard and the screen came to life.

An email from Ranolph McLaughlin - 8.38pm - 're. Coastal movements'.

*'Hi Scott, find attached. Glad I could help. Ronni.'*

Scott clicked on the attached file and a spreadsheet opened up on his screen listing four columns of numbers. At first glance it all just looked like gobbledygook until he noticed a second sheet entitled 'craft numbers'. This page referenced the names of boats against a list of numbers and, as he inspected the first page again, he realised that the first columns were time/dates, down to the second, obviously sent out directly from some specialist software.

He checked down the second page again, searching for one name in particular. Jouer Sur Mer.

The boat was numbered in a column headed SSR as OB3267, a reference to the fact it was registered in Oban.

Scott yawned and made himself a coffee, washing up the already cleaned plate in the sink at the same time. Something was swirling round in his mind and the nagging wouldn't go away. Why was Jess calling Julien de Runcy? He had tried to call her when he got home but it went straight to voicemail and he decided not to leave a message. As far as he was aware, the pair barely knew each other. Yet her number was stored in his phone. News from the hospital had last come through at 9pm, that the patient was stable after removal of a bullet from his left ribcage and on a life-support ventilator. As yet, no analysis of the bullet had been done, that would require resource from Inverness. As Scott saw it, whoever was in that car must have fired the shot, and left De Runcy for dead. If he didn't make it, that would certainly involve Glasgow, since the car was found down there, so the big boys could do the maths on that one.

Chucking a biscuit to Beth, he settled back down at the screen, his tired eyes scrolling down the entries. Sorting the spreadsheet by SSR number, he got a complete list of all the movements of Jouer Sur Mer for the last six months. On the face of it, nothing seemed out of the ordinary.

20211411:1322:23 was the last entry he found for the vessel, the fourteenth of November, four days before Jen-Luc's death. The boat went out at twenty-two minutes past one, returning just forty minutes later. More records showed previous short trips, usually once per fortnight until he got back to August when there had been many more comings and goings, some for a day or two at a time. Using the most basic of computer skills he managed to cut and paste the most recent entries into a word document, and saved it.

Next he fired up his email programme and replied to Ronni.

*'Thanks, pal. This is ideal.*

*Do you have CCTV records of vessels coming and going?*

*Could do with ones for the entries attached, pls. Scott.'*

It took Scott the next five minutes to fathom out how to attach the word file and send it off. Then he went back to the list. Now he checked the entries for boats arriving the same day that De Runcy's boat had been on the move, but there was nothing out of the ordinary there. Scrolling the figures a few more times and draining his coffee, he closed the lid and headed off to bed, Beth settling down on the rug by the fire.

Scott's stone bothy had been renovated three years ago, using the best materials, but still it was nigh on impossible to stop the Argyll wind getting in when the weather was bad. The tiniest of gaps around the Velux window, or where the wall met the roof joists was enough for it to get its little grip, and then quietly grumble its anger into the house at a varying pitch. Scott had got used to it by now to the point where he barely realised it was there, like a rural student moving into town and hearing traffic from the roads outside. Sometimes he found it soothing, while his mind whirled around his troubles or guilt. Tonight it was the latter, sweat forming across his chest as the failings of the day's events mixed themselves into a cocktail of fear, while the evils of restless sleep fuelled the flames with exaggeration. Somewhere a dog barked, distant enough to be ignored but close enough to feel the trail of blood coming from its side.

Beth raised her head, still drowsy from the pain-killers that the vet had administered, as the lock on the back door turned quietly, twice until the handle opened. Cold air arrived unwelcomed, as the intruder stepped on to the tiles, expensive walking boots calmly stamping off the snow. A gloved hand closed the door, causing Beth to wake again. For a second she wagged her tail as the visitor hushed her quiet. Then she let out a few barks in defiance until a scented dog-chew did the trick and she returned to her bed, half-heartedly gnawing at it.

A small lamp by the fire gave off enough glow to see into the shadows, as the intruder glanced around the room. Scott's laptop was on the table, and the prowler sat down silently on a kitchen chair and pulled opened the lid. Password required, password entered, the screen now showed a spreadsheet full of figures. With glove removed, red varnished fingernails scrolled the mouse pad down the list. 'What are you up to, you silly boy?' a voice whispered to herself.

Then she opened the email app and read the mails to and from the marina manager, noting Scott's request for camera footage. Quietly she closed the laptop again, removing her coat and hanging it on the back of the chair. His mobile phone had been left on charge in a socket next to the kettle, where he always put it. She picked it up, entering the simple four-digit password, and scrolled through the WhatsApp messages, the most recent one being from Jim, stating that De Runcy was still alive. Two or three others were from Megan. She read them all too. 'Oh, how sweet,' she said to herself, 'this might be fun!'

Pulling off her other glove, the intruder pulled her own phone out from the breast pocket of her heavy coat, typing a text message. 'He's getting close.' She waited for the message to confirm it was sent, then went back into the app and deleted it, standing up and turning to the work surface. She ran her fingers along the row of neat sharp Japanese knives clinging to a magnetic rail. Her thoughts ran to guilt as she selected one and lifted it down, checking its edge.

At the other end of the phone, a man in a dark blue

suit put his whisky tumbler down on a coffee table and lowered his cigar to the ashtray, before opening the message. He looked up towards another man, older than himself, who was half dozing in a red leather chair.

'Getting close?' he sniffed, laying the phone down again and retrieving the cigar. 'The fuck's that meant to mean?'

The older man spoke without opening his eyes, voiced like cracked ice. 'We running? Or fighting?'

'Never run from a fight yet.' Alfie looked around the wood panelled room, with its ornate gilt frames on the wall displaying art of bygone painters. 'Didn't get here without a fight, bro. It's what we do?'

Standing up, the other man's knees creaked quietly as he wandered to the large bay window, staring out into the dark night that was helped out by the yellow glow of a few streetlights. Deep in thought for a few seconds he eventually asked a question. 'You sure we got the tracks covered? What if the bastard wakes up? Then what? He gets in a corner, he'll sing like a fucking choirboy.' His hand ran over a forehead pockmarked with darker stains where the sun had taken its toll. 'This needs tidying up, Alfred. Or I'm off back home and leaving you to smell the porridge.' A few flakes of snow swirled around the empty street. 'Can't stand this bloody weather much more.'

'I'm on it,' Alfie stood up, draining his whisky and stubbing out the cigar. 'First thing.'


Next the intruder stood to her feet, took off her shoes and tiptoed to the bedroom door, listening for signs of life. Behind it she could hear snoring so she turned the handle very quietly. Scott stirred a fraction but didn't open his eyes. The woman held her phone up in the darkness, taking a snap but without the flash engaged. The photo captured Scott's naked body as well as the intruders face reflected in the mirror. She pocketed the phone, letting out a smile as she quietly closed the door.

# Chapter Thirty-Six

Beth sounded the alarm just after 8am, that someone was probably knocking at the door. Scott felt across the bed as he opened his eyes. He had had a strange dream, a recurring one where he was in bed with a naked woman, just out of reach. Outside the chapping on the door got louder and he pulled on a pair of check cotton pyjama bottoms and a fairisle jumper. It was still dark outside when he pulled back the kitchen curtain, but the sun was starting its glow somewhere in the far hills.

'Jeez,' Jim exclaimed when Scott opened the door. 'You look like shit. Had a busy night?'

Scott rubbed his eyes, checking his phone as he put the kettle on and seeing two missed calls from the uniformed copper now standing in front of him. 'Something like that, yeah.'

Jim grinned. 'You not been humping that vet, already, have you. Christ, you used the dog to get into her pants, you rascal.' The said dog wagged her tail as Jim stroked her head.

'Aye. I mean no.' He glanced at his watch. 'You wet the bed or something?'

'Big boss has been shaking the stick. Wants the goth girl brought in. Wants fucking everyone brought in. Even you.' He grinned again. 'Especially you!'

Through the night Beth had just about removed her bandage and had been licking at the stitches where Megan had taken out the shotgun pellets. He thought of her, and then of Jess, shook his head and pulled two cups from the cupboard. Absentmindedly he straightened the knives on the magnet. 'Now what have I done,' he said out loud.

'Thankfully the lads in Glasgow work night shift, and

they have a few leads that might open up a path to De Runcy.' Jim sat at the table, eyeing the laptop, blinking a red light to show it was low on charge.

'He still with us?' Scott asked.

'Aye, just about.' Jim eyed the coffee coming his way. 'Got any bacon?'

Scott ignored the remark. 'Will he talk?'

Jim shook his head, 'Not just now anyway. Still tubed up and out cold.' He stood up, opening the fridge and checking the shelves. 'Aha, you beauty,' he yelped, pulling out a half open packet. 'Knew you wouldn't let me down!'

'Couldn't you have just got a roll on the way?' Scott sighed, pulling a pan down from a hanging rail.

'What, on my wages!'

Scott headed to the bathroom. 'You want it, you cook it.'

'You want some?'

'Nah, packet's probably older than my dog!'

Jim checked the sell-by date, 'I'll take the risk, thanks.'

Ten minutes later, showered and wearing a navy-blue police jumper, Scott opened the door to let the dog out, leaving it ajar to let the smell of over-cooked bacon out as well. Gemma was at the gate and gave a roar when she saw him. 'You can bugger off, too,' he muttered. The cow raised her head as though understanding him. 'Alright, I'll be there shortly,' he added.

Back inside Jim was washing the pan under running hot water. He noted a single cup in the sink from the night before but the absence of wine glasses. 'So, the bird, what was she like?'

Scott snapped 'Fuck off with that, will you?'

'Only asking, mate to mate, like!'

'You want me to enquire whether Alice likes to be on top?'

Jim stopped, going a little red. 'Touché,' he said.

'So who's the guys we are looking at in Glasgow, Jim?'

'Matheson Brothers. Mean anything to you?'

Scott shook his head, pulling on his boots. 'Should it?'

'There's a briefing at ten, so we need to get the skates on. All may well be revealed.'

He fed the dog before leaving, checking on the packet of drugs Megan has sent him away with, and tipping a small sachet of powder into her food. 'I'll get back later, and get those bandages changed, OK. And no pulling those stitches out!' Beth wagged her tail furiously.

'You really think dogs understand humans?' Jim asked.

Scott sighed. 'About as much as we understand women.'

'That'll be a no then!'

Scott sat down in front of his laptop. 'Just need to check something.'

'Make it quick, we're under the cosh.'

There was no reply from Ronni, so he closed the lid, plugging the machine into charge. Jim fired up the Land-Rover, 'You're with me,' he shouted above the engine.

'Can't I just follow in mine, then I can get back here again?'

'Just get in, for fuck sake. Boss's orders.' On the way, Scott questioned why he was being brought in, and was he under arrest. Jim laughed, explained that they were taking Shauna in and that it required two of them to be in the car together. At the end of the lane, Scott checked his watch, and made a point of looking both ways.

In the distance down the valley he saw what he was looking for and pointed to the milk tanker. 'I'm sure that bugger has it in for me.'

'Just coz you're paranoid, doesn't mean everyone's not

out to get you,' Jim teased.

'I reckon my brother sent him.'

'Ah, yes, how is the sleazebag?'

'Shifty as ever. I could swear he's hiding something.'

'What, you think he's in on this shit? I thought he despised all these incomers?'

They swung left down towards the campsite. 'Just something not quite right with him,' Scott continued.

'Could've told you that years ago!' Jim pulled down the sun visor as the red glow glinted off the lake. 'And anyone who shoots his brother's dog, definitely isn't playing fair in the classroom. What was that about anyway? A warning maybe?'

'Well it was him that told me Liz was shagging Edis. So he must have an ear to the ground, that's for sure.'

Jim slowed as they reached the entrance to Ardnashaig.

'How we going to play this?' Scott asked. 'If this is an arrest? And if so, what for?'

'No arrest. Just bringing her in for questioning.'

'About McCarthy?'

'About McCarthy. But I ain't going to question her on her patch. She's too twisted for me. We'll let Heather have that option.' Jim pulled the vehicle outside her small chalet and marched to the door.

The girl opened it immediately and stood defiantly, reasonably well dressed for once. 'Shauna Edis, we would like you to come to the station, for questioning?'

'Oo, a ride in a Landy. Haven't ridden in one of those for ages!' she teased. When she saw Scott she added, 'And doubled up, too. What fun.'

Jim kept his calm. 'It's no laughing matter, miss. You are not under arrest, but my colleague here will be witness to anything you say until we reach the station.'

'I got time for a pee first?'

Jim nodded and she disappeared back inside. Scott took the chance to roll a cigarette, glancing down towards the office. Liz was watching them from the window, so he turned his back on her. He was half tempted to suggest they took her in too but decided that Boss's orders were just for the girl and he was not about to mess up another day trying to do the right thing.

Once they were on the road, Shauna in the back seat of the crew-cab vehicle with a small canvas bag at her feet, she quieted down a bit. The two men kept the conversation minimal, both agreeing that it was a braw day and how lucky folks round here were to have that view of the loch. As they passed the hotel she demanded that she needed to be back by three as she was working there today.

'I didn't know you worked at the Kilchrenan?' Scott asked.

'Just starting today.' She even sounded excited. 'Last girl couldn't stand the pace.'

Scott recalled the last girl and considered that even Shauna's attitude would be better than hers.

It was 9.45am before they reached the station at Oban, where Shauna was shown to an interview room and offered a statuary coffee which she accepted. The door was closed behind her and the room lay in silence.

All eyes turned on Scott as he walked into the briefing room, taking a chair at one of the Formica topped tables, avoiding eye contact with the others. Since his last visit the whiteboard had been updated, with lines below De Runcy leading to a few photos of men he hadn't seen before. He also noted that Shauna Edis had been underlined in red. Andrew McClatchie entered followed by Heather and the four policemen stood up.

McClatchie made a point of looking round the room.

'Donald,' he mused. 'Glad you could join us.' Scott said nothing. 'OK, let's get down to business.' He beckoned to Sandy. 'If you'll start, please.'

Sandy took up position at the front of the room. 'Since we found De Runcy's car, we have been working with Glasgow CID on the movements of these two men.' He pointed to a photo. 'One Richard Matheson, trained lawyer, traded the market, top dog in a firm dealing in property and finance. Now lives in Spain, but pops back and forth ad hoc, in the company chopper. The same chopper than brought De Runcy up here. Clean sheet, but suspected close contacts with drug gangs, in Glasgow, Manchester and London.'

He moved on to the next picture. 'His younger brother, Alfred Matheson. East Glasgow hard man. Been in more bare-knuckle fights than Mike Tyson. Carries a shooter. Been in the dock a few times, mainly for violence, but never been put away. We all know Glasgow can be a hard place but even the weegies are scared of this man. I think even some of the force. He's been on the radar for two years, and photo'd with some real bad bastards, but too smart to get caught. So far. We are pretty sure his connection with De Runcy is whisky trafficking. And/or drugs.'

Scott raised his wrist, before asking. 'So we think he is our killer?'

'A pretty fair chance, I would have said.'

'Would have said?'

'Forensics tell us the bullet from senior and junior don't match.'

Scott considered this. 'Could have changed weapons?'

'Unlikely. These hoods have a favourite. And the method was different, first one a definite hit job. Second wasn't so clean.'

'What about the car, who was in it with De Runcy?'

Heather asked. 'Scott, you chased him.' She cleared her throat. 'Well, sort of. Did you get a look at him?' Scott shook his head. 'All we know is the car was collected and signed for by this man.' She stepped forward and pointed to another photo. 'High-flying Glasgow lawyer, must have been staying around here some place, to get here so soon. Since gone to ground, nobody has seen him.'

'And we think he drove the car to collect Julien de Runcy?'

'Probably, but not certain. What if he had passed the car on to this villain? An easy switch. Smart guy would have done it away from the cameras. Probably out of town, somewhere.'

'The marina.' Scott stood up. 'Our Alfie could have been waiting for him there?'

Sandy scratched his chin. 'OK, feasible. So if the lawyer goes to ground after that, where would he go?'

'Could still be there, on the boat?' Scott announced. 'They have CCTV, might show up something?'

'I don't think so. Both men would be too smart for that. More likely collected and taken somewhere. Or had another car hidden.'

Heather recapped. 'So Alfie picks up De Runcy at the distillery, right under our noses.' All eyes stared at Scott. '

'Aye, and he sent me a distraction.' Scott gave as defence. 'Either didn't want us to know where he was going. Or to see who was in the car.'

'Heads off the road, gives you the slip. Pops the old man and dumps the car.' McClatchie spoke up. 'Sounds pretty professional.'

'For what it's worth, I think De Runcy was driving,' Scott said.

'What makes you think that?'

'Just the way he drove, devious move. Would know

the area better.'

'You saying they could have switched drivers? Any TV in the car-park at the distillery?'

'Not that I know of. No.'

McClatchie spoke again. 'Well if the victim pulls through he can confirm who was driving. Until then, let's move on.'

'OK. Glasgow has a mole in the whisky camp. Some barrels have come on the market recently. High value stuff, pushed out to investors, four or five grand apiece. They are pretty sure Matheson is in on it. Richard, the older one. But the source has been hard to trace, and it's a close lipped community. The numbers on the barrels don't match up with anything recognised.'

'De Runcy,' Jim piped up. 'Too much of a coincidence?'

'Bingo.' Sandy said. 'But that's where the trail ends.'

Scott moved seats, logging on to a computer. 'I have all the vessel records for the marina.' He signed into his email account and a mail showed up from Ronni but he refrained from opening it until he'd finished speaking. 'De Runcy's boat has been running out regularly, just for short trips, forty minutes or so. Up till just before he was killed.'

'And you were going to share this with us when?' Heather's eyes narrowed but Scott ignored her.

'I requested CCTV of the harbour, for the times when his boat was on the move.' He checked the mail, but Ronni said the files were too big to email, and could they be collected. 'I should have them soon.'

'What are you saying, Scott?' Sandy asked. 'You think he was shipping barrels out on the boat? Where the hell could he go in forty minutes.'

'That's what I am trying to find out. Is there someone who could run an errand for me please?'

'Not your bloody dog again?' Heather glared at him fiercely. 'Can't you just stick to police work, for once?'

'What do you need?' McClatchie diffused the situation and Scott told him about the files. He nodded, 'Send someone down Heather, please?' The woman turned away, annoyed at being overruled in her scolding of this incompetent officer.

'Is there footage from the day of the murder?' the senior officer continued.

'Nothing to see. We checked that,' said Bill.

'I rather hoped you had,' the man smiled a half smile.

Sandy picked up the reins again. 'We think that De Runcy has been shifting his whisky to Matheson, in return for bankrolling his business. But he wouldn't do it alone. Hence we brought in the girl. She was close to the son and could easily have been working with him. Her father was making the stuff so it stands to reason.'

'And where are we with the father, Edis?' McClatchie pointed to the board. 'Seems a hell of a long list of suspects and no proof of anything.'

'I'm pretty sure the girl didn't kill her father. To the contrary, she was trying to find out who did. And she was well away from the action at the time.' Scott took a cloth and removed the red line from under her name. 'And I don't think Liz Mills did it either. Too soft, despite her controlling ways.'

'Unless she shagged him to death!' Bill meant it as a joke but nobody laughed.

'McCarthy didn't do it, either. In fact, I suspect the scheme they have going on, Edis was paramount to its success, so killing him wasn't exactly a smart move by any of them.'

'And do we think Edis's little scheme was the same scheme that these big boys were playing at?'

'No, Sir. I don't. From his history he was more a small-time crook. Seeing what the bosses were playing with, thought he would pull a similar stunt himself, bringing the locals in for help. My guess is they pulled a decent barrel out for themselves and stashed it somewhere.'

'So who the hell killed him,' Heather dived in, 'in this theory of yours?'

Scott stayed calm, knowing he had the room now. 'It came from De Runcy. Not him personally. But one of his henchmen.'

'So we back to Alfie again.' The Super straightened his jacket. 'Jeez that man's a serial!'

'I'm not sure it's him either. That's not his style.' Scott stood and walked to the whiteboard. 'No. There's something we've missed.'

# Chapter Thirty-Seven

'Interview started, 10.42, Detective Inspector Downs and Detective Constable Young in the room.' Heather nodded to Shauna. 'Could you state you name please?'

Scott watched the interview through the window along with Jim who was relieved it was Bill in there. He checked his phone for messages. Nothing from Jess. He'd let her move first this time. In the thirty odd years he had known her, she had done a few odd things, but arriving in his bed in the middle of the night was up there with the best of them. And that certainly had left him with a massive guilt trip this morning, particularly as he had eyes for another woman. Did she know that? Had she found out about Megan? Not that there was anything to find out, really. Some jealousy, maybe? He had heard how woman like to control with sex. And she had controlled him. Always. Mostly just out of reach. Scott had liked to think they would get back together one day, but he had never quite breached that hurdle; something always just fell across the path. And now, just when he was moving away from that path, she steps back into it.

'We weren't really lovers. Just sometimes he got me to do things,' Shauna was saying.

'Got you to?' Heather was firing the questions. 'How?'

'Paid me.'

'What sort of things?'

The girl looked straight ahead, carefully forming her answers. 'Be places. See the odd person.'

'Which places?'

'On the boat. Sometimes at his flat.'

'With other men?' Shauna nodded, saying nothing, so

Heather continued. 'Did he pay you to have sex with other men?'

'He just paid me to be with them. Or him. He said I didn't need to have sex with them, not if I didn't want to.'

'And did you?'

Another long pause. 'Sometimes. If they were nice.' She raised her head for the first time, looking at Heather. 'Look there was drink. Drugs. Parties. I am sure you know about it? Add those up and sex usually happens. Better to be with a man you like than to be the last one in, so to speak.'

'Were there other girls at these parties?'

'Sure, loads of them. But never quite enough to go round.' She smiled. 'Sometimes we shared. Occasionally.'

Behind the glass Jim's jaw had dropped slightly. 'Bloody hell!' he said in a whisper.

'Are we talking orgies, Shauna,' Heather kept the girl's focus.

'If you say so,' she smiled again. 'I'd just call them normal parties, really. Fun, you know?' She returned Heather's stare. 'Or maybe you don't?'

'Ouch,' muttered Scott, 'that was a low blow!'

'That night, in Inverness, was there a party then?'

'The night Dad was murdered, you mean.' Shauna showed no emotion. 'No, just us.'

'Why that particular night, Shauna. Why did he take you to Inverness on that very night?'

'Don't you think I've been asking myself that question,' she reached down to her bag. 'Mind if I smoke?' Heather pointed to a sticker on the wall, and Shauna put the pack away again.

'Jean-Luc didn't stay all night, did he?' Bill picked up the reigns now. 'Where did he go?'

She didn't hesitate, 'He said he had to meet someone.'

'How long was he gone?'

'Oh, I dunno, four, five hours, maybe. I was asleep when he came back in. Done a pill, hadn't I. He tried to climb into bed with me, but he smelled of perfume, so I pushed him out.' She smiled again. 'Might have shouted at him, a bit. May have even kicked him in the nuts! The bastard.'

Scott renewed his interest when he heard the word perfume, but said nothing.

'And he stayed until morning?'

'Yeah, as far as I know. When I woke up he was gone. And I got the bus down home when I heard about my dad. End of.' She picked up the packet again. 'Can I go now?'

'Interview paused at 10.56. Defendant is demanding a cigarette break.'

Scott watched Bill escort Shauna outside. 'Defendant?' he said quietly, raising an eyebrow. Bill gave him the finger.

'Package for you, Scott.' Sandy looked up from his screen. 'How's that interview going in there?'

'Tight, I'd say.' He opened a jiffy bag just marked Scott in felt pen on the front. Inside was a silver USB memory stick. 'That was quick,' he said loudly, 'Thanks, whoever fetched this.' Sitting down at a desk he logged into the system again, and then inserted the drive. The screen showed just one directory but when he clicked on it, at least a hundred files appeared. A number at the bottom of the screen showed each file was at least 10 gigabytes. Scott went back to his email and opened the file he had sent to Ronni, checking the date and then selecting the corresponding file on the drive. There were two files on that date, each one for a different camera. The first one was inside the main office, come shop, showing a wide area from the door to main desk. He closed the picture and opened the second one which must have been mounted on a mast somewhere so high up that it just about covered all the boats and gangplanks between them. Scott checked the time on his document and slid the file forward, seeing a few boats coming and going, each one leaving a wake as they negotiated the hammerhead and set off out into the bay. This day had been dull and it was quite hard to distinguish which vessel was which, but using the spreadsheet he could at least cross reference the SSR numbers. Eventually he saw the Jouer de Mer leave her berth, going slowly backwards, and then chugging leisurely out to the open sea. He watched until it had disappeared from sight, never raising the sail. The timeline showed that it was in shot for only eight minutes. Checking the column of numbers again, he moved on to the time it returned and, sure enough, in it came, slowly into marina and back to its berth. The timeline matched exactly to the file he had. 'Where the hell have you been?' he said out loud.

'I could ask you the same thing,' Heather had walked into the room and was looking over his shoulder. 'What do we have here?'

'De Runcy's boat,' he was about to add, 'Ma'am,' but decided against it. 'Left the harbour and comes back forty minutes later.'

'Nice little cruise,' she nodded.

'In November? Look at those waves. Hardly a day for sight-seeing?'

They watched as a tall slim man in a baseball cap roped the boat back to the side of the mooring, pulling a sheet back over the deck. 'Maybe been dolphin watching?' Heather added. They both knew that made no sense.

Scott wound the frame back until the boat was leaving and then further than that until they saw the man in the cap arrive, pushing a small trolley loaded with a few things and a sheet over it. From such a distance the picture was fuzzy but they could make out him opening a metal gate to the pontoon and wheel it up to the boat. He lifted a few bags and then what looked like a drum of fuel on to the deck. Scott stopped the frame. 'How much petrol does one of those things drink?'

Heather shook her head. 'No idea, but that looks heavy, way he is struggling with it.'

'What if it isn't fuel?'

Heather patted him on the shoulder. 'Good work,' she said, her voice more enthusiastic.

Scott smiled inwardly already opening up a file dated two weeks earlier. 'Thank you, Ma'am.'

Heather left the room when she saw Shauna coming back with Bill Young, as they headed back to the interview.

'Why did you hit John McCarthy?' Heather was saying after they had settled back into the routine. Shauna stayed quiet, so she repeated the question.

'He hated my dad,' she said eventually. 'Everyone knows that. They even had a fight, once. Man was a bully. And he'd been up at the distillery that day.'

'You think he killed your father?'

She put her head in her hands. 'Yes. No.' A tear came into her eye. 'I don't know?' Sudden anger arrived from nowhere. 'You're the fucking police. Why don't you know?'

'He says he didn't. Why shouldn't we believe him?'

She cocked her head on one side, the tear spilling onto her cheek. 'Derr. He could be...ummm.. lying?' The tone had changed to patronising. 'Like the rest of them.'

Heather stayed calm. 'Seems to me you're the one telling the lies?'

Shauna stood up and shouted. 'I'm telling you the truth. But you,' she waved her arm around the small room. 'You only hear what you want to hear. And see what you want to see!'

'Shauna, sit down.' The girl obeyed. 'See what you want to see?' Heather brought her face down to Shauna's level. 'What is we are not seeing, then?'

# Chapter Thirty-Eight

'How you doing today, Dad?'

John McCarthy lowered his newspaper and raised a faint smile. 'I forgot how bloody awful these places are,' he replied grumpily. 'You come to take me home?'

'I hope so,' she dropped into a chair beside the bed. 'When we can get to see a doctor.' On cue, one rushed past the doorway, dealing with a commotion a few doors down. Another two nurses followed him, at full run. There were some raised voices and the high-pitched sound of an alarm going off.

They both listened to the sound of panic for a minute. 'Looks like they will be busy for a while. I'll be back in an hour.' She stood to her feet, pulling a baseball cap on her head.

'Clear!' shouted a voice in the far room, followed by the sound of a defibrillator being used. 'And again!' Jess looked down at the painted lines on the floor as she headed back towards the exit.


Scott freeze-framed the picture to get a better look at the man. Even zooming in it was impossible to see any features. The previous file was very similar, again a person in dark clothing arriving with a drum of fuel, taking the boat out and arriving back without looking up. It was as though he knew where the camera was. Scott checked the list of files again, to see if there was another dated the same day, hopefully overlooking the car park. There wasn't.

Sandy stood up and came over to his desk, a print-out in his hand. 'De Runcy's phone records.'

'Senior or Junior?'

'Senior.' He laid it on the desk, showing that some of the numbers had been run through with a highlighter, a few different colours. 'Recognise any of them?'

Scott looked. 'That one's mine. I phoned his phone when I arrived at the scene, so I could hear where it was.'

'And the next one up?'

Scott looked down at the table. He knew perfectly well who's that was. 'Jess McCarthy,' he said quietly.

'So that must have rung after you found the body?'

'I guess so.' Scot wasn't sure where to go with this. He knew he should have mentioned it.

As if Sandy was reading his thoughts, he asked. 'What else aren't you telling us, Scotty.' His eyes narrowed. 'You seem to have a few too many secrets.'

The conversation was broken up when a head poked around the door. It was Andrew McClatchie. 'Bad news. The old man didn't make it!'

Sandy threw his hands in the air. 'Three murders?' his voice raised. 'I'll be here for a fucking month at this rate!'

The boss waited for him to calm down. 'Hospital said there was something suspicious about it. One of you get down there and check it out?'

Sandy sighed. 'I'll go. I need to get out of this place for a while.'

'Land-Rover keys are at the front desk,' Scott muttered, still in shock from the news.

'A walk will do me good.' He reached for his jacket. 'I think we need to talk, when I get back?'


'Poor bastard,' Scott said out loud. 'You may have fallen on your own sword, but you didn't deserve to die.'

For half an hour he checked the videos, taking freeze-frame screen-prints. As the dates had suggested, the trips were regular but something about the gait in the visitor didn't quite add up. He called Jim over to take a look.

'On the first couple of files the man was slightly hunched when in the next few he was a little more upright. Maybe it was just the weather determining his walk or...' he trailed off.

Jim finished the sentence. 'Or, they're not the same person?'

'Exactly!'

Next he checked the video from the shop. There was no sign of this person coming inside but from one of the dates, he could see him walking past the window outside. The picture wasn't clear, but it definitely seemed like the same person. Again he snapped a freeze-frame and enlarged it. The man had unbuttoned his jacket revealing a bit more body shape. It was a shape he recognised and he pulled his hand to his mouth. 'Oh fuck!' he said quietly.

Jim looked at him quizzically from a nearby desk, but he refrained to speak, instead sitting in silence.

'Something just came in from Glasgow.' Jim stood up. 'Wanna see it?' He looked closer at Scott's face. 'You OK, pal?'

Scott shook himself and focussed. 'Aye sure. What you got?'

'They've been digging on these two brothers. It appears someone has overlooked something?'

'What?' he snapped.

Jim stopped. 'You sure you're alright? Looking a bit peely wally. Hangover, is it?'

'What?' he stood up, about to head for the door, phone in hand.

'Richard Matheson, that's the older one, is on the board of the whisky society, and just been voted chairman?'

'Good for him,' Scott made it through the door before

clinging to the handle once outside in the corridor. In his stomach he felt the bile rise as his face drained of blood. Thankfully the toilet was unoccupied as he bent over the bowl, throwing up for all he was worth.

Splashing cold water on his face, he took a long hard look at himself in the mirror, taking in deep breaths. He came back out just in time to see Shauna leaving the building. Jim was following, keys in hand.

'You running her back to Kilchrenan?' He asked.

'Aye, won't be long.'

Scott pulled his coat from a peg. 'I'm coming with you.'

Jim looked him in the eye. 'Boss won't like it. Wants to speak to you.' Scott was ignoring him. 'You sure you're alright?'

'Nah. Feeling a bit rough. Must be something I ate.' He put his hand on Jim's arm. 'Get me home, will ya?'

Scott was so silent on the journey back that Jim eventually turned on the radio. Shauna made him change the station to something a bit livelier and was singing along to herself to some boy band. Now and again, she chipped in some conversation about music and life in general. In fact her tone had been most pleasant since she had left the station. As they neared the village she said. 'Drop me off at the hotel, can you, please?'

'Aye. Me too,' Scott muttered. 'Or somewhere in the village.'

Jim pulled the Land-Rover to a halt. 'I thought you were going home sick?'

'I'll get some powders from Jeannie. And the walk home will do me good. Be right in no time.'

Jim waited until Shauna was out of earshot, throwing him a thank you for the lift. 'I cannae keep covering for you, Scott. Shit's piling up. Anything you want to tell me? Something I can use to calm the waves?'

'Chase down those bad bastard brothers. From what you just told me, there's a trail of spirit leading to their door.'

He stood on the pavement, watching the Land-Rover disappear out of sight, before heading to the hotel himself. Shauna was in conversation with the chef by the time he arrived, flirting in her usual way. She even winked at Scott as he passed, heading to the bar. Jess stood behind it with her back to him, changing a bottle of whisky on the optic.

'Good stuff, is it?'

She swung round. 'Hey, mister,' a smile on her face. 'You need a shot?'

'Nope,' he took a deep breath, 'I need a talk.'

'What? About you not taking me for a drink? Don't mention it, just thought it would be nice, you know....' She placed her hand on the bar and he grabbed her by the wrist.

'Hey,' she tried to snatch it away. 'Don't do that.' The smile was gone and her eyes narrowed. 'You love me. Remember?'

'We need to talk, now,' he said, again. He nodded to the storeroom behind the bar. 'In here, or down at the station?'

'We could always go back to your place?'

Scott considered the offer, returning her stare. 'Only if you promise to tell me what's going on?'

'Okay, okay. I'll tell you.' Her eyes lightened. 'But not here, and there's really no point driving back to Oban, just for a friendly chat, is there?'

'Will it be friendly? Because I think you have a lot of explaining to do?'

Jess grabbed her coat, and Scott followed her to the door. 'It's quiet in here,' she called out to the chef, 'so I'll be back in an hour? The girl can help you in the kitchen till

I get back.'

A WhatsApp message pinged on Scott's phone which he ignored.

# Chapter Thirty-Nine

As Scott's pick-up was back at his house, he suggested they walk down but Jess insisted they take her car. Her demeanour was chatty as she teased him about this and that in her usual way, especially when his phone rang and he still ignored it. Once at the house he unlocked the door, realising that the spare key was under the same stone it had been for the past three years. Beth greeted him at the door and then made a fuss of Jess as she always had done.

Jess went to the fridge, pulling out a half full bottle of white which had a stopper in it. 'Slowing down in your old age?' she said, raising an eyebrow. 'Most folks speed up drinking as they get older!' She pulled down two glasses and set them on the table, him already concerned that he had lost the upper hand in this interview before it had even begun. 'So, you want to talk?'

'No, I want you to talk, Jess.' He looked at her face, and the beauty she had always wooed him with, and then turned away. This had to be professional, not emotional. 'How well did you know Julien de Runcy?' He pulled out his phone, intending to record the conversation.

'Don't do that,' she smiled. 'We are friends, right? Not spies?'

He repeated the question, putting the phone away.

'I knew him. Of course I did. Everyone knows everyone around here. He stayed at the hotel; we had the odd chat.'

'About?'

'This and that. He liked his wines. Was very

knowledgeable, actually. Something we all share. You'd know, you had dinner with him the other night?'

'How long have you known him?'

Jess looked to the ceiling. 'Three or four years, I guess.'

'Sociably?'

'Aha. You want to know if we were shagging?' she sipped the wine, pulling a satisfied face. 'No. We weren't. You really think I have sex with everyone in the village, don't you?'

'No.'

She took a deep breath. 'If you must know, I did some work for him.'

'In what way?'

'Hmm. How shall I put this? I made a few contacts.'

'Were you shipping whisky for him?'

Jess stopped, momentarily, her eyes darting towards him, and then away again. 'Where did *that* come from?' Eventually she smiled. 'First I am a whore. Next I'm a smuggler.' She stood up and went to the sink. 'I thought you liked me? But those are unfriendly things to say, Scott.'

Another message pinged into Scott's phone and he decided to check it. 'I just need the bathroom.'

'Your house, pal!'

On the way through, he went to a cupboard in the bedroom, pulling out a pair of standard issue handcuffs. Flushing the toilet, he arrived back to see Jess topping up the wine glass.

'You going to tell me the whole story, Jess? I trusted you. I've always trusted you. Should I believe what you are saying now?'

'That's your problem, right there, Scott Donald. You have always believed me, haven't you?' She sat down, a smile appearing on her face, decision made. 'Ok,' she joked, 'I'll tell you, then I'll have to kill you!'

Again that was something she had often said to him, when they were kids. All the same, Scott shuddered.

'When Julien first bought the place he needed inside information, on the village and the local industry. He came to me for help and paid me well. Also, he introduced me to a few of his friends. We had a few meetings, on the boat. Jean-Luc took a fancy to me, and Julien encouraged that.' She looked to the ceiling again. 'They were some great parties, Scott. But not really my thing. All that sharing drugs around, and women. Jean-Luc used both, pretty heavily. One of the men took me to one side and offered me money to work for him. He'd pay me twice what De Runcy was paying, he said, just for information. Things were tight at the time, my old man's business wasn't doing great, so I took his offer. And, for a while I worked for both of them?'

'What was his name?'

'I can't tell you that, Scott, you know that.'

'Let me guess. Matheson?'

She smiled, looking him in the eye. 'If you say so!'

'So you were working for De Runcy and Matheson at the same time?'

'Kinda neat, eh? Didn't need to do a lot. Just help him along, him and junior. And occasionally report back to the big guys.'

'Help him along? With what?'

She took a deep breath and sighed. 'Junior was siphoning off some of the decent whisky, and Edis was mixing it into a cocktail of some sort. He would take it down to the marina, and meet a fishing boat a few miles off shore. Chuck the thing in the water, and they would retrieve it.'

'Who owned the fishing boat? Matheson?'

'To be honest,' she swigged the wine back, 'I didn't really care.'

'But you did the run a few times for him?'

'Julien had taught me to sail a few years back, and I really enjoyed handling the boat. So, when he asked me to do a couple of runs for him, it wasn't that difficult.'

'Did you kill Jean-Luc?'

'Me?' she looked him in the eye. 'No, you know me better than that, I'm not a killer.'

'So who did?'

Jess was still nervous about mentioning names. 'They did.' She said, sadly.

Scott poured more wine. 'Did you love him?'

'What, Junior? Sort of. But I never let it show.' She added 'Did I?'

Scott ignored that, feeling for the cuffs in his pocket. His was a tough gig. All the time he had known this woman she had been mischievous, controlling, and spiteful sometimes, but he had loved her. Now he just wanted the love to drain away, like someone pulling out of a sink plug. 'What about Edis?' he asked eventually.

The woman had her back to him again, and he seized his chance, jumping behind her and swinging the cuff over her one wrist. It wasn't a highly accurate move but he felt it close shut, just as an elbow bust into his ribs and then a solid pan hit him around the head.

Two or three minutes later, his eyes opened to find himself handcuffed neatly to the kitchen chair, both arms behind his back. Jess had lit a cigarette and was puffing out smoke rings as he focussed. She offered him a drag and he turned his head away. 'You never were as quick as me, Scott. I can sense your every move, you know. Always could. Even when you brought that bitch back here!'

'Is that what this is about?' Scott felt blood dripping

down the inside of his cheek. 'You not over that, yet? It wasn't my doing.'

'Yes, it fucking was, Scott.' Her anger ignited as she shouted directly into his face. 'You dumped me because of her. Dumped me after all we had built. How fucking dare you!'

For the first time, he noticed the sharp knife in her hand and his fear rose up a few notches but he tried to keep his voice calm. In all the years he had only ever seen her kill a few times. Rats mainly, when she would put a boot on their head and then stab them through the neck. She had killed a chicken once, slicing its throat from behind, down at the farm when Scott hadn't the guts to do it himself. She was holding the knife in the same manner. 'She was my wife, Jess,' he tried not to sound pleading but failed. 'She wanted another go at our marriage.'

'She wanted a go at me, you mean. Jealous bastard bitch!' her knuckles tightened on the handle. 'Why are women always so jealous?' He noticed that while he had been unconscious, she had opened another bottle of wine and was gulping at it now, reading her phone, until he realised it was actually his phone. 'And now you have another one?' her voice had calmed as she waved the phone. 'Why do you keep hurting me, Scott?'

Scott ignored the remark. There was nothing he could say about his new friend that would make this situation any easier. 'You killed Julien, too, didn't you?'

'Aha, so you did read your messages. Why didn't you say so?' She made a point of reading out loud. 'Suspicious woman seen on the ward. Tall, baseball cap, think it might be McCarthy's daughter. De Runcy's tube was cut through.' She looked at him. 'That what you mean?'

'You always were handy with a knife,' he mumbled. 'But why him?'

'Orders,' was all she replied. 'From on high. But I

didn't really kill him, did I? The bullet did that. The bullet he got after you chased him in a car. A bullet he wasn't supposed to get.'

Scot couldn't work out if she had gone delusional, or was there something else they'd missed. 'I don't understand? Who was it meant for?'

'I'm not sure you ever understand, Scotty boy.' Another glug of wine 'Revenge,' she sighed, and then looked him in the eye again, a tiny tear forming. 'You do realise I have to kill you, don't you. If I don't, they will kill you. And me!'

Panic started to set in when he realised she was under orders still. With one death on her case sheet, another wouldn't make that much difference. 'No,' he panicked, 'you don't have to.'

'You're getting stressed now, Scotty. You know you shouldn't get stressed, it's bad for your heart.' She sat down at the table again, as though deciding to unload all the information now. 'Julien had short-changed them in a whisky deal, something hugely financial, and the brothers had killed Jean-Luc because of it, to teach him a lesson. Julien wasn't going to stand for that, his son's life being taken for something he had done.' Jess looked up to the ceiling, a certain sadness in her eye. 'He never mentioned it but I knew he would go after the assassin, and make him pay.' She looked back at him, drawing in a deep breath. 'But he was no match for Alfie, the man is an animal. Very few people are. Not you, certainly.' She looked up as a car passed by the window. 'Me neither!'

'How do you think you'll get away with this one?' Scott considered all the mischief they had been up to over the years and how she had never seemed to get the blame, even when she was guilty. 'Killing a top businessman and then a police officer? They'll hunt you down.'

'What, your numpties in Oban. They'll be no match for my boss, I'm telling you. Anyway,' she lifted an envelope from her pocket, pulling out a striped piece of paper. 'I'll be sunning myself, thank you very much. Had enough of this cold weather for one lifetime.'

'Spain?' he gestured.

She ignored it. 'So, time to get this over with. Some of us have a plane to catch.' Silence filled the air, Scott blind with thoughts of death. And love. And guilt. And deceit. Eventually Jess pushed back her chair, steadying her hand on the table as she did so. 'Nice knowing you, it's been a blast!'

Scott battled for help in his mind. 'One more thing. You didn't answer my question? Who killed Charlie Edis?'

Jess smiled and looked at her watch. A few more minutes wouldn't hurt. 'Oh, haven't you worked that one out yet? Call yourself a copper, and then spend all your time looking in the wrong direction!'

'Where should I be looking?'

'Should have been looking, you mean. Past tense now, Scott. A bit too late.'

'Where?' he asked again.

'Straight ahead, would be as good a place as any? Bloody fool Charlie, not happy with getting paid for what he did, but trying a scam on the side. A pretty blatant one as well. Julien wasn't happy of being made a fool of, as you can imagine. And his partners none too happy having more whisky from the same distillery hit the market.'

'So you hit him?'

She nodded, 'Not bloody hard enough, though!'

Scott noticed the faint sound of a car coming back up the lane.

'If I'd gone there to kill him, I would have made a proper job of it. No, it was just to scare him, and shut down his little operation. That's when he wrote me a list of all those involved, with half the bloody village idiots on it.

He was drunk and thought he could over-power me. Even blackmail me. Ha, I've thrown men twice his size out the bar before now.'

A loud rap on the door took them both by surprise, but Scott was quicker with his reactions than Jess, and he lurched forward with the chair, knocking her off balance.

'Scott. Are you home?' a woman's voice shouted from behind the door. 'I left you message, you left Beth's drugs behind, at the surgery?'

Jess came back at him, knife in hand but as the chair rocked backwards he struck her hard in the stomach with both feet. At the same time he shouted out. 'Megan. There's a key.' Both of them hit the ground at the same time but with Scott's hands tied behind him, it was Jess who surfaced first. She held the knife to his throat, a drunken grin coming back on her face. 'Megan, there's a key, la la la.' She mimicked his voice and then her eyes narrowed. 'You really think I would leave you the key? What do you take me for, a bloody idiot?' Then the grin came back again. 'Maybe I should let her in, poor little mite, out there in the cold?'

Behind Jess, Scott saw a shadow pass the window. He didn't know whether to shout RUN, or HELP. Megan would be no match for Jess, but at least she would be sober. Jess came at him again, the knife held out in front of her. As he rolled sideways, it glanced his shoulder and he felt a jab of pain. Again using his feet, he swung his boots in the air, this time catching her in the face which knocked her sideways, onto the cold tiled floor, blood spilling from above her eye.

Scott tried to focus as the hollow sound of a gunshot rang through the room. Had Jess brought a gun with her as well? Maybe the hoods she was involved with issued her with one. The sound was followed by splintering wood as the door burst open, letting in a rush of cold air. Jess was up on her feet again but this time she wasn't going for Scott but the intruder.

Megan stood in the doorway, pointing the pistol right at her head. 'Back off!' her shrill words echoed around the kitchen. 'Back off and put the knife down!'

Jess pulled a smile and then up-righted a chair and sat on it. 'Well, lookee here.' She turned to Scott who was trying to get up. 'Where would you be without all these women fawning after you?' She still had the knife gripped in her hand as Megan advanced.

'Put it down!' she yelled again, helping Scott up with her other hand. Jess made an arc towards her, aiming for her throat and this time Megan ducked away, dancing to the sink in one move and grabbing the pan. Her turn to swing an arc now and it caught Jess right on the temple. This time the woman cried out as she swayed backwards, crumpling into a heap. Megan put the pistol down, picking up the knife, her hand shaking. 'You fancy telling me what's going on here?' Holding the knife to Jess's throat, she checked her pockets and retrieved the keys to the handcuffs. Jess had one eye open, the other swollen and filling with blood. She tried to speak but a couple of her perfect teeth were broken. Megan undid one of Scott's hands, allowing him to do the other himself.

As soon as he was on his feet, blood dripping from the gash in his arm, he rolled Jess over and cuffed her hands together.

'Time for that drink now?' he said to Megan, his eyes boring into hers. 'Bit early for dinner?'

'Should have shot the pair of you two idiots,' she smiled.

'Except you couldn't, could you?' Scott put his arms around her. 'Not with that thing?'

'Well, she wasn't to know that it was just a stun gun, was she?'

Scott inspected the pistol. 'These things only kill from

281

a two-inch range?'

'Ah. Sorry about your door!'

It was another ten minutes by the time a squad car arrived, by which time Jess had gained consciousness and Megan had wiped her down, as best she could.

'No,' she mumbled through her swollen mouth. 'I didn't kill Edis. Haven't you worked out who did yet?'

# Chapter Forty

'We come to lot seventy-six,' the auctioneer, a well-dressed man in his thirties looked down at a catalogue before beaming round the room. 'Mortlach, 1989. Who'll start me at five thousand? Five thousand is it. Come on you collectors, you know it's worth. OK, I'll take four to get on. Come on, investments like this don't come every day not at this price. Three then?'

A hand went up near the back row of the auction house.

'Three it is, three thousand, three thousand, two. Three thousand two, I have, four, on the internet, six, in the room, eight, four, four thousand.'

Richard Matheson tapped the computer screen again, sending in another bid. 'Four thousand five,' the auctioneer continued. 'My bid is on the internet. Is there anyone else? Or I'll sell. Five! Fresh bidder, just in time there. Five thousand I have, another internet bid, this one from China. Five thousand, five-thousand. Fair warning now. Five thousand for this genuine 1989 Mortlach. And I sell at five thousand. Goes to bidder number MT3721.' The computer let out a loud ping, and Richard a smile.

Richard spoke out loud to his empty office. 'That's it you eastern boys, you keep taking it, we'll keep making it.'

A few lots later, a bottle of Port Ellen, 1968 made eleven thousand, to the same buyer. Richard closed the screen and stepped out onto the terracotta terrace, bright Spanish sunshine washing over him, a glass of whisky in his hand. In front the landscape rolled hazily down to the Mediterranean Ocean, some 5 miles away. That was the great thing about Southern Spain, the villas in these hills concealed a lot of things, even in broad daylight. One thing Matheson had learned in his long life of crime, if you were going to hide something, plain sight was the very best place to put it.

Two days later, Scott and Jim sat outside the interview room looking in. With Jess now held in a cell in Inverness, awaiting a murder trial, Alfie Matherson had not been located over the last few days, despite half the force looking for him. And with no real evidence of any crime against him, even when they found him it was unlikely that they would get anything to stick with regarding the murder of Jean Luc de Runcy. So far information on Jess's arrest had been kept away from the newspapers, as well as the locals.

Their only chance of a conviction was from this man in the interview room. Scott had mulled over what Jess had blurted out about Edis's killer until he was sure he had the answer. After she stitched the wound on his arm he had persuaded Megan to drive him down to his old family home, her protesting that they weren't yet even dating so why would she want to see it. Leaving her in the car he had sneaked around the farmyard, trying to second guess his brother's movements. After taking a few photos they had made it back to his house undetected and Megan had tried to put him to bed. However, after a few glasses of wine, she had given up protesting and decided to stay overnight. Before she joined him in bed, she had put a chair up against the door, and wedged the sofa against that which Beth slept on.

With photographic evidence, the Oban team had agreed that the farm would have been an ideal place to hide a barrel and Heather had issued a search warrant of the farm steading, which had in turn revealed two barrels of whisky hidden in a dusty outhouse.

'Where's my chicken-shit brother?' were the only

words Fraser said when asked to repeat his name in the interview. Scott watched on, ignoring the remark.

Heather was conducting proceedings. 'Fraser Donald, we have had three confessions from witnesses who say you drove a forklift at Glenlachan distillery on the evening of Sunday 14th November.'

'What if I did?' Fraser looked to be sweating. It was pretty obvious the others had broken rank.

'We believe that you raised the body of Charles Edis and subsequently pushed him into a container of malted barley.' She straightened up, looking him in the eye while Sandy Lawson watched on. 'I am therefore arresting you for his murder.'

'You can't do me to that. He was already dead. I never killed him. She did that, she belted him. That woman. The bitch my brother was shagging. You need to find her, and she will admit it!'

'Ah, but Mister Donald, we already have.'

Behind Scott, Andrew McLatchie tapped him on the shoulder, holding out his hand. 'Well done, Officer Donald. Must be difficult having to convict your own brother.'

Scott stood and shook the man's hand, inwardly smiling his revenge.

**THE END**

Coming soon...

# Lord of the Hill

When Scott Donald finds a dead ram up on Ben Cruachan mountain, it turns out to be one of extreme value. Lord of the Hill opens up a whole world of corruption and deception amongst Scotland's sheep industry.

Published by
**Chauffour Books, FRANCE**

Editor
**Winskill Editorial, Aberdour, Scotland**

First print October 2022

Printed in Great Britain
by Amazon

16685247R00163